D0122085

To P. J.

on entering the years
in which billing have
preceded her but without
her riches.

Dick

THE
PARTNERS

Also by
Louis Auchincloss

The Indifferent Children
The Injustice Collectors
Sybil
A Law for the Lion
The Romantic Egoists
The Great World and Timothy Colt
Venus in Sparta
Pursuit of the Prodigal
The House of Five Talents
Reflections of a Jacobite
Portrait in Brownstone
Powers of Attorney
The Rector of Justin
Pioneers and Caretakers
The Embezzler
Tales of Manhattan
A World of Profit
Motiveless Malignity
Second Chance
Edith Wharton
Richelieu
I Come as a Thief

THE
PARTNERS

Louis Auchincloss

HOUGHTON MIFFLIN COMPANY BOSTON

Second Printing   v

Copyright © 1973, 1974 by Louis Auchincloss
All rights reserved. No part of this work may be
reproduced or transmitted in any form by any means,
electronic or mechanical, including photocopying and
recording, or by any information storage or retrieval system,
without permission in writing from the publisher.

A portion of this book has appeared
in *Cosmopolitan* magazine.

Library of Congress Cataloging in Publication Data

Auchincloss, Louis.
   The partners.

   1. Title.
PZ3.A898Par   813'.5'4   73-13633
ISBN 0-395-18279-4

Printed in the United States of America

FOR MY SON,

John Winthrop Auchincloss II

Contents

SHEPARD, PUTNEY
& COX

(formerly Shepard & Howland)

Announce the removal of their law office

from

65 Wall Street

to

One New Orange Plaza

January 1971

From *The New York Times* Sunday Real Estate Section:

"The single note of the past in the great glass cube that Joseph Lazarus, Jr., has constructed on the Battery is its address. A few readers may recall that our city was briefly known as 'New Orange' after the Dutch reoccupation of 1673."

I

A Kingly Crown

BEEKMAN, or "Beeky" Ehninger, had always known that his rise from clerk to partner in Shepard, Putney & Cox had not been wholly due to his legal aptitude. He was aware that he was a competent lawyer and comfortably conscious of his popularity with partners and associates alike, but he was also very much aware of the large and devoted family of sisters and cousins and aunts who, through the years, had faithfully made up a large part of his clientele. Such clan loyalty is not characteristic of New York, but it is sometimes found among the issue of "robber barons." Money can be thicker than blood, and the hundred-odd surviving descendants of Augustus Means, railroad magnate of the 1870s, contained several dozen still well-to-do individuals who remembered the common origin of their good fortunes and were glad enough to help each other out. Only a small number of the males had gone into law, and Beeky was the beneficiary of this statistic. It had helped to keep him youthful, right up to the age of fifty-six. Being "Young Beeky" to aging and aged clients seemed appropriate to his vivid check suits and bow ties, to his large, staring, lemurish eyes, to his diminutive, agile, "smart kid" figure. Beeky liked to think of himself as the naive young hero who always outsmarted the villain in the silent film comedies of his boyhood.

He was modest about his position but by no means humble. If he was not the administrative head of the firm, like Hubert Cox, or its great litigating light, like Ed Toland, or even a recognized expert in a particular field of jurisprudence, like many of his other partners, he had still a sound, round, general knowledge of law, and he kept comfortably abreast of every new statute or regulation affecting his clients. Beeky might have come to those by family ties, but he had nonetheless hung on to them. He never allowed any of them, no matter how specialized their problems, to fall under the jurisdiction of another partner. He always saw that the problem — a merger, a divorce, a will, a bankruptcy, a tax audit — was assigned to the proper technician, but that technician then worked under Beeky. Though his own work was largely supervisory, the combination of his attentiveness to detail with a certain shrewd common sense, not always characteristic of the legal expert, had given him a reputation for wisdom among his partners and clients. Beeky knew that life had dealt him a good hand. He also knew that he had played it well.

But his roster of clients was not what Beeky regarded, with an inner pride amounting at times to exhilaration, as his greatest contribution to the firm. No, this had been rendered twenty-five years before, in 1946, when he had saved the fading old firm of Shepard & Howland by converting it into its dynamic successor, Shepard, Putney & Cox. The memory of this success was the mainstay of Beeky's emotional life, the constant, comforting source of a timid assurance that he was, to himself anyway if not to the public or even to his friends — and that despite the disadvantages of his small size, his limited renown and his funny marriage — a leader of men.

What did it matter that hardly anyone now remembered or cared that it was he who had pulled it off? Had he not read somewhere that any man who was known as a great diplomat could not have been one? He had been so quiet and unobtrusive — with authority from no one, certainly not from poor old Judge Howland — in luring his classmates, Hubert Cox and Horace Putney, over from Sloane & Sidell that they had come in time to think that it must have been their own idea to remold the crumbling remnants of Shepard & Howland into a great modern firm. But if the cause was obscure, all downtown knew the result.

And now it looked as if the job was going to have to be done all over again. Beeky had had to recognize that he could no longer rest on even anonymous laurels. The crisis of the old firm, after a quarter of a century, had become the crisis of its successor. Hubert Cox was preoccupied with tax work, Horace Putney was always angling for another government job. The administrative center of the firm had weakened. Inconsistency was everywhere: in salaries, in raises, in vacations, in hours of work. The partners were forming cliques; the clerks felt exploited. For "Young Beeky," with his sixtieth year now a pale shape on the horizon of the only too visible future, there remained, as for Ulysses, a "work of noble note" yet to be done.

"What's new today in the office, Mrs. Bing?"

"They say Mr. Van Winkle is leaving. He's going over to Johnson and Knapp. At a salary hike of thirty-five hundred dollars and a promise of partnership."

Every morning, while opening his mail, Beeky discussed the problems of the day and the world with his secretary. So much of his work consisted of reading memoranda prepared for him by associates that Mrs. Bing had little to do. Never, however, did she take advantage of this circumstance to join the girls in the ladies' room or even to read magazines. A breathless, excitable, popeyed little bird of a woman, she kept busy, a tense acolyte, in constant readiness for a task from her

worshiped boss. Mrs. Bing, Beeky knew, had a Mr. Bing somewhere in Plandome, and even a married daughter, but the circles of her professional and private lives never intersected.
Beeky even suspected that she talked as little of him to her
husband as of her husband to him. Before she had been
Beeky's secretary she had been briefly secretary to the late
Judge Howland to whom she had shown the same exclusive
devotion. She was like a poodle, a well-clipped, well-disci-
plined, sleek and glossy black poodle, totally loyal to one
master — at a time. In their morning dialogue she sat opposite
him, smiling, like a client.

"Now how do you girls know that already?" Beeky demanded. "Van Winkle told Mr. Cox only yesterday."

Mrs. Bing's unaltered smile seemed to take this as an accustomed tribute. "And that will cause a rumble in the tax department. Mr. Cummings will think now he'll be the next
partner, whereas really it will be Mr. Carroll. Only Mr. Carroll won't know that, so he may leave, too."

Beeky threw up his hands. "What are we coming to, Mrs.
Bing? We used to be a firm. Now it's dog eat dog. And even
when somebody does want to treat the young men decently,
it's no good because he won't tell them in time." Beeky
slapped his hand on the desk and rose to roam the office. "We
need a leader. We need a leader desperately."

Mrs. Bing's eyes followed him admiringly. "I've always said
that's what you should be. You're the only partner with the
authority and the vision. The only one whom everyone in the
firm respects. From Mr. Cox right down to the lowest office
boy!"

Mrs. Bing was an enthusiast for law and order. She had a
photograph of the late Senator Joseph McCarthy lovingly
pasted to the inside cover of her office diary. Beeky was a
Democrat, but Mrs. Bing refused to take his now old-fashioned

New Deal liberalism as anything but the amiable, rather lovable eccentricity of a prince.

"You think I should be a dictator, Mrs. Bing?" he asked with
a self-depreciating smile.

"So long as you take the first position, Mr. Ehninger, I don't
care what the label is."

"So long, then, as I'm a despot, it doesn't matter if I'm a benevolent one?"

"Oh, you'd always be benevolent. Too much so, I'm afraid."

Beeky remembered with a little pang that it was the same
phrase that his wife had used the Sunday before when he had
refused to reprimand their old gardener for spilling water on
her card table in the conservatory. Annabel Ehninger and
Mrs. Bing understood each other. The difference was that Annabel did not share the secretary's admiration of her husband.
She left Beeky to Mrs. Bing, recognizing with a breezy scorn
that *that* was all he really wanted from a woman. Oh, yes,
Beeky had had it all out on the analytical couch, had faced it
hundreds of times! He and Doctor Fellowes had jointly recognized that he had married Annabel when he had been an innocent bachelor of forty and she a buxom, raven-haired, flashing-
eyed, loudly laughing, triple divorcée of fifty-three, with
grown children of different last names, only to prove to his
dying and infinitely disapproving old mother, with whom he
had always lived, that he was, after all, a man. Now Annabel
was sixty-eight and golden blond, and spent her days and
nights at the bridge table, a huge, rouged, laughing, terrible,
gorgeous old thing.

"I can't change my spots at my age, Mrs. Bing," he protested. "And for that matter I never had many spots to
change. If I could be anything, it would be a kind of gray eminence. I like power for what it can accomplish, not power itself." Here he had a momentary vision of what Doctor Fel-

lowes might retort to *that*, and he made a mental face at his mental image. "Some people can't believe in disinterested action," he continued in a sharper tone, as if rebutting the absent psychiatrist. "They are quite wrong. Even pathetically wrong, I'd say. What is it to me personally that the firm be saved? My clients are looked after. My little fortune is securely invested. What I earn here mostly goes in taxes."

"Oh, Mr. Ehninger, do you think anyone doubts that? Nobody is less selfish than you. That's true. It really is. You have no idea how you're looked up to in this office."

Beeky was a bit ashamed of his pleasure in Mrs. Bing's indiscriminate laudations. It was not a very keen pleasure — he knew too well that the woman was a goose — but it was like the misty spray of a high-powered fountain on a hot day. It cooled without really wetting. Beeky reflected ruefully how different his life might be if Annabel ever spoke to him in that tone.

"I thought we had found our leader in Hubert Cox," he went on. "He seemed to have all the qualities I thought we needed: he was liked as well as admired, and he cared about everybody, not just his partners, not even just the clerks — everybody. But he's too reasonable. Maybe too soft. He sees too many sides to every picture. Cox hates to say 'no.'"

"Who doesn't?"

"I have one partner who doesn't."

"Which?"

"Now why don't you tell me?"

Mrs. Bing's eyes sparkled. She loved a game. For a moment, turning her head sideways, she seemed to reflect. "Mr. Putney?"

"He'd like to say no. But he's not capable of so simple a conclusion. There'd have to be a qualification."

"Mr. Toland?"

"He'd say: 'Hell, no.' Or worse."

"Mr. Purdy?"

"Home run."

"But he's so unpopular, Mr. Ehninger!"

"From you that's unworthy. Why should a great leader care about popularity?"

"But still there are degrees!"

"I grant you, there are degrees. But Dan Purdy is not a dragon. There's some paper in him. The point is that he's the ablest corporation lawyer in the firm. At the age of only forty-one he controls more business than any other two partners. The administrator of a law firm has got to be its biggest man. Otherwise he won't be respected. He won't be obeyed."

"But . . ."

"Wait!" Beeky had his speech ready, and he had to get it all out in order to persuade himself. "Purdy's second qualification is that he wants the job. Everyone else, including Cox himself, loathes administrative detail. They're even proud of it. A great lawyer, they think, should be above such things. What rot! And Dan's third and final qualification is that he's ambitious. Once he is well shackled to the firm, he can be trusted to take us all up the ladder of fame with him. And for a guide and philosopher to tone him down, he'll always have me."

"I see." But there was a disturbing note of doubt in Mrs. Bing's usually trusting tone. "Of course, he'll have you."

"Precisely. He'll mind me because I put him there."

"Hmm. But if I may quote you, Mr. Ehninger, haven't you always told me that Mr. Purdy has created his own little group of henchmen inside of Shepard, Putney and Cox? Haven't you described it as a firm within a firm?" She paused to gather her courage. "Haven't you even described it as a . . . as a cancer?"

"Perhaps," Beeky conceded with a blush. "But that's just the beauty of my plan. The very boldness of it. I simply turn my cancer into a cure! By giving Purdy more than he could possibly expect, I render him at once harmless and useful. Because it will be to *his* advantage then, as well as ours, to have a great, well-organized firm. And he'll see it, too. He's not dumb, after all."

"I see." Perhaps there was a shade less doubt in her tone. "Well, it may be a brilliant idea. But I still think you should be number one and let Mr. Purdy be your gray eminence, if you have to have one. He even looks like a monk."

"You see that, do you? You're very keen. He's just the type to have been a political cleric in French or Spanish history. A Father Joseph or a Ximenes. Once he sees his way . . . well, wait till I show him!" He sat down, having made his decision. "Mrs. Bing, call Miss Thompson and ask if Mr. Purdy's free for lunch."

o

Dan Purdy, as Mrs. Bing said, looked like a monk. Austerity seemed to emanate from his tall spare frame like dry air from the desert. He was not, perhaps, a bad-looking man: his regular features and long, strong face might have been almost attractive but for an air of juicelessness that hung about him, a hard-baked clay quality that made one see his short stiff curly hair as a tonsure. Dan moved rapidly, abruptly, awkwardly. His voice was harsh and loud, and his laugh sounded like gravel on tin. But there was a tough humorousness in his cynicism, a trenchancy in his observations, a naked strength in his observations and actions that made him a leader, if not of men, at least of cliques. He had his following, consisting of two devoted clerks, who even affected his quick, almost running gait when they walked in and out of the office behind him. They hardly bothered to conceal their scorn for their fellow associates and made no secret of their opinion that Mr. Purdy was foolishly generous to support his "freeloading" partners.

Dan Purdy himself, however, had always professed a particular respect and liking for Beeky Ehninger, and it was on this rock that the latter hoped to raise his church, despite his suspicion that Dan's respect was based on snobbishness. Dan, the son of a stationery store proprietor in Newark, venerated such relics of old New York as the Beekmans and Ehningers. Beeky understood that the danger to his project was that Dan might see himself as building a new order on the stripped foundations of the old, that he might relish the fantasy of playing Mussolini to Beeky's Victor Emmanuel, but Beeky counted on his own astuteness to control this. When the new order was fixed, it might be a surprise to all to discover which was the puppet.

At their lunch Beeky opened the conversation diplomatically with a question about Dan's collection of porcelains. This collection represented what was probably the sole outlet for Dan's aesthetic nature. The law, only too evidently, provided one for his aggressions. But at home, in his little gilded box of a penthouse on Central Park South, looking north over the zoo, he would run the square tips of his fingers over his glass cabinets of Meissen and Lowestoft and sigh almost like a human being. Dan had a wife, a timid thin woman with a twisted mouth who laughed rather desperately at everything, but she seemed more a caretaker than a spouse. She had never been the same since their only child, a Mongoloid, had been committed.

"You ought to go to London," Beeky said. "Everything is sold in London today."

"Everything comes to New York," Dan retorted. It was notorious in the office that he never left the city, even in the worst heat of summer. "All I have to do is wait. And I can afford to wait a long time."

"I see there's a good auction coming up at Parke-Bernet."

"French Empire," Dan said with a scornful sniff. "I refuse to put so much as a toe into the nineteenth century. I think you know my credo: that all beauty expired with the fall of the Bastille. That's why I admire you and Annabel. You're old regime."

"Not that old, I hope."

"I'm sure your family were Tories in the Revolution."

"On the contrary. We were at Valley Forge."

Beeky fully realized that in never discussing legal topics with him, Dan unconsciously implied that Beeky did not know enough about them. But he also realized that the circle of Dan's contempt formed a comfortably large province, and it amused him, in his own turn, to consider how uneasy Dan would have been with the denizens of his chosen century — with Horace Walpole, for example, or Madame du Deffand.

"I have a plan today, Dan, of a different kind of collection for you. Not a collection, of course, that would be a substitute for yours, but an embellishment. It would be a collection of men. Mortal men."

"You don't mean you've found a man of flesh and blood who's finer than one of *biscuit de Sèvres!*"

"Ah, no. Nor woman neither. But what I've found is a group that, put together, might convey a harmony even greater than the loveliest group ever conceived in Meissen."

"And what, pray, is this group?"

"Shepard, Putney and Cox."

Dan's eyes flashed. "You interest me, my dear Beeky. You interest me. What bizarre proposition do you have in mind?"

Beeky proceeded to outline his simple plan. Dan conveyed the intentness of his attention by never once looking at Beeky, by preserving the immobility of his countenance, by shifting the fork and spoon by his plate twenty times. But when he looked up at last, there was a fierce little gleam in his cold stare.

"I have waited a long time for someone to see this," he said grimly. "If anyone can save the present situation, it's you and I, Beeky. We'll pick up this little old firm and run with it. To the very top of the hill."

Beeky was taken aback by such instant acquiescence. He had expected at least a few minutes of dozing between his dream and its realization. "Well, I guess we don't have to start this afternoon."

"Ah, but we do! I'm not sure we shouldn't skip dessert. There are inequities that shouldn't go unredressed another day."

"Inequities? What inequities are so pressing?"

"The partners' percentages, to begin with. Do you think it's equitable that Hal Gavin should receive a larger share of the firm profits than I? Or Burrill Hume? Or Alex West? An accountant friend of mine described our partnership agreement as a mutual fund for the benefit of the retired and disabled."

"You mean you discussed our partnership agreement with an outside accountant?"

"Certainly."

Beeky dropped his eyes at such shamelessness. "I suppose you think my percentage is too large," he muttered. "No doubt it is."

"On the contrary. If anything, it's too small. You're the only partner with any real sense of how to hold a client. You hold 'em, Beeky, and I'll handle 'em. We'll be the team of teams!"

Beeky reflected that Dan might not be overestimating himself. He probably could handle every client of Beeky Ehninger's. He might have lacked charm, and masculinity in the ordinary American sense of the word, but he still gave the appearance of being able to cut through to the ultimate reality of business: to the lowest cost and the highest sale. Dan, without ever putting a hand to a golf club or telling a dirty joke, Dan, who used first names with obvious constraint and never loosened his tie on the hottest summer day, could dominate a conference table of corporate executives as a priest might dominate a posse of Mexican bandits. They shared a basic faith.

"I thought one of the luxuries of our affluence was that we could afford to pay a good income to a man like Hal Gavin," Beeky suggested. "You don't remember, but Hal used to be responsible for half our bond business. It's not his fault that he has Parkinson's disease. I think it's heroic the way he makes it into the office every day."

"He doesn't do anything when he gets there. I'm surprised, Beeky, that you should fall for a grandstand play like that."

Beeky stared with astonishment at the yellow irises of his now frankly sneering companion.

"Dan," he protested softly, "the man's dying."

"Oh, there's a new miracle drug. He's no more dying than you or I. Now don't look at me as if I were some kind of a fiend, Beeky. I have no objection to pensions. What I object to is the ladling out of seventy thousand dollars a year to an old man who's pretending to be still practicing law. The day I get Parkinson's disease will be the last day you'll see me downtown. I hope I'll have the dignity to submit my resignation and accept gracefully whatever remittance my partners elect to send me. I think I can promise you I won't make a spectacle of myself as the grand old man dying in harness — while he picks the pockets of his foolishly admiring audience."

Beeky was beginning to feel the effects of his cocktail. He

had broken his rule of never drinking before lunch because Dan always drank two martinis at noon.

"Well, I guess it will work out somehow," he responded bleakly, turning his attention to the chef's salad. It occurred to him that his tone was depressingly similar to Mrs. Bing's.

o

That afternoon Beeky had an appointment with Doctor Fellowes. The psychiatrist had been his friend and doctor for twenty years. At first, while Beeky had been in intense analysis, their relationship had been strictly professional, but after Beeky's marriage and the completion of his formal therapy, it had continued on a more relaxed and personal basis. Doctor Fellowes and his wife dined with the Ehningers two or three times a winter and visited them each summer in Northeast Harbor. Beeky was a trustee of Saint Bartholomew's Hospital, whose staff the doctor dominated, and Fellowes had his will in Beeky's vault. Occasionally Beeky was happy to pay fifty dollars for an hour of Fellowes' time to discuss the further emotional progress or deterioration of Beeky Ehninger. Fellowes, a large, bald, grinning man of splendid health and giant aptitudes, was inclined to treat these sessions as pleasant smokers. It was painfully evident to Beeky that he believed that all that could be done for his patient had already been done.

That afternoon, however, as soon as Beeky had disclosed his plan for the reorganization of his firm, he felt Fellowes' immediate interest. Beeky sat, not on a couch, but in an armchair faced away from the psychiatrist. Only thus could he resist the full thrust of the latter's personality.

"Am I getting this straight?" Fellowes demanded. "You want to *impose* this man Purdy on your partners? Didn't I meet him at your house last year? Very snotty and uptight?"

Beeky had forgotten this. "Yes, that was he. But he's brilliant, Alan."

"Since when did brilliance qualify anyone for an administrative position?"

"What would you suggest instead?"

"Humanity, man! Something that tall drink of water obviously knows nothing about."

"How can you say that about Dan Purdy?" Beeky was almost hoarse with exasperation. "Really, Alan, it seems to me that for a psychiatrist you allow yourself some very flip judgments. What can you possibly know about Purdy after seeing him once?"

"Quite a lot. But that's not the point. Your firm is big enough to survive a little rough management. The real point is you. What's this ego act on your part? Why do you suddenly have to prove to a hundred souls at One New Orange Plaza that you're a man? They know it, Beeky."

"Has it ever occurred to you, Alan, that you might be wrong?" Beeky was now actually shrill. "Just plain wrong? Ever since I first came to you, you've been thoroughly convinced that my every breath, my every gesture, was to convince the world that I had balls. You were against my marrying Annabel because you said she was my idea of what the world considered a hot female. That she was a sex symbol to me, pure and simple. And you decided that I was making a fool of myself because the world saw her as you saw her. You never paused to consider that I might love Annabel."

"Go ahead. Get it off your chest."

"And now you won't believe that in trying to save my firm from the internal discord that threatens its very life I am doing anything but brandishing my arms like a petty King Kong. You can't see that I might want to act, for once in my life. To cease being an heir, a caretaker. To give back a part of all

that's been given me. You can't see me, or any man for that
matter, as capable of a disinterested act."

"All acts may be interested. But some may be interested
and sound. They don't have to be interested and nutty."

"What about you? Why do you sit back at that desk and
play God except to show what big balls *you* have?"

"At least I'm getting fun out of it."

"Oh, go to hell."

o

Beeky's interview with Hubert Cox proved astonishingly
easy. The acting senior partner, who cared much more for his
tax practice than for the daily headaches of office administration, was a tall, gray, soft, smiling man of constant charm and
infinite reasonableness. He saw too many sides to every question, and his tolerance just escaped being weakness. But it did
escape it. Cox was afraid of nothing in the world, including
any experiment. In his laughter there was occasionally what
struck Beeky as a Mephistophelean ring.

"We can consider this a formal meeting of the Governing
Committee," he said at once, right after Beeky had stated his
proposal. "Horace is in Washington, and two out of the three
members have power to call an emergency session. We also
have power to appoint a fourth member, subject to ratification
at a regular firm meeting. Therefore you and I can appoint
Dan Purdy to the committee as of now."

"But what do you *think* of it?"

"I'm aware that *you*'ve been thinking of it. Miss Vann and
Mrs. Bing, you know, are office buddies. And I'm perfectly
willing to admit that Dan is entitled to a shot at firm management. The move will be unpopular, but I think it had better
be tried. If only to convince you and Dan that it won't work."

"You think it won't?"

"*I* think it won't," replied the always exasperating Hubert. "But then I've learned I'm not always right. I've served under some strange leaders in my time. Don't forget I was with Patton in Africa. You never can be sure how much the mob will swallow."

Beeky felt his little plan drying up under the bleak sun of his partner's impartiality.

"You make me feel a bit of an ass."

"Not so, my dear fellow, not so. The whole pimple has been coming to a head. You may have picked just the right needle."

For the next week Beeky said little about the office and kept his ears open. Mrs. Bing reported to him the reactions of the clerks and staff. They were uniformly unfavorable and uniformly unsurprised. That Dan Purdy should take a seat on the Governing Committee seemed inevitable to most. That he should be backed by Mr. Ehninger, who was generally popular, was grasped at by an optimistic few as evidence that he might not be as bad as he seemed. Dan himself was totally occupied with a registration statement, and Beeky began to wonder if the inertia that had always seemed to invade the mental joints of each new member of the Governing Committee might not have already marked out even Dan Purdy for its victim. But he soon found it had not.

When he arrived in his office one morning and discovered that Mrs. Bing had placed his mail on the side of his desk so that nothing should distract his attention from the particular memorandum that she had placed in the center of his uncluttered blotter, he knew that he was in for trouble. Something in his secretary's arrangement of the document, placed so its sides were precisely parallel with the sides of the blotter, seemed to cry out: "I told you so!" He glanced about for her. She was not there, but he felt sure that she was lurking.

He picked up the memorandum. "To all partners, from Mr.

Purdy: Proposed changes in the partnership agreement." Yet it had not even been sealed in an envelope. It was unabashed, naked, visible to the mocking eye of every office boy.

And it was far worse than Beeky could have imagined. He sank into his chair as he read on. An immediate firm meeting was summoned to adopt (not even to consider!) the following resolutions:

1) That Messrs. Gavin, Hume and West be forthwith retired;

2) That Mr. Purdy's two principal assistants, Messrs. Prentice and Finley, be forthwith made partners;

3) That an accounting system be promptly devised whereby credit for every dollar of the firm's gross income be attributed to the particular partner or partners deemed responsible for earning it;

4) That the partners' percentages of the firm's net profits be revised annually to accord with this new credit system.

Beeky, crumpling the memorandum angrily in his fist, hurried down the corridor to Hubert Cox's office. He found the senior partner reading it. And he was actually smiling!

"Is it out then?" Beeky gasped.

"Didn't you get your copy?"

"I thought it might have been submitted for approval of the Governing Committee."

"Oh, no. It's been placed on every partner's desk. Including the unhappy three whose heads are so summarily demanded."

"I can't believe it. You mean he issues fiats like this without consulting his committee members?"

"Fiats? Let's be accurate, Beeky. This is a proposal."

"But the man must be mad!" Beeky cried, stamping his foot. "Here I am, stuffing the administration of the firm into his greedy jaws, and he can't even wait till I get my fingers out before he starts chewing."

"It is wonderful, I admit."

"It beats everything! It's not enough for him to be the big frog of the puddle. He has to rub our noses in the mud."

"Maybe that's the point of being the big frog."

"And I'm dining with him tonight." Beeky slapped his forehead in despair. "What a prospect!"

"That should give you the perfect opportunity for a cozy little chat. Because, let me tell you something, Beeky." Hubert's face became suddenly grave, although his eyes still smiled. "You got us into this. I'm going to count on you to get us out."

○

The dinner party, in Dan's apartment, consisted of six: the Purdys, the Ehningers, and the Prentices. Ned Prentice was one of Dan's apostles. He was a big, beefy, handsome blond man, without a trace of humor or mental lightness, and his wife Doris, very pretty, was also blond, but dry, ambitious, midget-souled. She was impressed by Annabel, and scared of her.

Annabel always enjoyed her success with the office juniors, although she admitted once that she felt like a toreador in a dairy farm. It had never seemed more so to Beeky than that night, as she sat between the innocent Ann Purdy and the naive Doris, large and chuckling, placing her empty glass on her round golden pate as the constant signal to her solicitous host that it needed replenishment. Annabel had always insisted that Dan Purdy was a "pushover." "He's terrified of women," she had theorized to Beeky, "but as soon as one of them pays him the least attention, he gets wildly excited. If he thinks she's seriously trying to seduce him, he may panic. But if he suspects it's only a game . . . well, that's just heaven! With me he's pretty sure it's only a game. After all, I could be his mother. But he's not absolutely sure . . . not quite. He can be safe and still dream of cuckolding Beeky Ehninger."

"What would you do if he made a pass at you?" Beeky had inquired.

"Sing my Nunc Dimittis!"

That night she was particularly noisy, and Dan seemed to be trying to match her boisterous mood. They even made a bit of fun together of Ned and Doris Prentice, both of whom were very ill at ease.

"I heard all about your coup d'état, Dan," Annabel said, raising her glass in a toast. "I drink to Purdy, Cox and Ehninger. A great triumvirate! Of course, Purdy must be Caesar." She giggled and shot a wicked glance at Beeky. "Caesar has crossed the Rubicon and is marching on Rome! When will the ravishing begin?"

"The ravishing, Annabel?" Dan inquired with a leer. "What does the ravishing Mrs. Ehninger need to know about that participle?"

Annabel squealed with delight. "Why, Caesar is actually gallant! But now that we have a leader, we cannot expect that to last. We girls must shiver in our slips. When our husbands are shipped off to fight the barbarians, we may look to a nocturnal summons to the palace. Ours not to reason why! Our consolation must be that Caesar's bed bears no disgrace. Even our husbands, averting their eyes, will calculate the profits in obliging Caesar."

Dan hurried to refill Annabel's glass. "The ladies need have no fear," he said with a chuckle. "Only superannuated consuls who have been feeding in the public coffers need apprehend Caesar's wrath."

"I don't know if I quite like that, do you, Doris?" Annabel protested. "Caesar had better not neglect matrons who seek a little maltreatment." She winked at Ann Purdy. "Saving your reverence, Calpurnia."

"My name's not Calpurnia, Mrs. Ehninger," Ann Purdy murmured in bewilderment.

"Really, Mrs. Ehninger, I don't know what you're talking about," Doris Prentice protested, blushing uncomfortably. "I'm sure I have no need of anyone but my husband."

"Oh, blessed virtue!" cried Annabel. "You make me feel like some shabby old Neronian tart who has survived into the reign of Marcus Aurelius. Handsome Ned Prentice, tell me I am not universally despised. Tell me you do not share all the severe principles of your admirable spouse!"

"When Caesar and Consul Beeky are away in Gallia," Ned ventured now, with heavy playfulness, "Consul Prentice may come to call."

Annabel clapped her hands in triumph. Beeky could stand it no longer. He knew that under his wife's showy bravura there were deep resentments: resentment of his own higher ideals, resentment of his passion for his law firm, resentment — oh, yes, most of all — of the patient good manners with which he charitably faced the long disillusionment of their ridiculous marriage. If she had thought him a callow fool for placing her originally on a pedestal, she still preferred the fool to the man she had educated. And yet he loved her. That was the dim candle in the darkness for both of them.

He went over to where Dan was standing by the bar table so that they could talk without being heard by the others.

"You might have shown me that memo before you circulated it," he said in a tight voice.

"Was there anything wrong with it?" Dan demanded, instantly aggressive. "Isn't it what I told you that day at lunch I meant to do?"

"Perhaps. But you should still have cleared it with Hubert

and me first. We might have devised a way of presenting it to the firm that would have spared some peoples' feelings."

"You mean Gavin, Hume and West? You can't get rid of freeloaders by subtlety. You've got to hit and hit hard."

"You still shouldn't have acted alone."

"We must agree to disagree about that."

"Very well. But let me make it perfectly clear that I have no intention of playing Lepidus to your Caesar."

"We're certainly very Roman tonight. I think, Beeky, you had better talk this whole thing over with Annabel. She has a wonderful comprehension of the ways of the world. She sees things you and I could never see."

Going home in the taxi Beeky was grimly silent, and Annabel was wise enough to leave him alone. She always recognized the rare moods in which something besides herself totally pre-empted his thoughts. She could cope with any defense that he set up against her, but she was powerless at those times when he had forgotten that she was the rival. Beeky, knowing this, had even learned on occasion to simulate the mood that she recognized as having nothing to do with herself. But that night this was not necessary.

Yet he was not unconscious of her. He knew that he had to be fair. Oh yes, even at the worst he had to be fair to Annabel. What, after all, was his firm to her but the thing men did downtown? In her great days that had not been the thing about men that had interested her. And he had to be fair, too, to Dan. What was the firm to Dan but a means of filling his pocketbook? His heart lay elsewhere, in his cabinets of Meissen or possibly even in the asylum where his idiot son spun out his useless days. What did Dan care about the free association of a group of civilized men dedicated to the practice of a noble profession and supported by the daily interchange of their ideas and philosophies? And by their devotion, too, their devotion to each other! Yes, why not? Why shrink from the word? There was money to be made, of course, but only incidentally. Oh, how Annabel would laugh at that. Well, let her laugh!

The next day, at the partners' lunch, Beeky requested Hubert Cox's permission to lay the matter of Dan's office memorandum before the firm. Dan sat at the far end of the table, aloof, silent, yet betraying by his very thunderous solitude how tensely he awaited the outcome of the discussion. Discussion, however, was just what Beeky had decided there would not be. Without any expression he read aloud the memorandum. Then, after a grave pause, in a voice that just hinted the suppression of tears, he continued:

"Mr. Purdy's appointment to the Governing Committee was at my suggestion and motion. I thought we needed a centralizing force in the management of our affairs. But I now see what others all along have seen: that one may pay too dearly for efficiency. I think I speak for all but one of us when I say that I want my partners to be my friends and not simply money machines. Gentlemen, I move that Mr. Purdy's suggestions be rejected *in toto*."

Dan Purdy rose without a word and left the room. The motion was passed unanimously, without discussion, and Beeky excused himself. In the corridor he found Dan waiting for him, like a warning ghost.

"It's only because of Annabel that I'm really sorry for what's happened, Beeky. Please tell her that I shall always regard her as a friend. It would have been the same with you, had you not been taken in by Hubert Cox and his gang. Poor Beeky. You'll never know who your real friends are. You're too desperately anxious to be on the right side."

Beeky simply stared at him without saying a word, and Dan strode off.

A week later Mrs. Bing came into Beeky's office to tell him that Mr. Cox had summoned a special meeting of the partners in the main conference room. Almost all were there by the time Beeky arrived. When the door was closing, Hubert Cox, after flashing on the group his small, wavering, sarcastic smile, made this announcement:

"Gentlemen, I have just been informed of the resignation from the firm of Dan Purdy. As of next Monday morning he will become a member of Donavan, Pettingill. Messrs. Finley and Prentice leave with him to become associates in the same firm. It is anticipated that Dan will take with him Hudson River Trust, Almorex, the Andrews Siding Company and Ossining Glass. Others may go, too. I am appointing a committee consisting of Messrs. Ehninger, Hodgson and Dulaney to see what action must be taken to prevent further defection of clients."

There was a burst of voices, and for several minutes nothing could be heard but an outraged babble. At last Cox's voice again prevailed:

"Gentlemen! I have one further observation to make. There was a time when we were a partnership of gentlemen — in the best sense of the word. Some time back — I don't know just when — we ceased to be that. The operation that we have just undergone has been a drastic one. We may not survive it, but if we do — and I for one think we shall — the practice of law at One New Orange Plaza may once again be a pleasure."

The applause that followed brought the tears at last to Beeky's eyes.

o

In the weeks that followed Beeky called on every friend and relative that he knew who had any connection with the defecting clients and related the story of what had happened. All his professional life he had been told that his position in the New York social and business worlds was close to the centers of power, but he had never before tried to tap that power. He now found himself as impotent as a file clerk. Everyone listened sympathetically, for Beeky was widely respected, but when it came to taking the smallest action, the answer was invariably no. It startled Beeky that none of these men even bothered to be evasive. Most candid of all was Hugh Wrickam, a second cousin and Harvard roommate of Beeky's, who owned a near controlling interest in Hudson River Trust. Hugh had the exaggerated admiration of "toughness" characteristic of many descendants of nineteenth-century tycoons.

"But did Purdy do anything actually wrong?" he asked. "Anything against your canons of ethics, I mean?"

"No. But I don't know what he may have told the clients about us. That's why I feel it's advisable to get *our* version of what happened on the record."

"I see. And I admit there's been some variation in the versions."

"Then don't you have to accept mine? This is me, Beeky, telling you, Hugh. Do you think I'd tell you a lie?"

"No, of course not. But these inside matters are like family affairs, very emotional and ticklish. It's better for outsiders not to get involved."

"You want a man like Purdy representing Hudson River Trust?"

"Why not, if he's competent? What's it to me if he's hard as nails? Look, Beeky, take a tip. Drop this thing. There's not a man downtown who isn't going to say: 'Well, I guess Purdy pulled a fast one on Shepard, Putney and Cox. He must be a pretty smart cooky to have got away with it.' Now, I ask you, Beeky. When a man's in a jam and is looking for a tough lawyer, is he going to the smart cooky who walked off with half the firm's business or to the firm that let him do it? Every time you complain, people are going to say you're on the skids. If I were you, I'd tell everyone you kicked the bastard out. They won't believe you, but it'll still sound better."

Beeky rose. "Thank you, Hugh. I may do just that."

Leaving Hugh's office he took out the list of other relatives to be consulted and tore it up. Then he went to his appointment with Doctor Fellowes.

"Why did you ever tell me I could be something I wasn't?" he demanded as he faced away from the doctor toward the bare green wall. "You seemed to be saying, back there behind me: 'Ask and ye shall receive.' Yet all the while you must have known that Beeky Ehninger was never going to be anything but an heir. That the most he could hope for in life was to *look* like a lawyer, to *look* like a husband, to *look* like the partner in a downtown firm."

"You were the one who wanted to look like those things. I never suggested that you be anything or look like anything."

"Because you thought I couldn't succeed."

"I only wanted you to be yourself."

"And what was that, pray?"

"How can we ever know when you wouldn't even try?"

Beeky jumped up and turned around to face his friend. "You've given me up!" he cried. "A psychiatrist should never ask a question as terrible as that!"

"But we're friends too, Beeky. And it's not too late to face what you have become. You wanted pictures, and you got them. And all in all those pictures are not too unlike the things they represent. You have happy times with Annabel. And happy times with your firm. Don't ask for the moon."

"But it all breaks down at the first real tussle with anything that represents reality. With Dan Purdy, for example."

"Well, maybe that's true of most of us."

"Not of you! I'll bet you'd welcome Purdy on the board of Saint Bartholomew's. Alan, you're a fraud and a quack!"

As he grabbed his hat and coat in the waiting room, he could hear the doctor's rumbling laugh in the office from which he had fled. They both knew that he would be back.

II

The Love Death
of Ronny Simmonds

Ronny Simmonds had believed in many of the things that men of thirty believed in in 1971, but his experience had nullified his beliefs. He had been in Vietnam for three years as an army lieutenant, and he had witnessed atrocities on both sides that he could not bear to talk about. He had had his trips with LSD and heroin, and he had traveled alone in communist countries and had seen things that had made him understand why there were men who preferred even fascism to that gray death. He was, in brief, an old-young man whose heart was sick at human folly and who saw no answers. After his military service he had gone to Tokyo and lived in a monastery for three months where he had written a volume of bad poetry. Thereafter he had spent three weeks in Osaka with an airlines stewardess. Then he had come home.

In New York he lived alone in a tiny apartment and avoided, as much as he decently could, the noisy attentions of his large family directed at him from Greenwich, Connecticut. They wanted to see him married and settled in the suburbs. His father was a lawyer, and his five sisters were all married to lawyers or bankers. It was their general feeling that Ronny had better hurry and catch up with them and get over his "morbidity." They loved and admired him, but they wanted to love and admire him in the context of their group. They were delighted when Beeky Ehninger, a college friend of Ronny's father, gave him a job in Shepard, Putney & Cox. Although it was not one of the biggest law firms, it was quite as good as Ronny at thirty, six years out of Columbia Law, with middling grades and no experience, could expect. And after he should have become a partner, everything would be all right. But *would* he become a partner? Would he get over his don't-give-a-damn attitude? This was a frequent family topic on Saturday night cookouts.

It made it harder for the Simmondses that Ronny *looked* so much the part they wanted him to play in life. It was as if nature had conspired with them to point the direction in which their boy should go. He was a trifle short, but he more than made up for this with his broad shoulders and splendid muscular build. Anyone who had seen him at the beach could not but regret that such a figure should be cloaked in gray flannel, particularly as Ronny's face, however handsome, somehow just missed any vital or even notable individuality. It was a kind face, a patient face, even to many girls an attractively melancholy face, with its crown of long, smooth blond hair parted way over and combed to one side, and its grave, seemingly protesting blue eyes, but like Ronny himself it was a bit bland, a bit sullen. Ronny's strength lay in a kind of passive resistance to life. He might be immovable, but would he ever move?

Mrs. Simmonds and her daughters might have been encouraged had they known that Ronny was not really interested in anything but sex. Such normalcy in a young man might have been expected to end in a church or at least in one of those fashionable outdoor weddings with sandals and folksongs and Shakespeare sonnets. But any such encouragement would have been decidedly qualified had they learned at the same time the peculiar value that Ronny attached to the act of love. To him it was only good if perfect, and then a rare boon worth giving one's life for. He would have preferred the love death in *Tristan and Isolde* to the happiest lifetime of mere average coupling. This attitude would have struck the Simmondses as not only unmasculine, but actually decadent. Ronny knew this and never talked to them about it.

The law, anyway, took care of his days. After a few months in which he was assigned to general office work, Beeky Ehninger called him in to review the situation. Beeky had the reputation of being the partner most helpful to the younger men, and because of his friendship with Mr. Simmonds, his interest in Ronny was quasipaternal. He asked him to dinner rather more often than Ronny cared to go. It was not that he minded Beeky, but he detested his merry, older wife who was always inquiring, with leers and chuckles, about his sex life.

"You must pick a department," Beeky advised him. "Otherwise you end up getting sucked into an antitrust case and spending the rest of your days in the files of a corporate client looking for letters to prove it's been competing. One morning you'll come back to the office and find you haven't even got a desk. Which kind of law do you prefer?"

"Litigation?"

Beeky started moving things about on his desk as Ronny had noted he did when expounding favorite theories. "No, that's passé, all silly motions and endless appeals to get settlements. We have to have a litigation department because clients don't think we're really a law firm without one. But if we break even on it, we're doing well. What else?"

Ronny shrugged. "I don't really much care."

"You veterans are all disenchanted," Beeky retorted with a sigh. "I suppose we mustn't blame you. But so long as you're so neutral, what about taxes?"

"I'm no good at figures."

"You don't need to be. We have accountants for that side of it."

"But tax questions are so picky."

"Modern life is picky."

"Not as much as the Revenue Service!"

"You're behind the times, Ronny. Everything today is taxes. Common law, constitutional law, even criminal law. They're all soaked in tax questions. What better seat on the grandstand of life can I offer you than that of tax counsel?" Beeky rose to pace the room as he enthusiastically expounded his conception. "Public and private morality, where are they? Submerged in a sea of exemptions and depreciations, of write-offs and loopholes, of fabricated balance sheets and corporate hocus-pocus. What is hospitality but deductibility? What is travel but business expense? What is charity, charity that was greater than faith and hope, but the taxpayer's last stand? Who is the figure behind every great man, the individual who knows his ultimate secrets? A father confessor? Hell, no. The tax expert!"

Ronny was perfectly willing to be guided by Beeky Ehninger. After all, it was something to have a member of the firm take such an interest in him. So he reported to Mr. Coleman, the head of the tax department, who assigned him to his partner, Mrs. Stagg. That august lady barely smiled when she came into her office the next morning and found Ronny waiting for her, gazing out the window at the Statue of Liberty.

"I guess you won't find the answer to what constitutes a private foundation under the sixty-nine act out *there*, Mr. Simmonds" was her greeting, as she settled herself before the neat stack of her opened mail and picked up the top letter.

"I beg your pardon, Ma'am?"

"Didn't you get my memorandum? I put it on your desk last night at six."

"I'm afraid I left a bit early last night. I thought there wasn't much point starting my new work before the morning."

"Let us understand at the beginning, Mr. Simmonds, that I have no concern with when you arrive at the office or when you leave. I never interfere with an associate's time. So long as he gets his work done, he can quit at noon, for all I care. Have you read the nineteen sixty-nine act on private foundations?"

"Not yet."

"Start with that. Then read my memo. I should like some sort of answer, if possible, by tomorrow night."

This was his first interview with the only female partner of Shepard, Putney & Cox. In the months that followed he had many dozen more, but they were all of the same pattern. Mrs. Stagg did not appear to recognize that there was any activity conceivable in a law office beyond the practice of law. She had no jokes, no stories, no complaints, no smiles, no compliments, no reprimands. She was the driest human being Ronny had ever known. Even with clients her salutations were cut to a minimum that was almost grim.

Yet Ronny was reluctant to consign any female to the dread category of sexlessness. There was a persistent gallantry in him that made him see that Thelma Stagg might have actually been pretty as a young woman. He could imagine — for, after all, he was a poet manqué — that with blond hair and large, limpid eyes and that tranquil face dropping to a small dimpled chin, and with a thin, slim, trim body, she might once have appealed. But sometime, presumably with the defection of Mr. Stagg (the office rumor was that he had left her on the honeymoon), the juice had run out of her, so that now, although a well-preserved quinquagenarian, the blond-gray curls, the dry skin, the staring eyes, the sticklike figure, the brusque movements, all suggested a being totally desexed, or at least one deprived of those chemicals designed to attract a mate. Thelma was not a masculine woman, but she had the will (if not the physique) of an Amazon determined to subsist alone. Ronny doubted that she had the smallest interest in the liberation of her sex. She seemed, indeed, to see no function in the sexual organs beyond their power to create six-hundred-dollar tax deductions. But had she no value judgments? Had she no morals? Had she no heart?

A case came up at last that made him wonder if he would not be relieved to discover that his new boss was simply neutral in matters of morals. She asked him to review one of her estate plans whereby the rich husband of an incompetent was enabled to set up a trust in such a way as to throw the bulk of his estate taxes on his wife's children by a prior marriage, leaving the trust principal intact for his own.

"But the widow's property will all be gobbled up!"

"I don't know what you mean by 'gobbled up,' Mr. Simmonds."

"I mean that Mr. Pierson will have shoved the taxes that properly belong on his estate off on his wife's. His children will end up rich while hers are bust."

"It's an odd situation, certainly. I think I have handled it to the maximum advantage of my client."

Ronny stared. "But does Mr. Pierson *know* about his wife's will and the effect of this?"

Mrs. Stagg smiled thinly. "One thing you'd better learn right away, Mr. Simmonds, is never to ask what clients know. Mr. Pierson does not come to One New Orange Plaza for spiritual advice. He wants to look after his incapacitated wife with the minimum injury to *his* offspring. I think that is precisely what my plan will effect."

"You don't care that it does a hideous injustice?"

Oddly enough Mrs. Stagg did not seem to mind his intemperate language. "Is it illegal?"

"No."

"Is it unethical? By our professional canons?"

"I suppose not."

"Then I suggest, Mr. Simmonds, that it is my simple duty to accomplish what the client wishes accomplished. If a man chooses to leave his money to one person and not to another, is it my business to tell him he shouldn't?"

"Maybe not. But a paltry trick like this! To take advantage of a poor woman's incompetence to strip her children of their inheritance! How can you, Mrs. Stagg? I'm shocked!"

Her thin smile broadened a bit. "Well, I guess it's something to have shocked a veteran from Vietnam. We won't discuss it further. Leave the outline there."

She turned to her mail, but Ronny still stood there.

"Is that all?" he asked.

"What else should there be?"

"Do you care to have an associate working for you who thinks so poorly of your estate plan?"

"I don't care what any associate thinks of *me*, Mr. Simmonds. I am simply glad that you saw the point so promptly and that you agree with my analysis. Surely, there won't be many cases where you have to resort to conscientious objection. I suggest you forget this one."

So they continued to work together. She proved to be quite right about the rarity of moral issues. Most tax cases were simple dogfights between Uncle Sam and his reluctant taxpayers. There were moments when Ronny yearned to reject the whole structure, both sides of it, the auditors seeking to catch the little ferrets in their traps and the ferrets sniffing about for exits. It was the great American indoor sport in which, as Beeky had pointed out, all morality seemed to have foundered. But how could he reject it with any satisfaction while he was still such an amateur at it, while Thelma Stagg, of all people, could retort that *it* had rejected him? How could he face a gravel-voiced female who might point out, in a tone of tried and trained patience, that if it was an indoor sport, it was one that *he* seemed unable to master? He could hear that voice even in his sleep:

"No, Mr. Simmonds, you miss the point. I was quite aware that the donor could not hope to recapture the principal without the consent of the trustee who has an obvious adverse interest. The question I put to you was whether his power to amortize investment costs does not render the capital gains of the "A" fund taxable to him under the peculiar language of Article Eight. Now you may ask what difference it makes. It makes this difference . . ."

At times the jungle hell of Vietnam seemed preferable to a world where the legal abilities of such a female took precedence over everything. In the early morning, after his shower, standing before his full-length bathroom mirror, he would run his hands up and down his thighs and ask himself why any sound young man should be yoked to the plough of this monstrous priestess of taxes. Love, where was love in all this modern ritual of collection and avoidance?

o

One morning, when he came to Mrs. Stagg's office to report his progress on a joint returns question, he found her uncharacteristically inattentive. She had a funny fixed smile on her face, and she kept removing and replacing the lid of a small china jar full of paper clips. At last she interrupted him.

"Let me ask you a personal question, Mr. Simmonds. Would you care to come to a cocktail party I'm giving? You don't have to, you know. It's not for a client or anything official."

"Why, certainly, I'd be glad to."

"It'll be this Thursday at six in my apartment. Miss Glenn will send you a memo with the address."

"That won't be necessary."

"She will, anyway." She spoke as if she were afraid that he might get away. "I should tell you that the party's for my daughter. Her name is Mrs. Lambert. Pauline Lambert. She was married to a man called Oswald Lambert, but he deserted her."

It seemed odd for her to use a verb so emotionally charged. Her tone was as flat as ever. "Are they divorced?" Some comment seemed expected of him.

"Not yet. We haven't been able to make him agree to a proper settlement."

"Do they have any children?"

"No."

"I suppose that makes it easier."

"Easier!" Mrs. Stagg uttered a funny little snort. "Easy for my child to go through the hell of being shackled to such a hound!"

"I'm sorry. I only meant it would be easier not to have to fight out the issue of custody."

She closed her eyes and touched the lids gingerly with her fingertips. For a moment she sat absolutely still. Then she folded her hands on the desk and tried to smile at him. "Forgive me, Mr. Simmonds. Perhaps we'd better get on with our joint returns. I shall expect you, anyway, on Thursday."

Ronny went to Beeky Ehninger's office later in the morning to describe this remarkable scene.

"Oh, hadn't you heard about the daughter?" Beeky asked. "But she's Thelma Stagg's whole life!"

"I thought taxes were Mrs. Stagg's whole life."

"Oh, taxes are only to support Pauline."

"But she never mentioned her before. She doesn't even have a picture of her in her office."

"That's because Pauline forbade it. There used to be a dozen of them, but Pauline said they made the place look like a firemen's locker room."

"What did Pauline know about firemen's locker rooms?"

"That's just it," Beeky cried with his high laugh. "Everything!"

"Her mother implied that she was a poor injured creature, deserted by a hound."

"Of course, that's the way Thelma likes to see it. Because Thelma herself *was* deserted by a hound. She's had to work all her life to support the beautiful Pauline."

"Pauline is beautiful?"

"Wait till you see her, boy! But watch out. She's cold as a fish."

"What about the firemen?"

"Cold of heart, I mean. Not cold of body. Far from it, I'm afraid. Poor Lambert! He could hardly believe his ears when his mother-in-law demanded alimony. He came in to see me; he sat right there where you're sitting. He cried out with a little groan: 'Tell me, Mr. Ehninger. Doesn't Mrs. Stagg know what her daughter *is?*'"

Ronny began to find himself irritated. "And what is she?"

"A nymphomaniac."

"I've always thought that was a very silly term."

Beeky smiled. He was not the kind of partner who wanted

the juniors to pretend to an equality while subtly deferring to him. "What then do you call a girl like that?"

"I call her a girl who hasn't met the right man. And who's still looking."

"Does she have to look in every bed?"

"Where is she more apt to find love?"

"Are there no limits? I know your generation doesn't believe in the double standard, but would you carry it all the way? Would you say there was no difference between a promiscuous woman and a promiscuous man?"

"None whatever."

"And you wouldn't mind marrying such a girl?"

"If I were what she was looking for? Why, what more could a man possibly want?"

"Nothing, I guess," replied Beeky, as if with sudden, remembered humility. "Nothing at all. Maybe you and Thelma are the ones who are right about Pauline. Let's hope so, anyway."

o

Ronny, in a new blue suit with a scarlet tie, arrived at Thelma Stagg's promptly at six on Thursday. Only a handful of guests, mostly from the office, were already there. Pauline Lambert was notably absent, as her mother's constant glances toward the door plainly indicated. Thelma looked quaintly formal and rather lost, with her hair just done and an inappropriate orchid pined to a rather sad little pink dress. Everything in the room bespoke her overelaborate concern for her party: the profusion of tulips and azalea plants, the damask-covered table with heaped plates of hors d'oeuvres, the tiers of glasses, the trays of bottles of soda and tonic water, the white-coated bartender, the unneeded maid. Yet under its special gala Thelma's parlor was still as colorless and bleak as a hotel sitting room. She had turned it into a cocktail lounge for the beloved daughter who did not come.

Pauline arrived, probably designedly, just as she was being despaired of. She stood in the doorway and glanced about at the little group like the star of a play on her first entrance. Beeky had been quite right. She was very beautiful, very grave, pale and dazzlingly blond, with the large, serious, unblinking eyes of a 1920s flapper. Her expression was faintly quizzical, and she was chewing what appeared to be a long straw. She wore a pink silk shirt and mauve velvet pants.

The bartender handed her a bourbon mist, taking the cracked ice from a bowl that must have been prepared for her known preference. She did not even look at her excited mother, but simply bent her head so that Thelma could brush her forehead with the maternal lips. Then she went over to Ronny.

"You must be Simmonds. Mother said you're handsome, and you *are* handsome. She hasn't lost her eye."

"I never knew she even looked at me."

"Oh, she looks. But you're not quite what I expected. Most of the guys from her sweatshop have that how-am-I-doing look."

"How *am* I doing?"

"You mean, will you make partner?"

"What else can we slaves look forward to?"

She studied him. "I don't know. It's hard to tell. Are you kidding? Do you really not care?"

"I don't care."

"Then why in God's name do you work for Mother? Didn't you get a medal in Vietnam?"

"Oh, I was a real Boy Scout."

"Aren't Boy Scouts supposed to do good deeds?"

"One a day."

"Only in the daytime? What about taking the boss's daughter out to dinner?"

"That's the first assignment I've liked since I went into taxes."

For a moment she seemed to consider the implications of this, but her expression was inscrutable. "Well, what are we waiting for?"

"Now?" He was astonished. "But you just arrived. You're the guest of honor."

She glanced musingly around the room. "Mother never minds what I do."

"Well, *I* do, then."

"Why should you?"

"I can't be seen walking off with the guest of honor five minutes after she's appeared!"

"How long do I have to stay?"

"At least an hour."

She made a face. "Maybe you do want to be a partner, after all."

"Maybe I care about not hurting people's feelings," he retorted, irritated at last by her callousness. "Your mother's worked very hard on this party. She wants to give you a good time."

"Why, you lovable old thing!" she exclaimed with a burst of laughter. "Can't you see it's all catered? I didn't cost Mother much time from her sacred taxes."

Pauline moved off to talk to her mother's other guests. Ronny found it difficult to do anything but watch her, his imagination aflame with the luminous prospects of his evening. He glanced from this radiant creature to poor Thelma and wondered how there could be any blood connection between the two. He noted that Pauline drank bourbon as if it were Coca-Cola, yet when she came up to him, after the allotted hour, leading her mother, she did not show the least sign of intoxication.

"Mother, tell him it's all right if I go now."

"Oh, darling, of course it is. But remember, Ronny, she's getting over a cold. Don't keep her out too late!"

Ronny observed that Mrs. Stagg had used his Christian name. It was the first time. But before he could answer, Pauline had slipped her arm under his and guided him firmly to the door.

"Don't worry, Mother," she called back in her mocking tone. "He's a Boy Scout. Make him help you across the street tomorrow!"

At dinner she refused wine but continued steadily to sip bourbon, still without apparent effect. Not once during the meal, by so much as a flicker of the eye or a twitch of the shoulders, did she imply that there could be a question of sex between them. She was very articulate and just a bit banal. She was appropriately serious about Vietnam, about pollution, about corruption in high places, but her views were conventional. She showed a polite interest in his war career, his family, his ambitions, yet her interest seemed impersonal. After the last drink he almost decided that he had been wrong from the beginning. But when he took her back to her apartment, she brushed aside his proffered farewell.

"Oh, you're coming up, of course," she said as she reached in her handbag for the key.

o

He had never had an affair like it. Pauline refused to fit into any female category that he had ever heard about. She seemed totally devoid of sentiment. She made love with the naturalness of a long and favorite habit. She gave him the flattering feeling that he was a competent partner, but at the

same time that she expected no less of him. Her only artificial-
ity was her detestation of the least dirt or disorder. She was
antiseptically clean: in her body, her clothes, her apartment.
It was as if she dreaded the spots and odors traditionally associated with vice.

"Do you think you could love me if I had body odor?" he
asked one night when she emerged, after half an hour in the
shower.

"I don't think I could love you if *I* had body odor."

It was the nearest she had come to talking of love. She scrupulously avoided the subject, as she avoided terms of endear-
ment. Yet it was taken perfectly for granted that each of their
dates should end in bed. It struck Ronny that they were more
like two schoolboys than a man and a woman, more like two
adolescent males whose afternoon stroll in the woods has ended
in an unsentimental physical encounter. Yet the difference between the actual and suggested couples, ironically enough,
was more in him than in her. He was afraid that he was falling in love with her.

In the office, meanwhile, he felt under considerable constraint with Mrs. Stagg. It was not that he felt that he was
hoodwinking her. Only too obviously, he wasn't. Thelma was
so grovelingly the slave of a daughter who despised her that
there was a bit of the madame in her covert smiles and
charged morning greetings. Ronny even began to make out a
weird resemblance between mother and daughter. Just as
Pauline never praised or criticized his lovemaking, so Thelma
never praised or criticized his law work. Both took for granted
that he would do his job. There was, however, one new and
surprising development in Thelma's method of supervising
him. She had begun — without telling him — to edit his memoranda of law. Ronny was not pleased one morning in the file
room, when he happened to be glancing over one of these that

had received the praise of Mr. Cox himself, to discover that five pages had been added at the end to modify his conclusion to accord with a recent tax court case that he must have overlooked. When he showed this to Mrs. Stagg, she actually apologized.

"I knew you'd been very busy, Ronny, and I just happened to have seen that case. I should have spoken to you about it, but you were at the Law Institute the day Mr. Cox asked for the memo."

"Did you tell him I'd goofed?"

"Of course not. We keep those things to ourselves."

Ronny did not like this at all. Mrs. Stagg's loyalty had always been totally to her partners. If she was making an exception with him, it could only be for one reason. He began to feel kept.

Another odd feature of the affair, unlike any of his others, was that it expanded, rather than contracted, his social life. That Pauline disliked her mother's cocktail parties did not mean, he discovered, that she disliked other people's. She found Ronny a suitable escort into the worlds that particularly attracted her: the women's magazine realm of "beautiful people" and literary Bohemia. Ronny thought he had never seen adaptability such as hers. Among bearded poets she could use four-letter words with the same precision that she showed in talking haute couture to the editors of *Vogue*. She had an uncanny sense of the prevailing mood in any group and adopted it with the diplomacy of an anthropologist attending a tribal rite among the aborigines or an American expatriate speaking rigorously idiomatic French at a Paris cocktail party. Ronny suspected that fundamentally she believed in nothing. As her body sought cleanliness, so her mind seemed to seek form. But whereas most formalists tend to copy the manners of an age just past, Pauline was entirely contemporary. She could duplicate, like a clever stage designer, the very form of modern formlessness.

He did not like all the parties she took him to, but at least they kept her from talking about her mother. This was her favorite subject when they were alone. At times he wondered if it were not her only one.

"What do you suppose she does for sex?" she mused. "Or has she suppressed it? Still, it oozes out. Watch her when she's won a tax case. It's like an orgasm. She even gives little screams. I've heard her."

If he ventured to point out her indebtedness to Thelma, she turned on him in fury.

"How can you talk about what Mother's done for me? Can't you see she did it all for herself? Can't you see it was my function in her life to make up for my father's leaving her? Well, she's lucky. She's got me, and she's got her goddamn taxes. What have *I* got?"

"You've got me."

Pauline simply ignored this. "Never, from the beginning, did she give a damn what I wanted or what kind of person I really was. Her mind was always too full of the vision of what *she* wanted me to be. And what an ordinary vision it was! The dream of every shopgirl in the thirties. I had to be the prettiest debutante, the loveliest bride. I had to win the richest, handsomest husband . . . oh, Christ!"

"But millions of mothers have that dream. The only test is: how do they act when it fails? Does she ever reproach you?"

"But she won't admit it *has* failed. She's still at it."

"Well, she knows *I'm* not rich."

Pauline stared at him as if he had spoken suddenly in an unfamiliar tongue. "You don't know what she is," she muttered. "Let's talk of something else."

He began to wonder if, deep down, she were not afraid of

Thelma. Her mother, after all, was a woman of great will power. He even speculated that Pauline might be resisting her mother's image of her future by turning herself into the very opposite of the *True Romances* bride that Thelma had envisioned. And suppose, despite all the daughter's efforts, she were to see her mother still ineluctably pursuing her single goal, obliterating her daughter's defenses by her very refusal to acknowledge them, holding her tightly by a cord about the neck and tugging her relentlessly in the same old direction? Might the daughter not become hypnotized? Hysterical?

Ronny tried now to dominate her with his passion, to overcome her resentments. As a gallant of another era might have sought to arouse his beloved's feelings in order to possess her, so now did he practice with every skill he knew on Pauline's body in order to arouse some sentiment. But he never succeeded. Pauline, if insatiable, was unarousable. Indeed, as he grew more fervent, she became cooler. Love to her was a complication, an unnecessary factor in an affair.

"No. I can't," she told him abruptly one afternoon when he telephoned about the time of rendezvous at their accustomed restaurant.

"Oh? Why not?"

"Why not? What do you mean, why not? I have another engagement, that's why not."

"With a man?"

"Well, do I usually go out with girls?"

"Oh, Pauline!"

She ignored the shocked misery of his tone. "Don't fuss, Ronny. I'll go out with you tomorrow."

When he hung up, after basely accepting her proposition, he covered his face with his hands. Then he staggered into the washroom to stare at his own gaunt countenance. Was that the face of Ronny Simmonds, who had wanted to find so sim-

ple a thing as love? Was that the face of the lover who was already prepared to share his mistress with the world?

o

Thelma Stagg continued to be helpful, even officious.
Ronny had now been assigned part-time to other partners, in
accordance with the office policy against overspecialization,
but even so she insisted on continuing to correct his memoranda. She suggested tax articles for his home reading and
marked new cases in the advance sheets that he might have
missed. One day he marched into her office to object vigor-
ously to the signatures on a tax court brief that she had anony-
mously rewritten.

"It's printed under Mr. Littell's name and mine," he pointed
out aggressively. "Don't you want to add yours?"

"No, no, that's all right."

"But Mr. Littell will think it's all my work. You should get
the credit."

"I don't want the credit. I want my own people to do well,
that's all."

Ronny noted that she was nervous. Her eyes roamed from
side to side, and she never looked straight at him. "Pardon
me, Mrs. Stagg, but why am I one of your people?"

"You're in my department, aren't you?"

"For some of the time, yes."

"Well, if you're going to get anywhere in the firm, you're
going to have to do it through me. I'm only trying to help
you, Ronny."

"Help me to get where?"

"Well, to a partnership, of course." She stared with what
struck him as a combination of hostile curiosity and alarm.
"Don't you *want* to be a partner?"

Ronny became cooler as she became more excited. "I'm not

at all sure that I do. I'm not at all sure that I want to spend my life representing your kind of client."

"And what kind of client is that, pray?"

"Big companies that pollute the environment. Rich people who'd rather break their necks than pay their share of taxes."

Thelma's hostility dissolved now into frank bewilderment. "I don't know what's come over you young people. You've gone plumb crazy, so far as I can see."

Ronny said nothing. He did not see Mrs. Stagg again that week, except to pass and repass her silently in the office corridor. On Saturday, however, when Pauline drove with him up to Greenwich to spend the weekend with his family, she asked him what he had done to her mother.

"She's always singing your praises. But now she's suddenly stopped."

"Maybe she doesn't like what she knows about us."

"And what does she know about us? What do *you* know about us, for that matter?"

If Ronny was mystified by his girlfriend, his own mother was more so. Mrs. Simmonds was a small, neat, fashionable, fussing woman, always touching some part of herself with her fingertips, always smiling, always suspecting heresy in everyone. Of course, she had done her research on Pauline, and of course she had not liked what she had discovered. On the other hand, she was impressed by Pauline's coolness, by her beautiful clothes, by the names she artfully dropped. Ronny was amused to see that Pauline adapted herself as easily to Greenwich as to Greenwich Village. But when he whispered to her later that night that he would come to her room after his parents had gone to bed, she gave him a pale stare that made him wonder if her social poses were altogether poses. And, indeed, when he went there, he found her door locked.

"I suppose I must wait till we're married," he observed, with heavy sarcasm, when his mother and father had left the break-fast table the next morning.

"Are you thinking of asking me?"

Ronny put down his coffee cup. "Would you have me?"

"I might. If I thought you could support me."

He was as startled by her qualification as by the unexpected possibility of her assent. His heart began to jump about. "We'd get by. Mother and Dad would help out. Do you think your apartment would be big enough? For a year, any-way?"

"Oh, I don't mean that kind of a start. I've had that. I don't want to be a dependent younger-married again, having to smile at every old cat of a relative who opens a checkbook. No, I'd have to be settled. Secure."

"How romantic."

Pauline had one of her rare bursts of temper. "Look, buster, who brought this up? If you don't like my attitude, shut up about marriage, will you?"

"I'm sorry," he murmured in a dry whisper. "If you'd only give me time, I might be able to provide the things you need."

"What do you need time for? Just play your cards right, and you've got it made."

He gaped. "What made?"

"A partnership, you dope! Mother says it's in the cards."

At that moment Ronny's mother came back into the room to discuss Sunday, and the subject had to be changed. Neither of them felt inclined to bring it up again that day, even on the drive back to the city, nor did either suggest that they go up to Pauline's apartment. The very speed with which she slipped out of the car seemed to concede that a serious breach had occurred. Ronny, distraught, could think of no one to help him but Beeky Ehninger, and he called him on the telephone from a booth near his garage. Beeky told him that Annabel had gone to bed, but that they could talk in the library if they were quiet. There, fifteen minutes later, a white-faced Ronny poured forth his tale.

"It fits, it fits," Beeky murmured, shaking his head. "I hate to tell you, but it fits."

"Fits what?"

"It fits what Thelma's been doing. Pushing everybody like fury to have you taken into the firm by Christmas. Frankly, Ronny, most of us think you're a fine fellow and a good lawyer, but not yet ready for it."

"Not only not ready!" Ronny cried, appalled. "I don't even know that I'm willing!"

Beeky got up, ostensibly to put more whiskey in his drink, but probably to avoid his visitor's eyes as he put his next question. "Do you really want to marry this girl?"

"I don't *know!* I don't know if she wants to marry me. I have the funniest feeling that she only wants me to be a partner in your firm. But why, in the name of God?"

Beeky paced up and down with his refilled glass before he spoke. "Forgive me, Ronny, but I've got to save you from those women. Hate me if you will, but listen to me."

"Hate you? Why should I hate you? Haven't I come here tonight to listen to you?"

"Very well. Here it is. Thelma's motive is simple enough. She wants a good-looking, respectable boy for her daughter. She can never get over the idea that Pauline, with the right fellow, will settle down in a cozy suburb and turn her into a purring grandmother. Now she's decided that you're the good-looking, respectable boy, and she'll break her neck — or yours, if necessary — to qualify you for the job. But Pauline is a far more complicated creature. Pauline's always had an obsessive hatred for her mother's law firm. We're the symbol of the debt she owes Thelma. A debt she passionately repudiates. All her life she's heard how her mother's slaved for her, and she's sick to death of it. Imagine the satisfaction of being able to show that Venus is the real source of a partnership in Mummie's sacred firm! And that little Pauline, swinging her hips, has more to say about that than Mummie swinging all her briefs!"

Ronny's eyes narrowed as he watched Beeky pace up and down. He felt oddly detached from his own story. It was all suddenly too queer to be felt. "And that's all she cared about?"

"Oh, I don't say that, my friend. I'm sure you were a great lover."

Ronny uttered a dry little sob. It was not to be expected that Pauline would come out of his heart without a rip. Yet as he sat there, feeling his hot sweaty palms against his eyelids, he became conscious of a faint surprise that the operation should not hurt more. He was depleted.

"What do I do now, Beeky?"

"Get out of the firm. Get out of the law business. You don't want to be a partner. You don't like the clients. What the hell do you think you're doing in One New Orange Plaza?"

"I guess I was looking for a girl."

"Well, if you came to Shepard, Putney and Cox to look for a girl, all I can say is you got the one you deserved."

Ronny's lips parted as if he were going to give into a wild laugh, but no laugh came. He got up and walked to the window to look out at the night.

"Don't worry, I'm not going to jump." He had felt Beeky's grip on his shoulder.

"I thought it would be better if I let you have it all at once. What you need now is to work for something you can't possibly *not* believe in."

"And what could that be?"

"Oh, good heavens, there are all kinds of things. Legal aid. Foundation work. I have plenty of contacts. But go home and go to bed. We can talk about it in the morning."

"How can I thank you?" Ronny saw now that he had only begun to plumb the depths of the older man's kindness. "But tell me one more thing. If I *had* been made a partner, do you think Pauline would have married me?"

"Does it matter whom Pauline marries? Or how many times?"

Ronny went silently into the hall. Beeky was kind enough not to bid him good night.

III

The Peacemakers

THE FACT that Horace Putney was perfectly aware that his case was a normal one did not make it any easier for him to bear. As he sat in his swivel chair gazing out at the incomparable view of New York Harbor from two sides of his splendid corner office, as he ran a chubby finger down the middle of his bald head and blinked his small, curious eyes, as he shrugged his round shoulders under Paisley's finest tweed and raised a claret-colored shoe for a quite unnecessary shine, he felt all through his plump, taut, washed body the ache and throb of his ennui. He knew that he would grasp at anything to postpone a return to those bond-closing papers that he had promised to review for Hubert Cox. Oh, yes, Hubert was only too right about him! He had been bitten by the federal bug and was good for nothing.

His fatal whiff of power had come under LBJ. Horace had been an assistant secretary of state. Except for the too rigorously smiling, too starchedly posed portrait-photograph of Ginevra, all the pictures in his long, bare, Japanese office directly suggested those years. On the wall was the President himself, brow-puckered and serious; on the table below a grinning McNamara descended from a B–52; between the windows Dean Rusk chatted with the inscrutable Hirohito. How was it possible for a man who had known such colleagues to come back down to the earth of bond closings? Particularly now, when his mind was just beginning to profit from the visions conceived in office, now, when he was beginning at last, recollecting violence in tranquillity, to grope his way toward a feasible scheme for world peace?

The shoeshine boy departed, and Horace turned to the Dictaphone for his speech to the Foreign Policy Association.

"Everyone agrees that universal concord must await the decline of nationalism. Yet no one believes that this decline is yet in sight. New nations proliferate; new prides and new hates are born. And yet, peculiarly enough, as Arthur Hugh Clough put it in the poem so beloved by Churchill, if you look west, not east, at sunrise, you will be struck by the brightening land. Look west now at America and see the happy rot of nationalism already started!"

He paused to glance at the portrait-photograph of Ginevra. "What's wrong with patriotism?" she seemed to be demanding, in that sharp, cawing, mock-dominating tone that she and all her family considered such clear proof of good breeding. "Isn't America good enough for you, Horace Putney?" Had *he* been the grandchild of a Vermont governor, the child of a Vermont senator? Oh, no, quite the contrary, he had been a poor boy from Bridgeport, who had got through Yale in a laundry and Harvard Law as a night stenographer, who had had to fight his way up the mountain of small print, line by line, to legal eminence, and then, through the rain clouds of a mere vulgar success, to the brief sunshine of federal power. And should such a one not bless the system that had made his rise possible? Ginevra could never see that patriotism might be something beyond a wild blue yonder, something beyond turgid phrases mouthed in a small-town graveyard on Memorial Day, something beyond a flag rippled by an artificial wind while an organ blasted. It was appalling the way Ginevra, intellectual and social snob though she was, still reveled in the hot-doggery of her Yankee pride whenever, as she jeeringly put it, he played "Dean Acheson." Dashing the image from his mind, he continued now, fussed, upset:

"Never before in modern history has so large a portion of the population of a great and powerful nation been so actively unpatriotic. It is not uncommon, even in affluent, educated groups, to find American citizens who refuse with impunity to drink to the health of their President or to join in singing the National Anthem or even to salute the flag. Enemy banners are paraded in our streets to cheering onlookers. Writers, athletes, movie stars sneer at our principles as the rankest hypocrisy. And because so many Americans brand their nation as corrupt, bellicose and decadent, all the world takes for granted that it must be so. For no Asian or European, still caught in the toils of patriotism, can believe that good citizens would say such things of their own country unless they were demonstrably true. And thus the real truth is lost sight of, the wonderful, terrible yet perhaps redeeming truth, that the movement which may save civilization has already been born — and, of all places — in the despised United States!"

He stopped to glare at the ringing telephone. What a vile little glittering piece of metal it was, to bring the cling and clang of clients' squabbling closings into his garden of thought. How was a man expected to prepare a speech if he was never let alone? Then he remembered that he had told Mrs. Murdock that he would take no calls. It had to be Ginevra.

"Yes, dear?"

"That couple from Chid or Chod can't come tonight."

"Chad."

"Well, I can't keep these new African nations straight. Anyway, it's not worth it. They're bound to gobble each other up. I'll wait till the next round and then learn. But

Cyril and Vanessa Norton happen to be free tonight. It's a rare chance. As long as you insist on cluttering the house with United Nations representatives, we might as well have the fun ones. Shall I ask them?"

"I wanted to feature the Indians tonight. The Vehtis. You know how chip-on-the-shoulder they are with the British. And Cyril is so old world, so conscientiously liberal, so condescending. No, no, it won't do."

"But I've seen Cyril with the Vehtis. They get on perfectly well."

"Oh, they get on. They have to. But the point is, I want the Vehtis to be at their best tonight."

"So they can bore us with their old lecture about how Americans have no spiritual values?"

"Now, Jenny."

"I loathe Indians!"

Horace visualized the big, green-yellow eyes flashing, the long, thin nose snorting. Ginevra, with her gray, tumultuous hair, would have the look of a ruffled hawk. Hawks were for bold flights, for soaring, for grandeur. But they were also, apparently, for screeches and messy nests.

"It's a question of understanding them," he suggested mildly.

"Oh, I understand them all right. It doesn't take genius to understand their smugness and fatuity. Or their yackety-yack."

"Jenny, we have to talk to them. We have to talk to all the nations. We have to keep talking and talking. Forever, if necessary. It's the only way, in an atomic era, for there to *be* a forever."

"And that's what dinner parties are for?"

"It's one of their roles. A small one, perhaps."

"Well, I don't get it. You talk about talk, but you don't give a damn about *good* talk. Cyril Norton is the best conversationalist in New York. As for the hot air that emanates from your UN parties, I'd rather face the hydrogen bomb."

"You take a very short view."

"As a good hostess should."

"Do this for me tonight, darling, and I'll go along with you at our next party. We might make a pact. One for one. One dinner party for peace, one for society."

"Society? Is that what you think of my friends? How contemptuous can a man be? And how thick? Honestly, Horace, at times I'm embarrassed for you. I cultivate the people who count. How can you think that just because a party's dull, it's going to promote world peace? And your UN *is* dull. Nobody pays any attention to it anymore. If you want to do anything for peace, you've got to go to Washington. I know what I'm talking about! I learned some things in Washington that you refused to learn. You talk about your diplomats. Do you know what Cyril Norton said? He said that Harry Hopkins, in the old days, accomplished more at a poker table than Cordell Hull at a world peace conference."

"I'm not trying to be a diplomat. I'm simply trying to get a few facts across to a few people who might be able to act on them."

"Oh, bull."

"Very well, Jenny, if that's the way you want it. *Ask* the Nortons."

"Oh, God, I'll give up the Nortons."

"Now that's hardly reasonable. I'm being perfectly fair when I . . ."

"All right, all right. No Nortons. But it'll be the dreariest party of the season. The things I do for world peace!"

The telephone seemed to tingle with the shock of her hanging up. Horace swept the bond-closing papers to one side and buried his face in his hands. Could any rational mind deny that he had married the most aggravating woman in the world? From the very beginning she had tried to boss him. During the war, when her father, a reserve admiral, had refused to release his aide, Lieutenant Putney, for combat duty, even at the latter's desperate urging, Ginevra had spread it all over Washington that Horace would be sent to sea if he didn't take her out. And when this had got back to him, and he had told her that he would gladly prefer an atoll to her tyranny, of course, like all bullies, she had collapsed. But even in collapse she had succeeded in making her point. The stricken, sob-torn, writhing body of that big, noisy, nagging girl had gained her a husband.

Oh, yes, he still loved her. It was odd, but he did. And she still loved him, in her bossy, possessive way. But what good was love to a man who had great things to do? After the war, when he and Hubert Cox had reorganized the old firm of Shepard & Howland, had she not objected wildly to his leaving government? Had she not made disgusting scenes? What did she care for money, she had cried, or for security? Had not her family always managed to live off politics? Indeed they had. They had been like misers running the big coins of influence and patronage through their greasy fingers, listening greedily to the chink and clink of authority. What was the vision of world peace to Ginevra but a gold medal to be pinned on her husband's lapel? And just because, more recently in Washington, she had made a social hit in administrative circles, just because her wit had amused the President, she now felt entitled to run everything!

How could he win? Even when he didn't allow her to rule, even when he kept her under control, he was still riled about it, always in a snit. Where in this was the clear, lofty vision of the lawyer, the statesman? And where was either the lawyer *or* the statesman if all he could think about, in the middle of a business day, was how aggravating his wife was? Would a great man be obsessed with such trivia? Could one imagine Gladstone thinking of his wife as he composed a speech, or even Disraeli of Mary Ann?

He jumped, with a start of alarm, when the telephone rang again. Ginevra's voice was now enthusiastic, even triumphant.

"I've just had a brainstorm!"

"Oh?"

"You know the twenty-five thousand I inherited from Aunt Julia, back in sixty-three?"

"What about it?"

"Well, I put it aside, as you told me. I haven't even spent the income. It must be up to almost forty by now. Let's give it to the Republican National Committee. Then they can make you an ambassador!"

Horace closed his eyes in exasperation. "Jenny, you know we don't have that kind of money. We've been over this again and again. Marie's and Isabel's children will be going to school. We've got to be ready to help out."

"I don't see why. We brought Marie and Isabel up. We put them through school and college, gave them coming-out parties and wedding receptions. Their husbands can look after them now. Why should we bring up two generations?"

"Because taxes are so high. Besides, there's your old age and mine to worry about . . ."

"I don't care about my old age! I don't want to scrimp all my life so our savings can be blown on some fancy nursing home when I'm a vegetable, the way your mother was! And I don't care if my grandchildren go to snobbish private schools. *You* didn't. Just give me five good years, and you and I can go right to the top!"

"The top?"

"Well, the State Department, the Defense Department, some special peace unit — I don't care how you put it. After we've done that, who gives a damn? The girls can stuff us into a state institution."

"Jenny, even if we had the money, and all this were possible, there's still the firm and my obligation to it. I've been away three years. I can't possibly leave now . . ."

"Oh, the firm, the sacred firm," she interrupted angrily. "Once you're off on that, I know I've had it." And once again she hung up.

Horace could sit no longer. He had to pace his office. Really, he had married a prime idiot. For all her vaunted common sense, she totally failed to comprehend her own motives. She could never understand — or perhaps never face — the simple little fact that she had to be one up on her husband. It was not the United Nations or even his law firm that she found dull and tedious. It was him! Horace feverishly began to assemble the arguments that he could use to her.

"You talk about a woman's intuition and a woman's point of view!" he cried aloud, shaking his finger at her summoned image. "Is it anything but a child's? What is history to you but a swashbuckling romance? A *Three Musketeers?* When you think of a treaty, you hear the clink of champagne glasses and the tinkle of laughter of beautiful women. You see cardinals in corridors and horse guards on the street. The Congress of Vienna! You're nothing but a schoolgirl, Ginevra Putney. And a very foolish little schoolgirl at that."

When the telephone rang again he ran to grab it. But before he could deliver his stinging rebuke, she obliterated it with another terrible threat.

"I forgot to tell you, I *do* have a way to save this ghastly party tonight. With a marvelous new parlor game. Cyril Norton told me about it. Listen. You write down everybody's name on a card with six personal qualities after it, and . . ."

"Jenny, the Indians don't *like* parlor games."

"They don't know this one. Nobody knows this one."

"Jenny, please."

"Can't you trust me in anything?"

"Not in this. Promise me. No parlor games?"

"What you don't know won't hurt you."

"Jenny!"

For the third time that morning she hung up.

2

Ginevra Putney did not believe in spending money on incidentals. The apartment on Park Avenue was large, in the style of the older buildings, but it was sparsely furnished, with commodious, old-fashioned pieces and dull prints of landscapes and animals never meant to be looked at. Ginevra always said that an exquisite décor was not important to a good party. On the contrary, things that were too good sometimes put people off, awed them. What guests liked, she maintained, was to feel that their own homes were as good, if not better. So long as they were comfortable, with nice big bathrooms available for easing bladders, they were perfectly content. Even the food did not have to be memorable. Ginevra always insisted that a small minority of gourmets had terrorized the world, that most people hardly noticed the difference between the best and the second best, particularly after their cocktails. But those cocktails had to be plentiful. Also the wine. Ginevra kept a little list of musts.

Mr. Vehti sat on her right and drank no wine. Nor did he switch his conversation to Mrs. Ehninger, as he should have, with the roast. He simply continued his dulcet, singsong murmur of the virtues of the East.

"We have seen the West rise, Mrs. Putney, and we may yet see it decline. We have a store of wisdom on which you Americans would do well to draw. Your husband is one of the few people who comprehend this. He told me once that your constitution was an exercise in self-restraint, a mental gymnastic not unlike the crossed legs and arms of the contemplative Buddha."

It sounded like Horace, all right. The world of words, sacred words. The world of concepts, cows even more sacred. In the early years how many nights had she not sat up with him, laboriously comparing the galleys against the typescript of his *Tax Aspects of Corporate Mergers?* An indelible lesson in the fantastic trivia of the male mind. Not a hint of passion, not a glance at life. Only a heap of little silver circles, elaborately intertwined. And as for his sacred constitution — one did not have to live more than two weeks in Washington to see what the powers that be thought of *that* revered parchment.

"Ah, ice cream. I love your American ice cream, Mrs. Putney. I hope you will forgive me if I observe that it is the one dish of your great nation where the role of ice is properly understood. I always marvel at your way of making iced coffee. You first boil it and then pour it on ice!"

"That is not American, Mr. Vehti. That is *cuisine. Cuisine* is international."

How could he know that when he knew nothing? He was as empty as a courtier in the memoirs of Saint-Simon that she had been reading. Now there was an honest world! No kidding oneself with eternal generalities. The King was it. That was that. So it had always been. The real decisions were always made in the same way by the same kind of men.

"I was distressed, Mrs. Putney, to see that we may lose Grand Central Station. Another great landmark gone! How sad that your fellow countrymen can never learn to respect the past. It should not be so difficult. They haven't that much of it."

Ah, now, he had gone too far!

"When I was young, Mr. Vehti, I was taught that East should be East, and West, West, and never the twain should meet. There was even an implication that if they ever did meet, the mysterious East might prevail. Well, they *have* met, and the mysterious East has gone up in smoke."

"Perhaps you will very kindly explain what you mean by this very curious statement?"

"Fly around the world, Mr. Vehti. Where are your temples, your pagodas, your ritual, your enchantment? Gone with the west wind, my friend. It's Newark, Newark, all the way, except when it's Hoboken."

"Mrs. Putney makes a very funny joke."

Oh, to hell with him. If she could only get Horace back, back where he belonged, in a good embassy, or higher, in State or Defense! *Then* all his learning, his words, his sacred concepts would grace him like a glistening robe. For she had nothing really against his imagination or his great ideas. He was all wrong about her not caring for such things. But one had to build a house, and build it well, before one decorated it with old tapestries and rare porcelains. She pictured Horace bowing gravely to a smiling queen at Buckingham. Not too grave, not vulgarly impressed, but the good-mannered Yankee with Yankee independence intact. And there he was again, chatting with the Pope at Castel Gandolfo, with such understanding, such vision and benevolent humor, the civilized agnostic. And now, still again, very serious, with puckered brow, dutiful, selfless, casting only a brief, preoccupied glance at the TV camera, hurrying into the Paris hotel for a secret talk with the North Vietnamese. And this was to be wasted?

"Ladies and gentlemen," she exclaimed, rising to her feet as she tapped her spoon to her glass. "We are going to experiment tonight with a new parlor game. I think it will amuse you. It is called 'Room Temperature.' After the gentlemen have joined us in the living room, you will each get a card on which are listed all the guests at this party. After each name there will be six columns under the headings: Dress, Deportment, Imagination, Wisdom, Looks and Sex Appeal." She paused here for the laugh that did not come. "You rate each person on a one to ten basis for each quality. You then rate yourself. The person whose rating of himself or herself comes closest to the room's averaged rating of him or her will be the winner."

In the astonished silence that followed and the immediate babble of questions, Ginevra, with a defiant little smile, faced her husband's countenance across the room. But he simply rose to lead the men into the library for cigars and liqueurs.

3

In the library, whose shelves were lined with all the statesmen's and generals' memoirs of the past two decades, still in their dust jackets, looking untouched, unread, yet all actually read by their unsoiling owner, Horace joined Beeky Ehninger, taking a recess from his touchy guests. Wine had mellowed his mood.

"What's this game of Jenny's? It doesn't sound exactly diplomatic."

"Experience, Beeky, has taught me to leave my wife to her own devices. I saw her once in Warsaw electrify the dismalest dinner party you can imagine by teaching everybody the twist. Do you remember the twist? Nobody does anymore, yet it changed our era."

"Oh, yes. Annabel was an early fan."

Horace firmly rejected the image of Annabel twisting. "Everyone at that party took a lesson from Ginevra. Even the wife of the Afghanistan minister, a great dark creature who spoke no known tongue. Afterward, her husband confided to me that he had been told there was no night life in Warsaw. He said that had he known there were going to be evenings like that, he'd have brought a different wife."

"He certainly would have, had he known there'd be games like 'Room Temperature.' "

Horace decided that Beeky was becoming offensive. What help had his ridiculous, bibulous wife been to *him?* Ginevra might be loud. She might be clumsy. She might even at times be shrill. But she had never made a fool of him by getting drunk. Love — what did Annabel Ehninger know of love? Ask Beeky *that* one! Yet here he was again, Horace Putney, the man of big thoughts, obsessed with Annabel, with Ginevra. It was infuriating. He finished his brandy in one burning gulp.

"Tell me something, Beeky. Do you think a big man should care what his wife thinks of him? I mean what she thinks of him professionally. As a lawyer or doctor or statesman."

"You mean, shouldn't her opinion in such matters be something too trivial for his professional consideration?"

"I guess so. I guess that *is* what I mean."

"Well, I don't suppose that Franklin Roosevelt was too concerned over what Eleanor thought of him. Or Napoleon over Josephine. But a great man of the deepest sensitivity — well, he's like the weakest of us. He can't help it. Take Lincoln. I always loved that scene in Sherwood's play after Mary has been particularly odious, and they're alone together, and he says: 'Goddamn you.' Very slowly and deliberately. And then repeats it."

Horace laughed in surprise. "You're beyond everything,

Beeky. You always know what the other guy is thinking."

When they joined the ladies Ginevra was already distribut-
ing the score pads. It seemed to take forever, for almost everyone had questions and protests about her unpopular game.
But their hostess was determined. She moved from guest to
guest, patiently, quietly, even a bit grimly, explaining, illus-
trating, translating. At last they were all settled, and Ginevra,
alone on a chair in the middle of the room, had started playing. As Horace watched her jotting down figures on her card,
glancing up hard at each guest in turn before entering, with a
slight shrug, what he surmised was a curt, contemptuous rating, he was perversely amused. Engaged in one of her terrible
parlor games, holding the inevitable score pad, she put him in
mind of a stubborn little girl, grasping a tattered teddy bear
with a fierce and unneeded loyalty. It was an image that he
found touching. Of course, he likened himself to the teddy
bear.

"I've got an idea," Beeky whispered to him. "Let's you and
I give everybody ten for everything. That'll help pull the averages up and avoid World War Three."

Horace's heart hardened against his importunate ally. He
recalled Ginevra's opinion that Beeky Ehninger had the soul
of a small-town New England parson who had confused the
Almighty with Shepard, Putney & Cox. When the chips were
down, and it seemed that they were very much down that
night, did anyone in the world (including his blandly preoccupied, baby-ridden daughters) give a single goddamn about
Horace Putney or his career but Ginevra? Surely no one cared
for her or hers but he! Between them, did they not add up to
one angry, battered person? Wasn't Ginevra, who was very
proud of her reputation as a hostess, preparing to ruin her own
party in order to get him out of what she called the dead end
of his UN life? He chuckled at the sudden vision of her

sprawled on her back on the floor before a full-length mirror. That had been the day when he had come home unexpectedly to find her practicing a court curtsy!

"If you're ever going to accomplish your goal of world peace," Beeky pursued, "you're going to have to get a UN ban on Ginevra's parlor games."

Horace's eyes dropped to Beeky's thin ankle, resting exposed on Beeky's knee. The sock was not an evening sock. It was of wool, simple coarse black wool. Picking up his scorecard, he entered a zero under Beeky's space for dress.

"Jenny may criticize the way I work for my goal, Beeky, but at least she cares that I attain it. Her motives may be personal, but she's still on my side. Together, who knows? Maybe we *will* attain world peace. That may sound crazy, but we live in a crazy world."

"What are you marking me?" Beeky tried to look over Horace's shoulder.

Horace covered his pad. "I was just giving you a top ten for that beautiful waistcoat." He glanced critically around the room.

"Mrs. Vehti's the one I most worry about. The Indians are so sensitive."

"So they are." Horace picked up his pencil and marked her zero for sex appeal.

"And her husband fancies himself the Metternich of the nineteen seventies."

Horace gave Mr. Vehti a goose egg for wisdom.

"Are you giving them each a ten?"

"Why do you sniff like that?" Horace asked him with a little burst of laughter. "Can you smell my burning bridges?"

He turned to meet Ginevra's stare across the room. He winked at her and she winked back, as they silently reaffirmed that tightest of treaties: a man and woman against the world.

But what, he wondered ruefully afterward, turning back to his score pad and regretting that he had not refilled his brandy glass before leaving the library, did so basic, so savage an alliance have to do with world peace?

IV

Agreement to Disagree

BEEKY EHNINGER did not go to the Patroons Club more than once every couple of months. If he happened to be in the midtown area at noon, it was a convenient place for lunch, and, if Annabel were playing bridge late, a pleasant one for a solitary evening drink. But what he really enjoyed, in these visits to its great, cool, faded, dusky interior, with its distinguished silence broken only by the distant, faint throat-clearing of dozing members and the clink of glasses on trays borne by ancient waiters, was the titillating tickle of his never communicated (and therefore not *really* fatuous) sense that he himself had gone beyond all this. He could look up at the drooping eyes of his great-granduncle Gerhardus Beekman, painted by Eastman Johnson in 1870 with the club charter in hand, and whisper with a chuckle: "You needn't look so grand, old walrus. I've accomplished more that you ever did!"

Not that he, Beeky, had accomplished so much. He tried to be perfectly clear about this. But then neither had Gerhardus Beekman. The latter had founded the Patroons Club, it was true. But his great-grandnephew, in addition to becoming a managing partner of Shepard, Putney & Cox, had served two terms as a Democrat in the State Assembly and was Chairman of the Board of the Colonial Musem. And all this, too, with the handicap of having started as an asthmatic child, brought up by a socially ambitious father to cultivate aristocratic pursuits for which he had neither flare nor inclination. No, there *had* to be moments — not too many of them, of course — when he could allow himself the luxury of administering a pat to his own back, particularly as Annabel so rarely offered one. And the perfect place to enjoy such moments was in the huge, high-ceilinged taproom, swimming with paintings of the naval battles of 1812, with the long bar before which, stertorous and red-faced, affable with the precarious affability of alcoholic ill temper, were always gathered three or four of his contemporaries who had once been beautiful bronzed athletes on the beaches of Newport or Southampton back in the bad old days when Beeky, an etiolated figure swathed in sweaters, had coughed away his summers on the club terrace.

"A club is as strong as its weakest bore," Annabel had said after a ladies' night at the Patroons. But on a cold winter evening in 1971, when Beeky, sitting cozily alone by the steaming radiator, was sipping with relish his iced gin, those figures at the bar struck him for once as simply pathetic. They had wasted their lives, that was all. So bland was his mood that it cost him nothing to recognize that they undoubtedly considered he had wasted his. What was he to them, after all, but a shabby little lawyer mated to a woman who was almost old enough to be his mother? Oh, he could hear them! But nothing could subdue his self-satisfaction that night. Nothing . . .

"Hey, Beeky! Join the fellas, you old fart!"

Beeky did not immediately recognize the voice. He made out a short, pear-shaped figure, inappropriately garbed in red pants and a sports jacket, standing at the bar with the others, but facing him.

"I'm quite happy here," he replied faintly.

"What's wrong? Are you ashamed to be seen with ex-clients? Do I remind you of something you'd rather forget?"

The figure approached him now, glass in hand, and Beeky made out the rough, blotchy features and small staring eyes of his younger second cousin, Bradley Smedburg. He might have known. Only Bradley would have dressed like that at the Patroons.

"Oh, hello, Brad. Sit down. Have one on me."

Bradley sat down and looked at Beeky with a haughty air. Sometimes he liked to play the mad emperor, sometimes the clown. He had been considered as a young man the most brilliant member of the whole family connection, but he had chosen to fritter away his talents in a small insurance business, leaving his individuality only the outlets of eccentric clothes and bad manners. Of recent years he had given himself over to the expensive habit of litigating with his ex-wife. Unhappily for him, he suffered under the fatal drawback of an ineptly drafted separation agreement. Unhappily for Beeky, this agreement had been drafted by Shepard, Putney & Cox.

"Do you know what that bitch Minny now claims?" Bradley started right off, as if unaware that a solid year had elapsed since his last discussion of the subject with Beeky. "She claims that I agreed to pay the taxes on *her* capital gains! Did you ever hear the like of that?"

"Surely she won't get away with it."

"There's no telling what she may get away with when she comes into court brandishing that crazy agreement which your criminal — or criminally insane — former associate, Tom Potts, dreamed up. Tell me something frankly, Beeky. Do you think Minny's shyster *bribed* Tom Potts to sell me down the river?"

Beeky looked at the angry, glinting eyes in the rough, red face and sighed at the prospect of having to go into all this again. "You know perfectly well what I think, Brad. Tom Potts was a bad lawyer, and he wrote a bad contract. We fired him, didn't we?"

"But you should never have hired him!"

"Of course, we shouldn't. But that kind of thing happens, even in the best-run firms. He was a Korean veteran, and one of my partners wanted to give him a break."

"But you should have supervised him!"

"Oh, Brad, quit beating that dead horse. We offered you compensation, but you had to turn it down. You had to sue us for malpractice, and you had to lose. So far as I'm concerned that wipes the slate clean. I'm still perfectly glad to see you — after all, we're cousins — but only on condition that you stop throwing Tom Potts in my face. I'm sick to death of him."

"You're sick to death of him!" Bradley's near shout did not cause a single head at the bar to turn. The members were conditioned to violent expostulation. "You sit there, Beeky Ehninger, a slick fat cat, purring over your bowl of gin, bored with the sight of a man whose life you've ruined!"

"Oh, ruined. Come now, Brad."

"I say, ruined! I repeat, ruined. Shall I specify?"

"Can I stop you?"

Bradley raised an ominous forefinger as he prepared to reiterate the long, familiar inventory of his wrongs. "First, my children. They're both of age now, but seven years ago, when I signed your deadly little paper, they were still schoolboys. Minny's lawyer took full advantage of the cryptic clause about the mother's 'prevailing right of decision' in questions of health to ship them off to a dreary little expatriate school in Switzerland where I couldn't see them for the three most formative years of their lives. Result: when they came back to take up their abode with their fond female parent, at the period of what I can only term the 'monsoon' of her menopause, they blew up, dropped out and joined the drug culture."

"Brad, I know that's terrible, but thousands of boys today . . ."

"Wait!" Bradley held up again that stern chubby forefinger. "Second, my business. Thanks to the arcane formula devised by your Mr. Potts to cover the division of property, Minny's unsavory mouthpiece was able to pick the nadir of the stock market as the time for distribution. As a result I had to give her, in addition to my stocks, forty percent of the family insurance company. For five years I tried to run my business with Mr. Shyster shouting directions at me from the back seat. Finally I threw in the sponge, and sold out — at a ruinous loss."

"It was never a great moneymaker."

"To be sure. No great shakes to a Wall Street lawyer. A small thing but mine own. It gave me an occupation. Perhaps a bit of dignity. But no matter. Forget it." Bradley finished his drink, wiped his lips with a large purple handkerchief and signaled to the waiter for a refill. "Third and finally, my income. Your inimitable Mr. Potts was a virgin in tax law. I had thought I had pledged only a third of my income to support Minny in the style to which she was determined to become accustomed. But thanks to a curious phrase slipped in by the shyster, and either misconstrued by Mr. Potts or wickedly connived at by him, it appears that I must pay her taxes on *all* my contributions, which in turn increases her taxes, which in turn increases my contributions, so that logically I am swallowed up altogether. One judge, it is true, gave me some relief in equity, but only to save me from total bankruptcy. I am lucky, Beeky, if I have six thousand a year clear to live on. I can only afford to come here because Uncle Adolph picks up my house charges."

Beeky reached for the bar bill, which the waiter had placed on the table. "Not this one, anyway." He glanced toward the door. "What can I say, Brad? You sued us and lost."

"Sued you and lost!" Brad's sneer was superb. "Of course, I

lost. Judges are lawyers, aren't they? They don't want to muddy those waters. After all, they may be returning to practice themselves one day. But you ask what can you say. *This* is what you can say. You can tell me one good reason why I shouldn't blow my bloody brains out!"

Beeky had already risen to take his leave, but now he paused. Supposing Brad did it? Supposing, at long last, he were just that desperate? Even allowing for the dramatization that his nature required, he was still probably not exaggerating much. Beeky remembered Hubert Cox's saying at a firm meeting how lucky they had been that Bradley Smedburg had hired as bad a lawyer for his malpractice suit as Tom Potts himself. And had Beeky himself not welcomed Bradley's suit as exculpating him and his firm? Oh, yes, Bradley had suffered. There was no doubt about it.

"Let's talk this over, Brad," he said in a friendlier tone, resuming his seat. "Who's your lawyer now?"

"I don't have one. Eben Feezer threw me out of his office when I refused to pay his last unholy bill. A thousand lousy bucks for one silly motion at special term! Hell, I'm an expert myself by this time in domestic relations law. I know when I'm being had."

Beeky moistened his lips as he debated the offer that he felt suddenly impelled to make. Was he simply masochistically making up for the mood of fatuous conceit in which he had been basking when Bradley had greeted him? Or was he, by putting such a question to himself, trying to get out of the muddy business of repairing an old wrong?

"Suppose you give us another crack at your case, Brad? Suppose you see what we can do about clearing up this mess?"

Bradley, a man who liked never to be taken aback, was clearly taken aback. "You can't seriously mean that you expect to get another fee out of *me*, Beeky Ehninger!"

"I never even got one. But no, of course not. We'd enroll you as a nonpaying client, like the Cancer Clinic."

"And put me at the mercy of another Tom Potts?"

"We don't have another Tom Potts. If you're interested in my proposition, I'll see that you get Ed Toland himself. He's our litigation chief."

Bradley, still surly, began to be tempted. "And I really pay nothing?"

"Only our out-of-pocket disbursements. Otherwise it would be champerty."

There was a long pause. "Of course, you really owe it to me."

"Put it that way if you like."

"Very well." Bradley nodded several times, as if he were trying to convince himself. "So long as it's on that basis, I accept."

Beeky ordered a second cocktail and ignored Bradley while he waited for it. He was thinking about Bradley's case, and the latter, sensing this, did not interrupt. Beeky remembered what his early mentor, Judge Howland, had taught him about "creative imagination." There was never a situation, the old man used to say, where a lawyer could do *nothing* for his client. When the waiter brought his drink, he spoke.

"Something struck me just now while you were talking about your situation, Brad. How much money does Minny have of her own? I mean, aside from what you give her."

"About twenty-five g's a year."

"And she has expectations, does she not?"

"Oh, yes. Her mother's a rich old bitch."

"So she doesn't actually need to fleece you as she does."

"Except she's avaricious as hell. You might say that was a kind of need."

"I'm beginning to wonder if she hasn't another. May I ask

you a few frank questions about the early days of your marriage?"

"Shoot."

"When you first became engaged to Minny, didn't you tell me: 'She's dumb, but she's not too dumb to learn to play a decent hand at bridge.' "

Bradley smiled, as if actually complimented by Beeky's good memory. "It was all I required of her, and I will admit she learned it. I couldn't have put up with a bright, gassing female."

"And Minny was quiet. She was quiet for a long time. And submissive. But she's not so quiet now, from all I hear. She's on the board of this and the board of that. Isn't that so?"

"Shall I tell you the kind of woman my ex-wife is? She found her tongue when she found the martini, and now she can't control her yack. But her trouble is that she bores everyone to death, even her own sex, so she has to have money to buy ears. She buys doctors, lawyers, hairdressers, charities. All to shoot off her big mouth at. And, who do you think picks up the tab?"

"The man who shut her up. Obviously, Minny spent fifteen years building up a raging resentment. Then she made a plan. It was a very simple one." Here Beeky paused. He, too, could be dramatic.

"And what was this simple plan?"

"She decided to kill you."

As Bradley stared at him, Beeky thought he could make out in his cousin's expression not only the gratification that his drama should at last be taken seriously by a lawyer, but something a bit like awe, perhaps even a bit like fear, that this same drama might be greater than even he had reckoned.

"Go on."

"Minny may not be avaricious at all," Beeky pursued, feeling the reins of his theory now firmly in hand. "Indeed, I should speculate that she might be willing to ruin herself to ruin you. Look at her performance in the insurance business. Wouldn't it have been more profitable for her if her lawyer hadn't badgered you into selling it?"

"But greed can blind people."

"And hate can make them very perceptive. Consider what Minny's done to your sons. Consider what she's done to your peace of mind. No, I think you've grossly underestimated her. She's no simple penny-grabber. She's out of a Balzac novel. A monster capable of demonic hate and infinite ruse."

Bradley showed himself a quick convert. "Would it make any difference if you could prove it? In a court of law?"

"I wonder. The life of the law is experience. You signed an agreement. You were sane at the time. You were of age. Presumably you're bound by it. But suppose fraud were exercised? Suppose it were not, as it purported to be, a contract for the division of property and the support of your family? Suppose these things were only blinds? Suppose we could show that the real intent behind the document was to drive you to suicide by destroying your children, obliterating your livelihood and harassing you in your every waking hour? Mightn't it be against public policy for a court to enforce it?" Beeky now held up an admonishing finger in the way Bradley had showed him. "Are the ministers of justice of organized society to make themselves the agents of a madwoman in her plan to destroy the lives of her husband and family?"

Bradley slammed a heavy fist down on the table. "Goddamn it, Beeky Ehninger, you're a great lawyer, after all!"

o

Ed Toland had thinning dark hair, a bony, ashy face and the beautiful soft eyes of Leonardo's favorite male model. His passion was brief writing. He would start his day late and lazily, after an exhaustive perusal of *The Law Journal,* and would not hit his real pace until the early afternoon. After that he would work intensely until midnight. His wife and six children in Brooklyn had presumably adjusted themselves to his schedule. Ed listened silently to Beeky as the latter expounded his theory. He smiled.

"And how do you expect to implement this bizarre idea?"

"Minny Smedburg is suing Brad over the tax clause in the separation agreement. We could simply move to reform the entire document. On the grounds I've stated: that it isn't really a separation agreement at all."

"Mightn't one say the same about *all* separation agreements? Where would the law be if hidden motives — assuming you could prove them — were allowed to upset the written word? Read your Freud, Beeky. We all have motives other than we express. Other than we even know."

"But this is different. This is a motive for a *crime.* I maintain that Minny and her lawyer entered into a conspiracy to destroy her husband and sons."

"And you can prove that?"

"I can try!"

Ed shrugged. "Well, I recognize that Bradley's case is an unfortunate one. And that our firm is at least partly to blame. And I suppose the mere pleading of such a conspiracy might make his ex-wife and her counsel pull up a bit. Maybe even settle the case. It's a very nasty allegation, particularly the part about the sons. But aren't we in a touchy ethical position, saying anything like that against a fellow member of the bar?"

"But if I believe it, Ed!"

"*Do* you believe it, Beeky?"

"Yes!"

Ed repeated his shrug. "I'll give you Fritz Wilbur. He's a smart young litigator. Put yourself in his hands."

"But will you promise to review the court papers yourself? I can't risk another Tom Potts."

"Oh, everybody's going to read those papers. In our department we like to share the laughs."

Beeky had to be content with this, but he found even less support at home. He made the mistake, being full of his theory, of expounding it to Annabel over cocktails that night. She had had a bad afternoon at the bridge table, and her mood reflected it.

"I admit your theory," she said with a shrug. "It even seems to me obvious. As your partner suggested, isn't it true of half the divorces you hear about? Minny's a standard bitch. She wants to annihilate Bradley. The way I wanted to annihilate my first husband. It's only natural."

"But surely you didn't hate Tom Barnes that way?"

"Didn't I?" Annabel gave him a cool glance. "When I found that Tom Barnes was sleeping with that waitress at the Wyanduck Bath Club, I could have easily killed him. But I remembered Ruth Snyder and the electric chair." She sniffed. "And they say capital punishment's not a preventive. Well, it saved Tom Barnes's skin!"

The telephone rang, and Annabel settled down to the daily rite of her twenty minutes' evening gossip with her sister Clara. Beeky was glad to be able to turn away from her and avoid showing the acute pain that any mention of Tom Barnes's sexual prowess always inflicted upon him. For Tom Barnes had obviously been a great lover. Each of Annabel's husbands, as she sometimes jokingly, sometimes testily, used to remark, had been cooler than his predecessor, right up to her last who, she seemed to imply, was little better than a monk. But why did this still have to hurt him so? If she accepted it, couldn't he?

He felt giddy and closed his eyes. He saw again the big Park Avenue apartment into which he and his mother had moved when his father had died, with its relics of the old Fifth Avenue house, banal essentials of wealthy living before the first war: tapestries, bronzes of animals, huge dusky landscapes. Somehow the move into the great shiny new building with all the old things had almost unbearably emphasized the waste of his emotional life. So long as he and the sweet, patient, accepting mother had stuck it out on the Avenue, an end had seemed possible. The house, one day, would be sold, and then, perhaps *then*, he would leave and marry and be like his four chattering, scolding, giggling sisters, redeemed into uniformity. But the sale had come and gone, and there were all the old things, remorselessly renewed, reupholstered, gleamingly fixed up and placed in seemingly eternal permanence in this gaudy new edifice, with no hope now for a quadragenarian Beeky.

"It's funny you should mention that," Annabel's voice came to him from across the room. "Beeky and I were just talking about Tom Barnes. Somebody saw him this winter in Pasadena. Yes, looking very well, the old bastard. With his new wife. That's right, she' only thirty-six. And he's seventy-four if he's a day."

Beeky took his drink to the window and looked out at the tulips in the flowerpots standing up defiantly against the rain on the penthouse roof. He saw Annabel as she had been that summer in Saratoga when she had saved him. He tried not to romanticize the image. Her figure had been full even then ("dumpy" his mother had called it), and her hair, now blond, had been raven black, and the thick powder on her round, full face had intensified the darkness of her snapping eyes, as the rouge on her large lips had accented their sensuousness. She had been dressed in white with a wide-brimmed black straw hat, and she had been very competent with binoculars and betting sheets while still able to bandy wisecracks and emit, over and over, that high, shrill, contagious laugh which had become to Beeky the symbol of a life that had passed him by.

"Oh, Tom's probably as good as ever, the old goat. And I'll bet not even faithful to this new wife. He's the kind they find dead one day in a brothel. The police have to be bribed to dress him up and take him home and leave it off the blotter."

How they had all fought her: his mother, his psychiatrist, his sisters! "She's thirteen years older than you! She's fifty-three! She's after your money!" And he had seen her, too, at times, through their eyes, seen her clearly enough and ruefully enough, but he had also seen something they could never see. And one morning, after a sleepless night, he had stared at his haggard reflection in the shaving mirror and cried out: "You crazy fool! Don't you see it's your last chance? If you let *this* one go by, you may as well jump out the window." And he had opened the bathroom pane and stared twelve stories down to the garbage pails in the yard.

"Well, then, you're like Beeky, Clara. You always take the man's side. But I will tell him what I now tell you: that if you'd had the bad luck to know as much about the 'stronger' sex as I have . . ."

Oh, Annabel had been fair in her dealings with him, damnably fair. And why not, really? What more had she wanted, in her fifties, a three-time loser, but a respectable man, a trustworthy man, a well-to-do man, to neaten up her life and take care of her multitudinous domestic problems? What had she needed that other thing for, the thing Tom Barnes was so good at, damn him? She had her cards, her jewels, her drinks, her laughs. Oh, those laughs! Would he ever forget the one on their wedding night when, after all his ineffective fumbling, she had pushed him good-naturedly aside and said: "No, sweety, that's not your department. You don't care for it, and I don't need it. You want to show me you're a great big man. Well, let's agree that you are one and relax." And then he had relaxed — or at least had tried to — for sixteen years.

Annabel, who always seemed to know what he was thinking, put down the telephone now and turned back to him to resume the argument. "You heard what I said to Clara. It's perfectly true. You resent the woman in a divorce case. You resent her because you always put the blame on her."

Beeky was chilled by her brisk, hard, almost commercial tone.

"The blame for what?"

"The blame for your sexual inadequacy."

"But, Annabel, I thought you didn't *mind* about that."

"I don't. I'm an old woman. I couldn't mind less. But the point is, you can never forgive my sex for minding or for not minding. It doesn't matter which."

"You're very cruel tonight," he said in almost a whisper.

"I'm not in the least bit cruel. I only mention it because you may be going to be cruel to Minny Smedburg. You ought at least to know why you're doing it."

o

For the next six months Bradley Smedburg turned up as regularly in the offices of Shepard, Putney & Cox as if he had been a clerk. Indeed, some of the staff began to think that he was. He made himself a nest in a corner of the library where he read all the drafts of the papers to be filed in his suit and piled up the volumes with the cited cases, all of which he read and reread. He was constantly popping into poor Fritz Wilbur's office, driving him crazy with questions and suggestions, and it was only after Beeky threatened to drop the case altogether that he agreed to consult nobody but Beeky and then only at stipulated times. Matters were not made easier by Hubert Cox, who always took a wicked joy in teasing his partners and who purposely made the new client's acquaintance, read the court papers and restored Bradley's worst suspicions by pointing out holes in them. But the tables were turned on Cox when Bradley then began to haunt *his* office. The senior partner, after having had to resort to near force one morning to close his door against the intruder, became as anti-Smedburg as any of the litigation department.

"The guy must have you hypnotized," he complained to Beeky. "Why don't you kick him the hell out of the office?"

"I will. I will," Beeky muttered. "It's only a matter of weeks now, anyway."

Indeed, Beeky was beginning to feel that he *had* been hypnotized. Like Bradley himself, he seemed to be becoming obsessed with the case. They had lost in the trial court, and the Appellate Division had sustained, but to the astonishment of the bar Justice Rosenberg dissented. He was a young judge with a reputation for brilliant and independent thinking, and his long minority opinion was printed in full in *The Law Journal*. The paragraph that caused the most comment was this one:

> In a time when every precedent is being scrupulously re-examined in favor of the liberty of the individual, I see no reason why this laudable concern should be limited to criminal and constitutional cases. I maintain that it behooves the courts to carry the fight against exploitation of human beings into every field of jurisprudence. Why should we close our ears to the complaints of the great throng whose lives have been turned to

ashes because they failed to comprehend the small print of malicious contracts?

Beeky became almost a hero to the younger lawyers in the office, but he was far from that to the others or, indeed, to himself. He had no desire to subvert the base of commercial society, and he was constantly tortured in his mind by what Annabel had said. *Was* there some twisted sexual motive for his opposition to Minny Smedburg? Was that why they were fighting all the way to the Court of Appeals in Albany? He, Beeky Ehninger, the exponent of common sense, the soundest of family lawyers, the high priest of the life of reason?

When he went up to Annabel one evening at a cocktail party given by a Beekman cousin to ask if she were ready to go home, she pointed to the bar table where a tall woman with long red hair was standing alone having her glass replenished.

"Do you see your victim? She's probably drinking to forget. See if you can persuade *her* you're not a fiend incarnate."

Beeky recognized Minny Smedburg, just as she turned and recognized him. Walking over toward him, she carried herself with a self-confidence that he did not remember. She was too big and too bony to be handsome, but there was a grace in the way she now seemed to accept her own size, no longer hunching her shoulders and half squatting as she had when married to Bradley.

"Annabel said I'd better talk to you."

Beeky looked desperately around for his wife, who had already deserted him. "I'm sorry, Minny. It's not ethical for me to talk to you unless your lawyer's present."

"I didn't suggest that. I said *I* had to talk to you." She was certainly a very different woman from the one Bradley had married. Sipping the drink that she held in one hand, she used the other to grip Beeky's shoulder. "You can tell the Bar Association I used force. Does that make it all right?"

"I guess it helps."

"This theory of yours. About the conspiracy to destroy a family. It's a perfectly valid one. Only you've got the wrong conspirator. Bradley is the one who's determined that none of us shall survive. It was *he* who maneuvered me into sending the boys abroad by violating his visitation rights so flagrantly that it proved impossible to educate them in any place where he could get at them. It was *he* who ran his insurance business on the rocks despite all my lawyer's valiant efforts to save it. And, finally, it was *he* who insisted on selling his securities at the bottom of the market. Do you begin to get it?"

Beeky stared up at the ceiling without replying.

"It's perfectly true that I've tried to get hold of as much of Bradley's money as I could. I don't deny it. But it was only to save it for the boys. We're all dependent on it. My mother's wealth is another of Bradley's fictions. Would you like me to prove it? Call my lawyer."

Beeky's eyes met hers now for a moment and then glanced away.

"I've known from the beginning that I was dealing with a lunatic. I've had to learn to use every weapon I could get my hands on. I've watched Bradley go through lawyer after lawyer, never paying their bills, screaming that they were incompetent boobs or worse. I thought at last he was coming to the end of his legal rope. I thought I could see a patch of blue in that darkened sky. The last thing I dreamed of was that he'd find a lawyer to go along with his madness and not charge him a penny for it!"

"I'm sorry, Minny. I can't discuss it."

"You don't have to discuss it," she retorted in a voice of contempt. "I shouldn't really care to discuss it with so poor a creature as you've turned out to be, Beeky Ehninger. But if you have any conscience left at all, you'll think over what I've said. And then you'll kick Bradley Smedburg the hell out of your office!"

As she stalked off, Beeky reflected that it was curious that she should have used the same phrase as had Hubert Cox.

o

Bradley Smedburg put down his fork at the Lawyers Club and stared with an ominously gaping mouth at Beeky.

"Settle the case? You must be out of your cottonpicking mind! Settle the case just as we've finally got that bitch on the run?"

"One dissent is hardly a hue and cry. Of the six judges who have heard our argument, five have sided against us."

"But Rosenberg's the smart one! And the Court of Appeals loves to reverse. Particularly when they have the opportunity to make a great ringing reinterpretation of the common law which they imagine will be printed in textbooks for generations. How else can a poor beetle of a judge find immortality?"

"Bradley, listen." Beeky covered his eyes with his hands as he desperately summoned up his patience. "It's no use. We've had a meeting of the whole firm on the subject. That's never happened before in my experience. The entire partnership was consulted. If you won't settle — and we have what we consider a very fair offer from Minny's counsel — we cannot continue to represent you."

Bradley was briefly silent, breathing heavily. "You talked to Minny the other day at that cocktail party," he said hoarsely. "Cousin Tetine Loring said she saw you."

"Certainly I talked to her."

"Did you discuss our case?"

"No."

"You lie!"

"I'm not lying, Bradley. *She* talked about the case. Neither you nor she, obviously, is capable of talking about anything else. I simply listened. I said nothing at all."

"But she convinced you."

"Of what?"

"That I'm mad! It's the final phase of her plan. To get at *you*, my own lawyer and cousin, and turn you off. To leave me without children. Without money. Without friends. And finally without counsel! Oh, my God, can't you see it? It's your own theory, you jackass. To the last comma and semicolon!"

Beeky stared at him for a long moment. "I have no more theories," he said, with a desperate shrug. "And no more ideas. I don't even want any more lunch. Think over the settlement. It's out of my hands. If you won't take it, you've got to find other counsel."

He rose quickly and left the table. As he hurried toward the lobby, he shuddered to hear Bradley's high scream behind him: "Coward!" He took a taxi uptown and walked around the reservoir for an hour, his mind a near blank. Then he sat for another hour on a park bench. At last he came home.

Annabel was in the hall, her eyes alight with news. "Where have you been? Have you heard?"

"What?"

"Bradley Smedburg tried to kill Minny. He got into her apartment and came at her with a knife."

"My God! Is she dead?"

"Oh, no. She got away and locked him in her bedroom till the police came. They're holding him at the Sixty-fourth Street Precinct. They want you to come right down."

Beeky was surprised to hear his own sharp laugh. "So *that's* how he hangs on to a lawyer! Well, he wins, I must admit. I'll call Ed Toland."

V

The Diner Out

WHEN MISS FREER had died, leaving a fortune of ten million, and Burrill Hume, the next morning, had submitted a petition for the probate of her will (prepared with commendable foresight in the last days of her antemortem coma) to Mr. Everard of the Equitable Bank, only to be handed without comment (Mr. Everard was always very tactful in such matters) the copy of a subsequently dated will prepared by another law firm, Hume's mortification and anger had been in proportion to the facts. How cowardly, how typical of the rich New York old maid, for all her bluster of pride and independence, not to have the guts to tell an old friend that she was changing counsel! And next, when Austin Cassidy, with a crude honesty that was perhaps even harder to bear, had bluntly put it to his old college roommate, Burrill Hume, that the latter must agree that his new will would be better drawn by Messrs. Sloane & Sidell, experts in the oil interests of which Cassidy was so richly possessed, and had proceeded to expire just six weeks after that firm had prepared the necessary new testament, Hume's mortification and anger had been tempered with a rather shameful glee. *That* would teach clients what happened to those who glibly abandoned a faithful attorney after decades of devoted service! But when the same arcane sequence had continued, and Lloyd Cassidy had followed his brother across the street to Sloane & Sidell, without even the excuse of oil interests, but simply in the contemptible need to abandon the abandoned, to kick a hole in a ship that must now be deemed to be sinking, and had met his unexpected end that same week in a routine prostate operation, Burrill Hume had been neither mortified nor angry nor gleeful. He had simply been awed at this grim evidence of an invisible force that seemed bent on supplying him with such unsolicited vengeance.

These coincidences of death and discharge had been less obvious to his partners. All three decedents, after all, like Burrill Hume himself, had been in their seventies. But there had been lively concern about the falling off of estate business in Shepard, Putney & Cox. Hubert Cox himself had come to Hume's office to discuss the matter. Cox had achieved his position of senior partner quite as much for his talents as a diplomat as for his genius as a tax lawyer. He was so constantly good-natured that even when he lost his temper, people thought he was putting it on.

"When I read poor old Lloyd Cassidy's death in the paper," he began, "I hoped it might be a cloud with a silver lining. But now I hear the silver's all for Sloane and Sidell. What happened, Burrill?"

"Lloyd always did everything his brother Austin did. If Austin was going to fire me, then Lloyd was." Hume shrugged irritably.

"Did he have to die because his brother died? What do Sloane and Sidell do to new clients? Take them to lunch after the will's signed and put arsenic in their soup?"

"No doubt I should learn how it's done."

"Somebody around here should. And old lady Freer? It was the same with her, too, wasn't it?"

"Except she went to Hicks, Dale and Simon."

"There has to be a reason, Burrill." Cox got to his feet now and strolled about Hume's office with a roving, appraising stare, as if he were seeking his answer in the decoration. "And it's up to me to find it. But don't think *I* think it has anything to do with your brand of law. Everyone knows you're one of the best estate attorneys downtown."

Hume was so surprised and touched that he felt the tears start to his eyes, and he quickly went through the motions of cleaning his glasses. *Could* it be in the decoration? He had refused to give up any of his old things when they had moved to the glass cube at One New Orange Plaza. His sturdy mahogany furniture, still gleaming with its big brass fixtures, hardly fitted the long wide corridors, the abstract paintings, the prevalent transparency. Neither did his prints, very fine in themselves, of Lords Mansfield and Eldon.

"Perhaps you should redecorate," Cox suggested. "The era we live in, for all its cant of rebellion, is still remorselessly fashionable."

"I have to be myself, Hubert. I can't change now. After all, I'm seventy-three."

"Gosh, man, you don't look it!"

Hume sighed. Of course, Cox knew the exact age of each of his partners. If he were insincere in this, might he not have been insincere in calling Hume a good estate lawyer? But no, damn it all, he *was* a good estate lawyer! And just as good a one as before the wretched heart attack that had so aged and wasted him. Before that — ah, yes, he had been a fine enough figure of a man, thickset perhaps, but with strong features, what he secretly liked to think of as "leonine" white hair, and a way of holding his head that made people sit up and listen. Hadn't it been so? "Why did Burrill Hume never marry?" people asked. But now, well —

"I look my age and more, Hubert," he said gloomily, "and

that's the trouble. There's only one way to counterbalance age in a client's eyes. You should have set me up for it."

"And how, my dear fellow, should we have set you up?"

"Why, as the grand old man, of course! The sage. The voice of experience. The Nestor who separates the central snarl of the client's problem and then tosses the unraveled skein to eager younger hands to be finished. How does it look to a man like Austin Cassidy when he sees me working out every last routine clause of the powers of trustees in his will myself?"

"He ought to be glad."

"He ought to be, but he's not. He thinks I'm just an old hack. He thinks I'm as senile as he is."

"Or as he was," Cox corrected him. "But darn it all, Burrill, you do have assistants. You have Hermione Stoutenburg full-time and Mr. Bartram whenever you need him. You're not back in the days when clerks were getting twenty-one hundred dollars a year, you know. We can't turn them on for you like a chorus in *Aida*."

Hume sighed. What was the use? Cox was perfectly right. Miss Stoutenburg was an excellent will draftsman, and Mr. Bartram, though old himself, was even abler. But oh, how different had been Hume's picture of his old age! He had seen himself, in the image of their founder, the late Judge Hobart Howland, a great, gaunt figure, with a wondrous deep frog in an oft-cleared throat, arriving in the middle of a morning to preside over a conference of tired, brilliant young men who had worked late the night before. As each young man reported his findings and conclusions, Hume, or Hume-Howland, would supply a hint, a correction, a gruff commendation, perhaps a sarcastic but not really unkind reprimand. He would be the one who held all the threads, saw all the schemes, embraced the forests yet took in the trees! It would have been a performance to have elicited such whispered interchanges among the awed young men as: "The old bastard's still going strong," or "Jesus, who'd have thought he'd have remembered *that?*"

But now, who was even going to believe that the young men would have so reacted had he had them to react? What good was the survival of all his legal aptitudes if only the senior partner recognized them?

"And even if we gave you a hundred clerks," Cox remorselessly pursued, "even if you had enough for the grand march, do you think you could get new clients like those you've lost?"

"You don't pick up new clients at my age, Hubert. No matter how good you are."

"Then, my dear Burrill, there we are."

"Where are we?"

"At precisely the point that I came in here to discuss." Cox folded his hands and leaned forward to beam at Hume as if it were positively good news that he was about to impart. "Whether the time hasn't come for you to move over to the right-hand side of our stationery."

Hume uttered a cry of distress. "Retire?"

"You know we never use that word," Cox replied with mocking, if amiable cynicism. "You keep your office and have a stenographer whenever you want. You receive a small fixed salary under our formula. We all know you have substantial savings. I don't see that it's such a bad arrangement."

"That's the way it starts, Hubert. But you know as well as I do that after six months all your partners glower at you. They're thinking: does he need all that office space at nine dollars a square foot to read his mail in? Why can't he stay home and pocket the money we pay him for doing nothing?"

"We old farts have to know when to move over. In most of the big firms you'd have had to retire eight years ago."

Every partner over sixty knew Hubert Cox's "old fart" approach. With jaunty camaraderie he appeared to put himself in his interlocutor's boat, but when it came to the execution of the point discussed — a drop in percentage of profits, a smaller office, a part-time secretary — Cox himself was never affected.

"You know how I feel about the law," Hume said, wretched. "I have no family. No hobbies. I hate travel. I don't play golf. What am I to do with my days?"

"You have your dinner parties."

"But they're at night, Hubert!" Hume did not understand the laughter in Hubert Cox's eyes.

"Come on, now, Burrill, let's be honest. Considering the shabby way you feel the firm has treated you, you ought to be glad to retire."

Hume looked sadly again at each object on his desk, and then up at Lords Mansfield and Eldon. But obviously they would not help him. How could he make Hubert Cox see? It was not simply that he loved his craft, that he had a passion for making each will and trust deed fit precisely to its family's requirements, that he delighted in rescuing his estates from Uncle Sam's greedy jaws. It was also that he loved the firm itself, despite its horrible faults, that he craved the daily interchange of views and jokes with partners and staff, that he could not imagine forgoing the pleasant lunches at the firm table at the Lawyers Club and all the human stories of what was happening in a society of a hundred souls. Of course, it was true what he had told Cox about resenting the partners' failure to accord him the tools and trappings of a legal Nestor, but such omissions were true everywhere today. They were part of the spirit of the age and had to be accepted.

"Do you know what you're seeking to deprive me of?" Hume demanded in an anguished tone. "Of life itself."

"Burrill! Let's not be dramatic about it."

"I mean it, Hubert. This firm is life. Life for me, anyway. Maybe life to others. Look what happens to my clients when they leave. Look at Miss Freer and the Cassidy brothers. All dead within six weeks of giving old Burrill Hume the sack."

Cox's eyes showed a gleam of concern, and Hume saw at once that he would have to go easy. It was bad enough to be old without being considered crazy.

"I don't mean to imply that those deaths were anything but coincidental," he added hastily. "But it illustrates my point. I shouldn't survive in retirement. Reduce my percentage as much as you want, but let me stay in the firm." He paused before frankly pleading: "Please, Hubert."

Cox looked at him for a quizzical moment and then rose. "All right, Burrill. You can stay if you want. I, for one, shall be glad. But I'll have to dock your percentage, you know. To placate the Young Turks. They didn't all leave, I'm afraid, with Dan Purdy. Just be sure you hang on to Mrs. Bloxham. So long as you do, they may snarl, but they'll never bite."

"Thank the Lord for Fanny Bloxham, then."

Cox paused in the doorway. "Look here, Burrill. Why don't you dine with Sophie and me tonight?"

"Sorry. I have a dinner."

Cox nodded, as if this were only to be expected, but he kept his hand on the doorknob. Then he tried again. "Couldn't you get out of it? We have one of the Young Turks coming. Jerry Lord. He hardly knows you, Burrill. It would make things much easier if you and he were friends. Come tonight and charm him."

"But, Hubert, I told you. I have a dinner."

"God, man, are dinners so sacred?"

"When you've accepted one!"

"All right, all right." Cox shrugged as he turned to go. "You

say you have no hobbies, Burrill," he threw back at him.
"What do you call your social life?"

o

Burrill Hume was very serious indeed about his social life.
If Shepard, Putney & Cox represented indispensable work, his
dinner parties represented indispensable pleasure. If one was
duty, the other was rest, diversion — sex, as the young people
might put it. Hume loved to put on his dinner jacket and
make his way into the social world where for three hours he
could be sure of good food, good wine, the bliss of general
amiability and the heavenly relaxation of freedom from unpleasant surprises. The law and the dinner party were like the
contrasting themes of day and night in his favorite opera *Tristan*. The former was bold and hard and blindingly bright, the
latter soft and dark and soporific. One needed both, of course,
but now, after the long office hours, he looked yearningly forward to dinner at — where was it? Mrs. Trane's? — with a deli-
cious anticipation of candlelit rooms seen through half-closed
eyes, of the glint of glass and silver, of the anesthetic of gin
and wine, of the scent of powder and perfumed candles, of the
throaty tones of old women saying nothing, of a murky, sub-
marine world of fantasy.

When he arrived at his apartment, his housekeeper of
thirty years, Mrs. Mullally, followed him through the dark little vestibule into his bedroom that, like his office, was full of
his long-dead parents' large mahogany furniture.

"You're not going out tonight, Mr. Hume," she announced
grimly.

"Who says I'm not?"

"That pasty face of yours says you're not. That pasty pale
face says you're going straight to bed and have your supper on
a tray."

"Mrs. Mullally, you're *ultra vires.* You're exceeding your jurisdiction. Will you kindly leave my room now so that I may dress? I'm perfectly well enough to go to Mrs. Trane's."

"If I was sure of that, I'd let you go."

"Mrs. Mullally!"

As she simply continued to stare at him defiantly, he placed his hands on her large round shoulders, faced her about and propelled her from the room. Closing the door after her, he sat down for several minutes and contemplated his reflection in the full-length mirror in the *Empire* frame. He *did* look sallow, and his heart was pounding. But after a period of willed stillness he felt almost himself again.

He could not remember Mrs. Trane's address while he was dressing, and he tried systematically to recall it as he again faced the mirror to button his black silk vest and stiff shirt. What nonsense it was, this business of being ashamed of forgetting numbers! How many men twenty years his junior could remember a fifth of the telephone and street numbers that he carried daily in his head? There should be no humiliation in looking up Mrs. Trane's apartment house, as he now did, putting on his glasses and leaning over very close to the page: Trane, Mrs. E. P., 1065 Park Avenue. Of course. Yet, twenty minutes later, when his taxi had pulled up at this address, and he entered the familiar lobby, still tingling from his final conflict with the obdurate Mrs. Mullally, a suspicious Irish doorman roundly denied that any Mrs. Trane lived in the building and as roundly refused him the loan of a telephone book.

"I'll find out who manages your building and have you fired," Hume snarled at him. But the man only laughed.

Hume walked over to Madison Avenue in search of a telephone booth and then realized his error. There were no pay booths on Madison Avenue. All the old shops had become art galleries and were now dismally closed. He looked at his watch. It was eight. He was already fifteen minutes late! Something like panic seized him. It suddenly seemed to him that if he missed this dinner party, he would never again be asked to another. "Burrill Hume?" Mrs. Trane would tell her world. "Well, of course, I adore Burrill, but you can't count on him." Why was he trapped on cold, stony Madison Avenue, shut out, damned, when somewhere, in bliss, at Elsa Trane's, the old friends were already sipping iced drinks about a cheerful fire? What wandering soul in Purgatory had ever suffered more?

Hume hailed a taxi and offered the man five dollars to find a telephone booth and to wait while he made a call. It was too much. The man was suspicious.

"Ten!" Hume cried and stuck the bill in his hand.

"Okay, Grandpa, hop in."

In a booth on 86th Street Hume frantically turned the pages of the directory. No, there was the address that he had looked up at home. He had been right. He dialed the telephone number and received the recorded answer: "The number that you have dialed is no longer a working number." She must have moved: And he remembered now that she *had* moved, but where, where? He called information and, with unexpected ease, obtained the new telephone number. In a frenzy now he dialed it, and to his almost painful relief, the maid answered:

"Mrs. Trane's residence."

"Yes, yes," he gasped, "but where are you?"

"Beg pardon?" came back the suspicious tone. Oh, why were people always so suspicious?

"I mean, where is Mrs. Trane's apartment?"

"Who is this, please?"

"It's . . ." He could not think of his own name! In another

second the remorseless Norn would cut the thread that connected them, and he would be left in the black void of outer Hades. He was like a man in a pit desperately shouting up at the white hole of light above him, the white hole, smaller and smaller, that would soon be merged in the total darkness. "It's a guest of Mrs. Trane's. A dinner guest!"

"Oh, Mr. Hume!"

"Yes, yes!" he cried. "Mr. Hume. What is her new address?"

"Madam was just asking about you. I telephoned your apartment and found you'd gone."

"Where *are* you?"

"At ten fifty-five Park."

It was only two blocks away. Exultant, Hume hurried to the street and scrambled into his taxi. Before five minutes had passed, the door of the apartment, of Paradise, had opened before him, and the horrible dream of frustration was over. Mrs. Trane's new apartment was like the old one, but smaller. He made out the same dimly lit interior, the Piranesi prints, the profusion of silver, the prevailing note of inherited, comfortable, ugly things. And there were all the neat and washed old friends and the blessed cocktail tray!

"We thought you'd forgotten," his hostess murmured.

"Forgotten? As if I could ever forget."

Because he was late there was time for only one drink before they went into the paneled dining room, candlelit, with more silver, much more silver, even silver service plates glittering at each place. There would be wines — oh, heaven — three glasses. A sherry. A burgundy. A champagne. Next to him was his old friend Fanny Bloxham.

Fanny was older than he; she had passed eighty, but with the loss of taste that assaults some octogenarians she now made herself up like an aged tart. Her short, sparse, tightly curled hair was a ludicrous gold, and she gazed at him with big black watery eyes that seemed to be melting under the fire of her ruby necklace. She was like a fish in an aquarium, bumping against the heavy glass of her tank.

"What luck my being next to you, Burrill dear," she was saying. "There's been something so on my mind, and I didn't know how to tell you."

"My dear Fanny, you know you can discuss anything with me anywhere. We have no line between business and pleasure."

"Exactly. No line. Which is why it's going to make no difference between us. You know that my daughter Amy's boy, Tommy Moore, has been doing very well in the Heslin firm. He's going to be a partner, of course, but Amy tells me the competition is very stiff, and if he can give them a hint that his grandmother is going to move her estate to his firm, it would do the trick very nicely."

Hume's fish had become a shark. One drop of blood, and he would be torn to bits. He sat so still that he thought he could hear his mind ticking. "Well, let him give the hint, then," he said judiciously, "if a hint is all they need."

"But, of course, I'd have to *do* it," she went remorselessly on. "I'd have to change lawyers. I hate to leave an old friend like you after all these years, but Amy says you'll be retiring anyway, and that all the fees on my estate would be going to partners of yours I don't even know."

"I shan't retire while you're alive, Fanny."

"Maybe you think I haven't so long!" she exclaimed with a little cackle of a laugh. "Oh, I could fool you, Burrill!"

Hume understood perfectly that she wanted to put him in the wrong to ease her own conscience. There was no possibility of appeal. Oh, yes, he knew his New York dowagers. No friendship, no loyalty would prevail against even a disliked grandson. Hume was being invited to consent graciously to his own elimination, to be the gentleman who concurred in the myth that he had nothing to gain from Fanny Bloxham's estate. How little it meant, after all, to Fanny Bloxham.

"It's not the fees I mind, Fanny."

"Why should you, at your age? It's not as if you had a son or grandson in your firm to carry on."

"Of course not," he agreed blandly. "But there's something you don't see, Fanny. Something you couldn't possibly see."

"That it's a matter of pride? Amy tells me you don't have to tell your partners. As a matter of fact, Amy said I didn't even have to tell *you.* I could simply have made a new will with Tommy's firm. So you see how frank I'm being."

"And I appreciate it. I know these things aren't easy for you."

Of course, he knew just the contrary. To women like Fanny money was an entity totally distinct from their own wishes or pleasures, a kind of national banner demanding strict duties of patriotism. If Fanny's fortune required the betterment of a grandson and the liquidation of an old friend, then there had to be a grandeur in Fanny's rising to the challenge. For Hume to appeal to her mercy would be to show that he had no sense of the greater issues in life.

"Amy thinks I've been very good to stay with you as long as I have," she continued now with a suddenly revealed spitefulness. "Considering how many years Tommy's been practicing."

Hume decided that he was glad she had said this. If she needed to ease her conscience, so did he need to ease his. She had made herself fair game.

"That's perfectly true, Fanny. But it's not of myself that I'm thinking. As you so rightly observe, I'm about to retire. I have more than enough in the bank for such little time as I may have left. My heart, you know, is not all it should be."

"Well, there you are, my poor old friend! It's time we all made changes. You see it now, don't you?"

It was the second time that day that Hume had been told where he was. He contemplated the white, eager, oft-lifted face of his old friend with a wry smile. Her eagerness for reassurance, at the expense, if need be, of his very life, removed his last compunction.

"It's you I'm thinking of, Fanny. Only you."

The watery eyes narrowed the least bit. "You don't think the Heslin firm is good enough? You don't think they could handle my affairs? Amy told me you might abuse them."

"Amy should have her mouth washed out with soap!" Hume retorted angrily. "For me to abuse a fellow lawyer would be bad enough, let alone a fellow lawyer my client is leaving me for."

Fanny's eyelids immediately drooped. "I'm sorry, Burrill."

"You should be." He allowed a silent, dignified moment to pass while their reversal of positions was established. "The Heslin firm is perfectly competent to represent you. There's none better. I've told you, Fanny, that I was thinking only of you. I mean it. And as a friend, too, not as a client at all. When I tell you that I am violating a canon of legal ethics in giving you the warning I am about to give you, will you believe that I am sincere?"

Fanny's countenance was awe-struck. "What warning?"

"The warning that something most unpleasant is very apt to happen to you if you leave Shepard, Putney and Cox."

"Burrill Hume, are you threatening me?"

"On the contrary. It is immaterial to me what you do. *I* shall be retired."

"You mean your partners would do something to me?"

Hume chuckled with pleasure at the idea. "No, we're not

Mafiosi. Whatever our rivals may think. No, Fanny, this threat comes from elsewhere. From another world, perhaps. A world of elves and goblins. I don't pretend to fathom it. A year ago I should have laughed at the idea. But not today. Not having seen what I have seen."

"My poor friend, are you imagining things? You should see a doctor."

"Would you rather I didn't tell you, Fanny?"

"Tell me what?" There was a hint of outrage, the ghost of a screech in her tone.

"What I have seen happen to our ex-clients. It's very weird. Very uncanny. I've never told anyone before. It wouldn't have been ethical for me to do so. But all the rules and canons must bow to my friendship for you."

"These are *facts* you're talking about?"

"Absolute facts. Facts that you can verify tomorrow, if you wish. Facts that all the world knows. But what the world doesn't know is the connection between those facts and my firm. And that is what I feel duty-bound to reveal to you. If you wish it. For your sake and for your sake alone."

Mrs. Trane was vaguely visible at the dark far end of the table signaling to Fanny that it was time to shift the conversation. But she might as well have tried to catch the attention of Andromeda as the monster approached. Fanny's mouth hung open as she stared at her terrifying neighbor.

"Tell me."

Hume proceeded, in quick, lawyer-like fashion, with a liberal sprinkling of dates, including days and months, to tell her the story of the deaths of his three other principal clients. The effect on Fanny was even greater than he could have wished. She continued to gape at him, as she moved her head slowly from side to side.

"It's lucky I knew in time," she murmured.

"Of course, it may be nothing but coincidence," he concluded briskly. "You can see it's not a thing I can talk about. Only to someone I absolutely trust." He paused. "Someone I trust and care for."

"I see that, Burrill. I see it, and I'm very grateful to you for telling me. It's the most scary thing I've ever heard! Of course, there can be no idea of my changing lawyers now."

"You don't think I'm superstitious?"

"I don't care if you are." Fanny shuddered. "What difference does it make who draws my will? Imagine, taking the smallest risk over something as trivial as that. No. Amy must find another way to make Tommy a partner."

Hume smiled. "She might even decide to let him do it on his own. It's not a bad way, Fanny."

o

The men had coffee and brandy in the library, a room into which the Widow Trane rarely penetrated. There were no candles there, and a harsh yellow electric light illuminated the shabby old standard sets, the big bronze animals and the expostulating old men. Hume, puffing a cigar, roamed the room and pretended to be interested in the books. His heart was beating too fast to make talking much fun, and he dreaded already that the discomfort in his stomach might be a herald of the pain that had preceded his last attack.

And then a dreadful thought struck him.

As it did so, the hand that he was reaching out to the butler's brandy tray shook so that he upset a glass. Without even apologizing he seized another and turned away to take a burning swallow. For what he had suddenly taken in was that Fanny Bloxham's nasty daughter Amy would never leave her mother alone until she had uncovered the reason for the latter's refusal to change counsel. And when she found out, would she stop at anything to destroy Burrill Hume? Of course she wouldn't! She would send her wretched son Tommy to the City Bar Association with a screeching complaint. How would it look that Burrill Hume was trying to save his dwindling practice by scaring his old lady clients with threats of death if they left him!

"I hear Austin Cassidy kicked the bucket just after he walked out of your shop to go to Sloane and Sidell," one of the men was now saying to him. "Served him jolly well right, I'd say." There was crusty laughter from the others, who were mostly fellow lawyers. "I wish I had that kind of power over sneaky clients. I'd certainly exercise it. I . . . Look here, old man, don't you feel well? Was it something I said? I'm awfully sorry. Damn bad taste on my part."

"No, no, it's not that. I just remembered something."

He hurried out to the parlor where Mrs. Trane greeted him with surprise and pleasure.

"Why, Burrill, are you bringing the men in already? How flattering!"

"I want to talk to Fanny."

"But you had her all during dinner! You didn't even change the conversation."

"I'm sorry. We were having a most important discussion."

Mrs. Trane sighed with the philosophy of one sadly accustomed to the vagaries of her senile contemporaries. "Of course, if you wish," she said, shrugging. She walked past him to greet the other men who, imagining him to be acting at her behest, had followed him out of the library. Hume found Fanny sitting alone on a sofa. She looked almost panic-stricken when he sat down beside her.

"Fanny, everything I told you at dinner was a lie. I did it to save my skin."

She gasped. "You mean those people didn't die?"

"Oh, they died all right, but so did millions of others who hadn't fired me. Plenty of people have fired Shepard, Putney and Cox and prospered afterward. I should say it's rather more common that way."

Fanny shook her head in bewilderment. "I don't understand."

"It's simple enough. I deliberately tried to frighten you into remaining my client. I knew my partners would make me retire if I lost you. And I couldn't face retirement."

Something almost like concern flickered in those watery old eyes. "But, my poor friend, perhaps then I should stay."

"No, no!" Hume was appalled. "No, for God's sake, that would never do. I've got to retire, anyway. I was only kidding myself."

"But supposing there was something in your theory, after all. Supposing there was a jinx . . ."

"Look." Hume was definite now as he saw his solution and as promptly seized it. "If there's a jinx, it has to be on the people who fire me. It can't be on the ones who are loyal. And you're loyal, Fanny. It is I who fire *you!* Because I'm retiring, as of the first of the month. So you see, you're perfectly safe. And I strongly urge that you take your business to your grandson."

"You turn me out. You turn me out."

"It's just what I do."

Fanny reached over her old jeweled hand, brown and black-veined, and placed it on his. "Very well, old friend. It's as you wish. But it's my bedtime. My doctor says I must be home by half-past ten."

"I'll go out with you."

"I have my chariot. I'll drop you home."

While both, well-wrapped, were proceeding slowly across the lobby below to the front door, Hume sensed with a numb resignation that he as well as she was now beyond the reach of the life-giving force of his firm. When the doorman pulled open the grilled portal he peered into the wet night and saw at the end of the marquee the big black glistening limousine that belonged to Mrs. Bloxham. It might have been a hearse! The chauffeur opened the back door, and the luxurious uphol- stered interior was brilliantly illuminated. Hume shrank back.

"Are you coming, Burrill?" his friend asked as she stepped forward into the dark.

VI

Beeky's Conversion

To BEEKY EHNINGER as a boy, the wealth of his mother's family had been a source of perennial embarrassment. In this he had taken his cue from her. "Nobody lives like my family," Elise Ehninger used to say, with a faint, contemptuous shrug that repudiated the least idea of hidden pride on her part. The multitudinous clan of the Meanses, her siblings and cousins, her uncles and aunts and nephews, had covered the east side of Manhattan with their pompous Beaux-Arts mansions and filled two generations of tabloids with their loves and sports. Indeed, the publicity given the descendants of Augustus Means had made the unsophisticated think that they must constitute a kind of special plutocracy in themselves, greater than less gaudy Rockefellers or Mellons. And when, as Beeky grew older, they began to disappear from the urban scene, taking their papier-mâché temples with them and leaving their heirs, for the most part, with only modest competences, they made their young relative think of the two silly pigs who had danced and fiddled while the wiser third, one of those less gaudy rich, no doubt, had laboriously piled brick on brick.

But if Beeky's mother, remote, detached, swathed in her long mysterious semi-invalidism, had been a constant dissenter, her husband known to the men's clubs as "Duke" Ehninger, had been more like a Means than the very grandest member of his family-in-law. It was Duke who dominated the home, the children, the social schedule, the tone of life — everything and everybody but Elise herself — with an eye that missed no detail, a voice that penetrated shrilly to every cranny and an energy that seemed to expand in inverse ratio to the importance of the issue presented. Beeky from the beginning had tended to see his father as it was only too plain that his adored mother saw him: as bristling, bustling, bossy, officious. Why could he not go downtown like other daddies and leave them be?

Not so, however, did Duke appear to Beeky's four older sisters. To them he was a beaming, sly, joking, gift-bearing, easily cajoled, lovable daddy whom it was fashionable fun demonstratively to adore. And they in turn were all that he wanted them to be: pretty, giggling, teasing, frivolous, worldly, the colorful fluff and feathers in the foreground of the Renoir family portrait in his mind's eye. They learned his gossip as they might have learned their catechism; they accepted his social evaluations of their friends, even of their young men; they allowed him to pick their clothes, and they blandly deduced, from the odd blend of scorn and awe in his constant references to "your mother's fortune," that if it was somehow low to have earned it, it was nonetheless admirable for such old stock as his to have married into it. Duke hypnotized them with his vivid sense of the wickedness, the crudeness, the vulgarity of their long-deceased maternal great-grandfather and his "robber baron" partners. He was a mine of information about the source of every fortune in New York or in the Southampton of their summers; he would rub his hands with delight at the iniquities that he adored to relate. There was a kind of worship, almost of love, in his ferocious contempt of the new and newest rich. He was a satirist who was perfectly happy to live and die among the targets of his own satire.

It was inevitable that an only son should have been regarded by Duke as a heaven-sent instrument to resurrect an aborted ambition. For unsuccessful men always know that they are unsuccessful, and Duke Ehninger was far too clever to see his career as the *arbiter elegantiarum* of the Southampton Beach Club in any light other than that in which it was viewed by the bankers and lawyers who admired his wine and feared his tongue. Society to such men was strictly a women's affair; it had no more reality for them than finger bowls and doilies. But Beeky was to remedy all this. Beeky was to do better than his father. He should, of course, be reared to succeed Duke as President of the Patroons Club, but why should he not be President of the Stock Exchange as well? Why should he not even be a congressman — like Ham Fish?

Duke tried to be subtle. He did not make the mistake of picturing the future as too awesomely demanding, nor did he ever imply that such glories simply fell into a man's lap. He constantly emphasized, lightening his discourse with witty anecdotes, that if a man remembered who he was and what he was, if he acted like a gentleman and dressed like a gentleman and talked like a gentleman, if he learned the proper balance between work and sport and gallantry, why then, given his inherited advantages, it should be almost impossible for him to fail. How Beeky hated it all! Walking in a new sailor suit up the beach to the club to meet his father's friends, driving in the old Packard town car on Sunday afternoons to Montauk, sitting on the terrace at the tennis matches, even deep sea fishing in the family launch, he heard his father's endless undulating tone.

"Never believe, my boy, because Americans prate so much of democracy, that traditions and inherited advantages do not count. They do! I have seen a lot of things in my day. I saw the crowds of New York waiting in the streets to see Consuelo Vanderbilt's duke. I saw the same crowds only last year when I was on the committee to greet Queen Marie of Rumania. I tell you, Beeky, never toss away a good card because somebody who hasn't got it in *his* hand tells you it won't take a trick. You'll see how quickly that somebody snaps it up, the moment you drop it."

Elise Ehninger was little help to her son. She offered sanctuary — that was all — and the sanctuary of a rather chilly chapel where the praying figures seemed intent on praying for themselves. Outside, in the world of his father's limitless jurisdiction, Beeky had to develop the protection of illness, of asthma, and build walls between himself and his intrusive parent manned by head-shaking doctors and thermometer-shaking nurses. And when his native health, surviving every such onslaught, betrayed him in his teens to the enemy, he had to adopt the protection of the "Beeky" manner: that of the bright, unruffled, ironical, wide-eyed, constantly questioning, precocious brat. To avoid the paternal challenges he affected a snobbishness even vaster, even more comprehensive than Duke's. He steeled himself to scale the very heights of odium!

"You know it really was the greatest luck, Father, that the doctors wouldn't let me play football. You wouldn't have felt as you did if you'd seen how the social climate has changed at Saint Andrew's. Today the *gratin* of the sixth form go in for tennis, which helped me to get in with the Boston set who are always a bit hard to know. They don't distinguish between New Yorkers, you know. There are some 'beans' who don't even know a Barber from a Barbey or a Rutherfurd from a Rutherford. And after the trouble we've taken to learn about their 'blind' and 'seeing' Gardiners! It's too provoking. By the same token, Father, if you had to live at Saint Andrew's, as I do, your fine sense of what's what would keep you from the egregious error of thinking, as I fear you once did, that I should try to be school monitor. Perish the thought! Last year the senior monitor was an Irish boy from Worcester, one O'Brien, if you please."

At such moments, Beeky, like the fool of yore, would glance slyly at his morose and distracted monarch, pretending to cower before an anticipated whip. Sometimes Duke would laugh drily; sometimes he would simply turn away. Sometimes his small reddish eyes would even betray a faint hint of apprehension, as in a Frankenstein who wonders at the ultimate nature of his creation.

In the fall of 1933, at the lowest point of the great depression that marked the twilight of Duke's gods, he came up to Boston to take Beeky, then a Harvard freshman, to the automobile show. He led his son to a glittering silver-yellow Hispano-Suiza roadster with red-spoked wheels.

"Slump or no slump, my boy, I promise you this. The day you're taken into the Porcellian or the Fly, I'll buy you that car."

"But, Father, what on earth should I do with a club? During the week I have my *cercle Français,* and on Saturday nights there's always the play. Besides, clubs aren't what they were. Perky Lowell says he'd never join one."

"I'm quite aware of your social schedule, Beeky. And I know a good deal more than you think I do about your fine-feathered friend Lowell. That's why I'm offering this bribe. I'll make it easier for you. Even if you're not taken into the

Porcellian or the Fly, I'll buy you that car if you'll only promise me that you'll *try* to be elected."

"Oh, try? Really, Father, I think not. How can one properly try for that sort of thing? Would you have me osculate every derrière in Cambridge?"

"All right, Beeky. I'll make it easier yet. If you'll simply give me your word that you won't do anything to *prevent* yourself from being elected, that car is yours."

Beeky made a face and shook his head, and the battle already won many times over, was won once more. But this time it was different. Duke did not try again. At least he did not try in any way that his son could see. And, as is always the case, Beeky began to miss their conflict. It is never very pleasant to be given up by a parent, even by an importunate one.

Beeky now lived in a moral vacuum. With his wit, his affectation, his large allowance and his easy good will, he achieved, on the campus and at New York dances, if not a real popularity, at least a recognized position. He became the favorite confidante of the most beautiful and publicized debutantes, a pet rather than a lover, consulted on matters cosmetic and concerns of the heart. He was a "personage," someone to be reckoned with, admired even by his sisters, the prince imperial of the Southampton Beach Club. Not surprisingly, he was thoroughly wretched.

o

A few miles east from the Ehninger's big, white, porticoed summer villa on the dunes, in a charming old black shingle house on the main street of the village of East Hampton, with geraniums in blue window boxes, lived their family lawyer, Judge Hobart Howland. The childless and widowered old ex-

jurist lived alone, surrounded by his collection of early English
law reports, a gnarled symbol of Yankee independence, his
back squarely turned to seashore sybaritism. It was not, however, that the judge held himself apart from the marketplace.
He and his partner, Elias Shepard, had made modest fortunes
as Wall Street lawyers, and nobody on the south shore of Long
Island, including Duke Ehninger, had a more sophisticated
idea of how the latter's friends conducted their businesses.
But if the judge knew how they worked, he cared nothing for
how they played. He despised neighboring Southampton and
made no secret of it. He was old enough to have belonged to
the era where the golf course, the country club and the martini had played no role in the development of a law practice,
and where an attorney did not have to be even on a first-name
basis with a client. So great was Howland's reputation as an
"old bear" that business leaders did not feel humiliated to
come to his office even when they knew that he would decline
to dine at their tables.

The judge had little enough sympathy with Duke Ehninger,
but he had always been fond of Elise, whose indifference to
the social world he construed as congruent to his own disdain,
and he had a grudging pity for Beeky, whose early ruin by an
indulgent yet domineering father he grimly predicted. But
when he learned, in a professional conversation with Elise, of
the now established division between father and son, he wondered if he could not make out an added responsibility for the
family counsel.

"If you're not going to some dizzy debutante debacle this
Saturday night, my boy, how about dining alone with me?
I've got some decent venison and a Burgundy that even your
father wouldn't despise."

This was growled at Beeky as the old man crossed the ve-
randah after a call on Elise. Beeky jumped up from the ham-

mock on which he had been reading *Les Liaisons Danger-euses.*

"Do you mean *me*, Judge?"

"Who the hell else would I be talking to? Or do you think, like the senile, I chatter to myself?"

"Well, of course, I *am* committed for Saturday night. Or at least it's far too late in the week for me to admit I'm not. But I'll chuck it for such a legal luminary. Who cares that my abandoned hostess could sell the Pacific and buy the Atlantic? It's worth it. I accept!"

"Oh, come now, I don't want you to get out of anything."

"Ah, but I insist."

"Your father would be furious."

"*Raison de plus,* your honor!"

The judge stared at this cocky response, but the engagement was made and kept.

They stayed up as late over their drinks as Beeky would have had he gone to his party. Their mutual sympathy was immediate. Howland sat puffing his pipe and sipping his port as Beeky poured out his doubts about the Meanses and Ehningers, the social life of New York and Southampton, the economy of the nation, the state of the world. He confessed his low esteem for his father, complained of the little help that he received from his mother and excoriated his sisters for fools. He couldn't write; he didn't want to teach; he had no aptitude for the sciences; he was too shy for politics and he loathed the very idea of business. What was he to do with his life?

The judge's answer was prompt and firm: the law. The law was what the church had been in the Middle Ages: the only ladder available for the elevation of the reflective, the introspective, the noncompetitive in a society of brigands. Beeky was to go to law school that very fall and eventually to come into Shepard & Howland. When Beeky brought up his ethical doubts and pointed out that absolute straightness had not invariably been associated with a Wall Street practice, the judge burst into a violent homily that he was never to forget.

"The great lawyers are all decent men. Never doubt that, Beekman! People who say they aren't are either vicious or ignorant. I have practiced law on Wall Street for half a century without having once done a thing that I should not be willing to cry out before the assembled bar association. I have, it is true, on occasion had to tell a client — even an important one — to take his dirty business elsewhere. But the man who can't do that is not a man. Now, of course, there are times when the borderline between right and wrong may be difficult to make out. But the number of those occasions is absurdly exaggerated by lawyers who want to excuse their own reluctance to give up a good fee. What the evil temptation usually boils down to is that you are asked to misrepresent a fact. A good way to avoid it is to avoid too many professional intimacies. Most of the easy camaraderie in American business life is intentionally designed to create intimacies that can be taken advantage of. Half the crooked things men do are done because they're afraid to be disagreeable to their so-called 'pals.' Learn to *hate* the man who asks you to do a wrong thing, Beeky. And then you'll find that your simple duty becomes your simple pleasure!"

Beeky felt like a citizen of ancient Alexandria, sated with the pleasures and sophistication of the town who hears in the rude tones of a desert anchorite the note of an unmistakable and liberating truth. He had found no solace in the church. Somehow that area had been rendered tasteless by his mother's placid preoccupation with it. If one parent thus tended to occupy, to the exclusion of offspring, the seemingly overdecorated and overheated spaces of the spirit, the other, by a process of more direct antagonization, had soured the temptations of the world. What was there left but the vision of Hobart Howland?

VII

The Marriage Contract

THE VISION, or fantasy, of which Marcus Currier could never quite rid himself was that of coming home to his apartment on Madison Avenue, as tired as any lawyer who had worked to midnight ought to be, yet vibrant with the glow of knowing that the bad point in the tough brief had been worked out at last, to find Felicia, radiantly fresh in her silver negligee, waiting up for him (the two little girls long healthily sleeping) over a tray of whiskey and ice and light little sandwiches, ready to hear about the toil of his day in Shepard, Putney & Cox and to give him in exchange, more amusingly and more briefly (oh, yes, he faced the implications of such condescension!), the happier trivia of her own. But each night when he had worked late, as he turned westward after mounting the subway steps, on darkened and deserted 77th Street, he had to adjust his image to the drastically different domestic scene that he was about to encounter.

Yet the very less Felicia realized his silly dream, the more tensely he clung to it. Even in his most resentful moments he still acknowledged that he did not want her to be like his mother or grandmother. Was it not her very deviation from this norm that had constituted her original attraction? His mother had always been so insipidly, so antiseptically pretty, with such a sexless slip of a figure, so afraid of not doing or saying just the right, the genteel thing, yet so ready all the same to be fed to the biggest lions for the smallest principles. Marc felt impatience, almost anger at times that his father's early death and her wonderful courage in bearing it had always protected her from the natural rudeness of her sole offspring. His grandmother had also survived his grandfather, and in much the same heroic way, so that they seemed, the two of them, widows of the bar, relicts of brilliant advocates who had "burned themselves out young," like two brave Brittany peasant women whose fishermen husbands, as in a Loti novel, had been lost at sea and who survived in gaunt chorus, grim symbols of resignation to the risks of their trade.

Marc, of course, knew that they both detested Felicia. They did not say it; they did not even imply it. They simply showed it in the intensity of their demonstrations of affection for his two little girls, as if to make up for noted maternal absences, and in their solicitude for his own health, so that whenever on a weekend he dropped by the apartment that they frugally shared, they seemed to be waiting with hot towels ready for his presumably aching head. Their Marcus might have been on leave from wars to which as a good Roman he would have soon to return, like his slaughtered father and grandfather before him, with the likelihood of a similar fate. It was almost too much for the women of his blood to bear that he should lack a Virgilia to pay him a proper attention and to guard his lares and penates while he fought the Volscians.

"You know, they're absolutely incredible," Felicia once remarked, with the detachment that always characterized her observations of his family. "They couldn't have existed anywhere but in their own place and time. Your grandmother can talk about nothing but a woman's domestic duties, yet she hardly knows how to boil an egg. She seems to think that we do our duty to one man by making ourselves unattractive to

all others. And, so far as I can make it out, your mother's
credo reduces itself to the principle that a woman aids her
loved ones just by brooding about them. It's a pity she's not
religious. At least then she could pray."

"Well, Mother can cook. And clean, too."

"She certainly can clean. That roast chicken last Sunday
was positively scrubbed."

Coming out of the dark street into the lighted lobby, Marc
asked the old doorman if his wife was home.

"Not yet, Mr. Currier."

Upstairs in the apartment he found Ida, the nurse, reading
the newspaper by a single light in the living room.

"Mr. Herring came by. They went to a lecture at the Metropolitan."

Ida, with heavy Swedish imperturbability, was lethargic to
the point of denying suspicion. Herring lived with his old
mother in the building, the harmless bachelor friend who only
dreamed of not being harmless. Felicia could have done far
better — had she wanted. And even as Marc made his way to
the bar table in the dark dining alcove he heard her latchkey
and turned to see her framed in the light of the elevator lobby.
She had leaned down to pick up a circular that a neighbor had
dropped and was now glancing at it, fluffing out her long dark
hair with her left hand. He reflected, half in pain, that she was
as white and thin and strong as when he had married her, as
direct and bold and beautiful.

"Go to bed, Ida. Oh, is that you, Marc? Make me one, too.
How's the brief? Did you work out that point?"

"Well, I have a draft."

"May I read it?"

"It's in my briefcase. On top."

When he brought her the whiskey she was already reading
it, seated on the sofa, and she reached out a hand for the glass

without taking her eyes from the page. Ten minutes passed.

"I think it's good. Only I wonder if you don't make too much of the independent engineer. After all, the company certified to counsel that the vats were for an antipollution purpose. Aren't you getting rather dangerously close to the position that your opinion on the bonds guarantees the facts?"

He sighed, in reluctant admiration of the speed with which her mind darted to the dead center of any tangle of circumstances.

"I'm going to bed. I'm bushed."

"Oh, darling, I'm sorry. You work too hard. You ought to cut down."

"Everyone can't be as quick as you."

"But what's the point of our both working, if you have to put in so many nights?"

"The point?" He paused on his way to the bedroom to stare at her in resentful surprise. "Why, isn't the point that you're entitled to your own career?"

"Oh, that of course. But isn't there still a way it can be *our* career?"

"How? By my staying home and looking after the girls?"

"You *are* bushed. Go to bed."

But he held his ground. "I'm perfectly serious, Felicia. What were you driving at?"

She got up to get a match. Her quick stride to the mantel and the brisk way she turned back to him as she lit the cigarette seemed to repudiate the morbidity that he knew she felt to be oozing from him. "Simply that if there are two lawyers in the family, neither one should have to break his neck."

"*His* neck?"

"Well, I'm not breaking mine."

"I quite realize that. But do you suggest that the partners of

Shepard, Putney and Cox should give *me* credit for the beautiful work you're doing in Sloane and Sidell?"

"Don't be cranky. These firms aren't the end of the world. Why should we work for rivals? Why shouldn't we practice together? Then we could set our own pace. You wouldn't have to kill yourself for Mr. Ehninger. We'd have our evenings together. We might even go away on weekends. Travel, sometimes. Oh, Marc, think of it!"

She looked very beautiful as she came up to him and placed her hands appealingly on his shoulders, yet he stepped back churlishly from the embrace. "What happens to my career? I'd be Mr. Felicia Currier!"

"You would not. You'd be one of the Curriers of Currier and Currier. Nobody would know which! Can't you see any other goal in life but a partnership in Shepard, Putney and Cox?"

"No!"

"It's an obsession, honey. Shake it. A law firm is only another tool to make a happy life with."

"What's unhappy about being a partner in a corporation law firm? It was good enough for my father and grandfather."

"Oh, of course. And I suppose you wish I were like your mother and grandmother."

"At times."

"Did I ever give you reason to think I would be?"

"Never. You were always scrupulously fair. You never gave me the occasion to develop the smallest illusion that you weren't a genius."

Their long exchanged stare, the product of her shock and his mulishness, tensed the atmosphere.

"You're so bitter tonight."

"I'm bushed. I've told you."

"Then go to bed."

"Aren't you coming?"

"I think I'll read a while." She paused and then, in a final effort, went up and put her arms around his waist, under his jacket. "Unless you feel you're not too tired for something else. I had hoped the evening might end differently. Poor Sam Herring. He makes me think of the great guy I have at home."

"I'm sorry. I am too tired."

Of course, after such loutishness he could not sleep, nor did he feel that he deserved to. But he could not have made love to her that night had they been floating, Cleopatra and Antony, down the Nile on a barge of gold to the twanging of languorous harps. Now Felicia would sit up late, perhaps even sleep on the living room sofa. Lying alone, he reviewed monotonously the catalogue of her perfections.

Could he even console himself that she was deficient as a mother? Certainly not. She came home every evening at half-past six to read to the girls and help them with their homework. She never went out before both were in bed. Surely there must have been countless nonworking mothers who saw their children less. And then Felicia used her time with the girls so imaginatively; she seemed so on top of their every interest and hobby. Small wonder that with such versatility, and without even working at night or on weekends, she was doing as well in her firm as he in his.

Her final triumph was that she seemed to have no ambition. She shared none of his dreams of partnership and professed to value her clerkship only as an apprenticeship to some broader, more publicly useful, practice of law. As Marc began to doze off he half dreamed of her as Portia, prevailing over Shylock. He, of course, was Shylock, a scuffling, mumbling, snarling rag of a creature, cowering before the tall female figure in

white raiment with upraised, condemning arm. But what was
the flesh that he was so excoriated for seeking? What was the
real shame of his cannibalism? What did he want that plain,
normal men weren't supposed to want? How could the world
survive if all the males were Antonios and all the females
judges?

o

The next morning, in Beeky Ehninger's office, they discussed
the brief. Beeky fixed his large, staring gray-green eyes on
Marc.

"You don't think we're making too much of that independent engineer?"

"That's what Felicia asked."

"Oh, does Felicia read your briefs?"

Marc flushed. "Sometimes. When there's no conflict of interest with Sloane and Sidell."

"I wasn't critcizing. I'm sure she's a mine of discretion. But
it seems to one of my generation such an odd relationship to
have with one's wife. I can't conceive of Annabel reading a
brief, much less writing one. But I suppose it's fun. Another
way of sharing."

"There are times when I wonder if I may not have a bit too
much of your generation in me."

Beeky stared at him even harder. "So it's not all rose-
colored then. You look tired, Marc. I'm afraid you've been
overdoing it."

"I hope my work doesn't show it."

"Not really. Although I thought I could detect just a trace
of staleness in your last draft. Maybe it's just my imagination.
Is everything all right? If I seem too curious, perhaps I
should tell you that I'm backing you for partner in the firm."

Marc felt suddenly dizzy. It was as if he were looking down

at this worried little man from the top of a high ladder. The sensation was followed by the horror that he might be going to weep.

"It's very kind of you, sir," he murmured. "I hadn't expected anything so soon."

"It's not kind of me at all. I'm looking after myself and looking after my firm. But you're not going to make things any easier for me if you work yourself into a nervous breakdown. Next weekend is Columbus Day, and you and Felicia will be asked to the Coxes' in Oyster Bay. See you accept. Annabel and I will be there. I've put Hubert up to this because I want him to know you better."

Marc felt that he would die for Beeky Ehninger. "Gosh, sir, that's wonderful, but you know I have to finish this brief. I'm sure Mr. Cox will understand."

"I'm sure he won't. Look, my friend. This brief is not due for two weeks. I know something about overtime work in the law shops. A lot of it's necessary, but some of it's compulsive. With you I'm beginning to wonder. If you care about your career in Shepard, Putney and Cox, you'll come to the Coxes'. What about Felicia? Will she be able to get off?"

"Felicia can always get off. That's the thing about Felicia."

"Well, why can't you borrow a page from her notebook?"

Marc was surprised into a laugh. "There's no guarantee *that* would land me where you say you want to see me!"

"Oh, I'll take my chances with Felicia."

o

The Hubert Coxes' house in Oyster Bay was, like everything else to which the senior partner put his hand in private life, "overimproved." That is to say, he could never have got his money out. Brilliant as he was at One New Orange Plaza, brilliant as he was reputed to have been in government, he was nonetheless a notorious failure as an investor, a father, a house planner and a gardener. His ventures in oil and in mines had all collapsed, his many offspring were lamentably unable to hang on either to their jobs or their spouses and his Oyster Bay black shingle house, purchased at a bargain price as part of an old estate in one of his "poor" periods, refused to respond to the money that he had thereafter lavished on it. The swimming pool looked too opulent, the greenhouse too metallic, the rose garden too pompous. But Hubert's sustained curiosity and enthusiasm for new things and people made him a lively host. Felicia was enchanted with him.

"I've made arrangements for you and me to ride this afternoon," he told her. "There were only two mounts left at Mac's Stable, but they're ours."

"And how did you know that I ride?"

"I figured that a securities lawyer at Sloane and Sidell had to be able to do anything."

"Haven't you got your quadrupeds confused? It's the camel I'm paid to get through that needle's eye."

"Confused? But what do you think we're riding? Your dromedary is called 'Become Effective.'"

"Aha. I thought the senior partner of Shepard, Putney and Cox would at least treat me to an ass!"

So the two of them went off with great hilarity. Marc was proud of Felicia for being so little the submissive associate's wife. His own mission for the afternoon seemed less venturesome. He was to walk with Mrs. Ehninger. Annabel had prepared for the autumnal woods with an elaboration that revealed her distrust of them. Her plump figure was clad in rich red tweed, her feet encased in shiny new boots, her blond hair concealed under a mink toque. These casings, however, only intensified the hard white look of her round face and the beady blackness of her eyes. Against the red and yellow of the foliage she looked her age.

"I think your wife's enchanting, Mr. Currier," she began. "But, of course, she's a riddle to me. In my generation there were women who worked, but they were apt to be big and brassy and unfeminine. Thank God, Mrs. Currier's not that type."

"No, and none of her friends are. They manage to work and still be attractive."

"*Very* attractive. If I were Sophie Cox, I'd have gone riding today. But tell me, do you never mind her working downtown, with all those men?"

"I don't mind the men." Did he not? But the climax of being at the Coxes', with all it presaged in the way of partnership, and with Felicia's still not caring, suddenly excited and angered him at once. He felt like shouting.

"Isn't that rather complacent?" Mrs. Ehninger inquired.

"Perhaps. But I've never been jealous of the men around Felicia."

"What are you jealous of? Surely not the women?"

Marc did not try to smile. He was too absorbed in facing what he *was* jealous of. "I'll tell you something, Mrs. Ehninger. Something I've never told anybody. Not even my mother. I *hate* her practicing law."

There it was, out of his mouth, out of the fetid little cell of his smothered resentments, escaping to the red and yellow woods, the sapphire sky, to be oddly dignified, curiously ennobled by the afternoon air. Annabel paused and looked blandly around, as if to take in the event, and Marc recognized his exhilaration as relief.

"My goodness," she murmured.

"I want my wife home, damn it all! I want her to look after me and my kids. I don't care if I sound Victorian. Every

working woman just enslaves another. How could Felicia do
what she does without our nurse? I wish she'd do the job herself for a while."

"Have you never told your wife how you feel?"

"Never. She'd scorn me."

"I wonder. She might be glad to know how much you de-
pend on her. I saw the way she looked at you at lunch today.
You're a very attractive man, my friend, with that curly lock
of premature gray hair and those big hurt gray eyes. And that
blush! If I were twenty-five years younger, I'd have found a
better occupation for our afternoon than a country walk. And
then Mrs. Currier would have had to look up from her law-
books! You must forgive a bawdy old bag. Tell me, how is
everything between you and her in the bed department?"

"Well . . . I don't know . . . I guess I've had no complaints."

"And you guess I'm one hell of a nosy bitch."

"Oh, no, Mrs. Ehninger, I . . ."

"It's all right. I had to check. Now listen to me, young man.
You tell that girl you want her home. Tell her she's got to be
a wife. Before anything else. Before a mother, even. Of
course, you've got to be fair yourself. You've got your obligations, too. You can't come home at midnight and be too tired
for you know what. You must keep your figure and your mus-
cles and your zip. And remember this: when the woman
wears the pants, the man ends by wearing the skirt. You may
think yourself a long way from having to buy your clothes at
Bendel's, my boy, but the time could come!"

"She'd just call me a male chauvinist pig."

"She may call you a lot of things, but never mind that.
Deep down, she'll like it."

Marc decided that Annabel was Mother Earth herself.
Perhaps he had allowed himself to lose sight of fundamental

values. Later that evening, as he showered and dressed for dinner, while Felicia was still out riding, he reflected that his mother and grandmother had never properly taught him the true role of a woman. Poor creatures, how could they? They had been simply slaves, without even being sexy slaves. Indeed, it might have been their sole integrity, fished up from who knew what murky depths of unrecognized sex antagonism, *not* to be sexy. Felicia, with her beautiful body and her happy use of it, had originally struck him as a goddess to whom it would have been presumptuous to offer anything but equal rule on the heights of Mount Olympus. Only the plain Jane should mind the hearth. Didn't that theory *have* to be crazy?

When Felicia came up, flushed from her long ride in the cold, he told her peremptorily to wear her red, not her black dress. Then he hurried down to the parlor and drank several cocktails. During dinner, which was attended by many neighbors, he held forth with what he considered remarkable brilliance on the unconstitutionality of antibusing statutes. When he and Felicia went up to their room at the end of the evening he felt little doubt that he was a great lawyer, a great jurist and a great husband.

Less than half an hour after he had turned off the lights, however, he developed at least a temporary doubt about his rating in the last category. Felicia rose, put on her robe and turned on the light by the chaise longue. Then she settled down with a book.

"I get the point," he muttered.

"Well, who told you to play Romeo after six martinis? Mrs. Ehninger? Go knock on her door."

"I'm sorry about the bum performance. I'd planned it as a kind of herald."

"To what, for God's sake?"

"To my great demand."

Felicia looked up, waiting. He knew the time was out of joint, but he could not stop himself. He sat up in bed and cleared his throat.

"I want you to give up the law."

"You're not serious!"

"I want you to give up the law and stay home. At least till the girls go to boarding school." Under the reading light her face had become pale and set. Marc couldn't make out any expression at all in her eyes. "Please, Felicia, don't turn me down flat. I'm going to be a better husband, I swear. We'll do some of that traveling you spoke of."

"Is this what you discussed with Mrs. Ehninger?"

"No!"

"You expect me to believe that?"

"What does it matter what I discussed with Mrs. Ehninger?"

After a pause, she shrugged. "It doesn't, of course." Her tone was now level, detached. "I must admit, the timing is curious. I had been meaning to tell you tomorrow I was going to resign from Sloane and Sidell."

"Felicia!"

"Wait. Brian Leonard, one of our litigation partners, has great pull with the NAPL."

"The what?"

"The National Anti-Pollution League. Oh, you know it, Marc, we've talked about it dozens of times. It brings suits against corporations and municipalities that pollute the environment. Mr. Leonard had recommended me to head up the section on inland waters. It's all too good to be true except for one thing."

"*One* thing! What, pray, is one thing?"

"I'd have to go to Washington for a couple of months. Until they set up the New York office."

"You mean, it's not just a question of refusing to give up law? You won't practice in the same city? I can't even settle for the status quo? My God, Felicia!"

She had risen and was standing at the end of the bed. There was no superiority or condescension now in her expression. She was obviously much troubled. "Oh, Marc, I want you to go with me. The NAPL has a job for you, too. It isn't quite as good a one as mine, but all that can be adjusted later. You'd be in the electric power department. Between us, we'd be making a thousand bucks a year more than we're making now. But that's not the point. The point is to get out of our stuffy life and do something big. And we'd be working together and fighting together and growing together. Oh, darling, say you'll think about it, at least!"

Marc reached down to pull the quilt up. He had suddenly felt the autumn night air through the open window, and he shivered, tucking the folds together under his sides.

"You say that yours is the better job?"

"But that's just the way we start. After we've been there a bit, we could switch."

"Why should I want to take your job? But tell me something else. Even leaving aside all questions of my own preference and my own career, how can you justify my throwing away the income I'd be making if I became a partner in my firm?"

"What would we need it for? Half of it would go in taxes. And this way we'd have such *fun*."

"You would, I guess. I'm tired, Felicia. I think I'll go to sleep."

"Marc! Won't you at least consider it?"

"I won't consider leaving my firm, no. If you can't understand what that means to me, there's very little point my trying to explain."

Oh, she was cold now, as cold as he, as cold as he had imagined she might have been when the conversation started. It was always a bit exciting and sickening to find how easy it was to break things.

"And by like token, I suppose I was a fool to try to explain what my opportunity means to me. But let's at least be clear about facts if we're not about reasons. I intend to take this job, Marc."

2

Felicia lay awake for an hour beside the sleeping body of her husband. It was a deep sleep, induced by cocktails, shaken by snores. It represented the simpler side of his nature, similar to the nature of an air force pilot who can catch twenty winks before a raid. She remembered reading of an aviator who had walked out of the flames of his crashed plane with a normal pulse. Had he been, the article had queried, heroic or neurotic?

But that was just an article. She *knew* that Marc was neurotic. She had long recognized as a symptom of his ailment the compulsion to keep on doing the thing that he happened to be doing. He hated, for example, to stop playing tennis or golf, or to leave a drinking party, or to turn off television. He could even be a bore in the length of his lovemaking. Friends had observed that it was fortunate that such persistency should have found its ultimate outlet in law, for that otherwise Felicia might have found herself, on his behalf, consulting a heart specialist or Alcoholics Anonymous. But she was not sure. She feared and distrusted the dark cloud of industriousness that seemed increasingly, as time went by, to envelop him. She thought she could even make out that it had nothing to do with his professional ambition or with his love of the law. It appeared to her more a miasma exhaled by some fetid, evil presence, some agent of a disdained, malignant deity. It seemed to have darkened the air between them so that he could hardly distinguish any longer, if he still cared to, her pleading eyes, her outstretched arms. He was drawn instead to the gaunt spectral figures of his mother and grandmother, looming in the background, stripped of their individuality by the same arcane curse but still endowed with power to lure him to their fate.

So anyway she was dreaming when she awoke with a gasp to discover that it was brilliant morning and that Marc was still asleep. She dressed quickly, ate her breakfast alone downstairs and then drove over to visit her mother. Letitia Bruce, separated from her third husband, spent her weekends alone in a small white cottage attached to a large greenhouse where she cultivated begonias. During the week she worked as feature editor of a fashion magazine. She was a big, plain, gray, simply dressed woman with a crinkled face and intelligent eyes which offered a sympathy that she seemed never able to deliver. She sprayed her pots as Felicia told of her plan.

"Work in Washington? With the children here?" Both hands being engaged, Letitia mumbled through a cigarette. "You'll crack."

"It's only for a couple of months."

"What does Marc say?"

"He doesn't like it. But he hasn't said no."

"Would it make any difference if he did?"

"Oh, Tish."

Letitia shrugged. "Well, I never can tell with your contemporaries. Not that I can boast about my own success with husbands — that's for sure. But at least mine all left *me*. If even one of them had so much as left a forwarding address, I'd have gone crawling after. But you're better than that. No, don't look at me that way. I'm not being sarcastic."

"Not much!"

"Well, what do you want?"

"Maybe to be treated as a daughter for a bit, and not always as an equal or superior. Oh, I know I've made it hard for you. But I'm all up in the air. I don't even know how much Marc cares."

"Is that what you don't know? Or is it how much *you* care?"

"Oh, Tish, help me!"

"I'm sorry, dear. I don't think I can. You've always been so in charge of yourself. It's a bit late to change all that."

"Why does everybody hate an independent woman?"

"Now you're feeling sorry for yourself. May I point out that it was *your* idea to take this job? Not mine or Marc's. If it makes you happy, go ahead. If it doesn't, chuck it. Perhaps being a hedonist is the practical answer."

"Ah, if I knew what I wanted!"

When she got back to the Coxes', she found that Marc had gone into the city with their host. Beeky Ehninger explained it in the hall.

"They had a call on the opinion letter about the engineers. It's got to be cleared up before the conference with the attorney general at nine tomorrow. I'm sorry, Felicia."

"Why? I don't give a damn."

"About the opinion? Or about Marc's leaving?"

"About either."

"I find that hard to believe."

"Do you, Mr. Ehninger? Ask your wife. She knows that I'm simply a frustrated female who's jealous of my husband's law practice. That's why I practice myself. Didn't you know? To make him jealous."

"Perhaps you've succeeded."

"Oh, I'm sick of the bunch of you."

She drove back to New York before lunch. That night she had to wait up until 1:00 A.M. for Marc to come home. He was tired, almost groggy, but she insisted that they discuss her plans.

"I've mapped out the details, Marc, and I want to talk now."

She told him that she was going to resign from Sloane & Sidell that same morning. As she had just completed a registration statement, she should be free to leave for Washington by the end of the week. She planned to stay there for two to three months, coming home every Friday night to spend the weekend with the girls. Ida could manage the rest if she had two days a week off. Felicia was clear, cool, precise. Marc answered in grunts or shrugs. Only in ending did she contribute a vindictive note.

"Don't worry. You will still be able to work every night. I'm going to leave things so you needn't even notice I've gone."

It was the giddiest self-indulgence, but her need was so great that she might have been taking the new job simply for the opportunity of getting this meanness off her chest. Of course, it was fatal to the last chance of a happy settlement. The sulky silence with which Marc received it characterized his conduct for the rest of the week. When the day of her departure came, she wondered if he would even kiss her goodby so she avoided the issue by going before he came home, leaving one of those notes about hating farewells. The whole thing was about as bad as it could be.

○

Felicia was surprised by her reaction to life in Washington. She had expected to be miserable. She had anticipated that she would worry constantly about the little girls and Marc and be jumpy with guilt; she had imagined that the emotional ambiance in which she would go through the motions of living would be hollow, dreamlike, scary, that she would pay the full penalty of giving in to the integrity of her mulishness. She had even feared that she would be in no condition for effective work. But things did not work out that way.

In the first place, the work was stimulating as she had never known work to be. She found herself deeply involved in finding practical answers to nationally important questions. There were no clients to please, no partners to placate. She had a boss, but he was congenial. The organization was new, fresh, idealistic, backed with a large foundation grant and the blessings of the forward-looking. Oh, it was the honeymoon, to be sure, but honeymoons could be fun. Hers with Marc had been.

Secondly, she found that her daughters adjusted themselves easily to her absence. After all, they were at school most of the day, and she came home for the weekends. But what was oddest of all — even rather shocking — was the relief she felt in not being angry anymore with Marc. When she did not know that he was working at night, she thought of him almost without resentment. He was her beloved husband, of course, but her beloved husband in New York. She did not go out with other men, but she went to cocktail parties given by lawyers in the office, and although she tried to make clear that she and Marc were only temporarily living apart, she suspected that this was not generally believed. After a while she did not insist upon it, fearing to protest too much. Anyway, it was nobody's business.

In the fourth week of her absence the oldest girl, Ruth, came down with flu, and Marc telephoned to say that his mother had moved into the apartment to help take care of her. Felicia was incensed, but she did not see how she could validly object. Mrs. Currier moved out on Friday before her daughter-in-law had returned for the weekend, but Ruth's room was full of little evidences of her grandmother's plan shortly to return.

"I trust your mother's not coming back," Felicia told Marc before her departure on Sunday night. "Ruth's perfectly well again."

"But she can't go to school before Wednesday. Mother can play games and read to her."

"She doesn't have to move in to do that."

"She and I find it more convenient that way."

"But *I* don't. I've got this apartment set up, and I don't want your mother interfering with my arrangements."

"She doesn't interfere."

"Oh, doesn't she? The first thing you know, Ida will leave. She doesn't want your mother always peering over her shoulder."

"If you want to run the apartment I suggest you live in it."

"Do you mean that, Marc? Are things that way between us?"

"How else do you expect them to be?"

"Then I'll take an apartment in Washington and move the girls down there."

"What about school?"

"They'll have to change."

"What about me?"

"You can be totally happy here with your darling mother."

"Haven't you forgotten something?"

"What?"

"Your law. And a little thing called the matrimonial domicile. You can't move the girls from New York without my consent."

"So you've looked *that* up."

"Don't you think it was time?"

"What have we come to, Marc? Is this a separation?"

"Haven't you made it one?"

When she left to take the shuttle half an hour later, it had been agreed that when she came home the following weekend he would go to his mother's. The next morning Ida telephoned to complain to Felicia that Mrs. Currier had moved into the apartment with two bags of clothing and that Marc's grandmother expected tea every afternoon when she called on the children. Hostilities had begun.

Felicia had an instinctive sense that the Currier women were challenging her directly, as females of an enemy tribe, and not simply as worshipers of a son and grandson. It was all very well for them to have built their lives on the premise that they lived in a man's world, but was not this premise based on another, namely that the so-called stronger sex depended as vitally on the administrations of the weaker as had the cotton kings of old upon the institution of slavery? Marc might have been Coriolanus, but what was Coriolanus without his woman but a poor ranting fool who might be expected to prove a victim to his own pique and bad temper? If his mother and grandmother loathed Felicia and condemned her conduct as abominable, did they not also consider that her principal crime lay in having taken with her to Washington the machinery that kept her husband going? Certainly it never crossed their minds to suppose that *she* might be faring any worse without the company and consolation of a spouse.

And was she? Was it their divination of this that aroused her anger? Was it her resentment of them that she took out on the unfortunate Mrs. Ehninger when she met her in Beeky's suite at the Mayfair Hotel where they were staying on a business trip to the capital? Beeky had telephoned to ask her for lunch, and she was disagreeably surprised to find his wife alone by a coffee table covered with cocktail things, wearing the same tweeds that she remembered from the Cox weekend.

"Beeky will be right out. Have a drink."

"Thanks, but not on a workday."

"I hope you're going back to that handsome husband of yours."

Felicia, still standing, stared with indignation at those small, squinting, ogling eyes. "I haven't left him, Mrs. Ehninger."

"Then what are you doing in Washington?"

"I hardly see that's your affair. But I don't mind telling you that my being here is entirely with Marc's consent. It's not desertion, if that's what you're getting at."

"What *I'm* getting at! You, my dear, are the one who's being legal. I don't understand what you young women want out of life today. In my time, if a girl had a good-looking husband and everything was all right in the bed department, she knew when she was well off. Now from what I gather everything *is* . . ."

"Annabel, please!" Beeky Ehninger came hastily in from the bedroom, pushing a handkerchief into his breast pocket. "I'm sorry, Felicia. Annabel has never got over a comparison that somebody once made of her to Chaucer's Wife of Bath. Shall we go down and lunch?"

To Felicia's great relief Annabel did not accompany them. In the dining room, as soon as they had ordered, Beeky came gravely to the point.

"I'm very much concerned about Marc. Do you know that he's been drinking heavily?"

"Heavily!" Felicia's voice rose in a cry more of repudiation than distress. "What are you talking about? A man doesn't become an alcoholic in a month's time."

"Doesn't he?"

Beeky proceeded to round out the dismal chapter. Marc

was supposed to be working in the evenings but he had not been. Ronny Simmonds had told Beeky that he had come twice to his apartment, late at night, drunk, and begged Ronny to go out with him to a bar, with that irritating assumption of younger married men that their bachelor compatriots spend all their evenings in riot and dissipation.

"Ronny Simmonds is jealous of Marc's success in the office, that's all! I'm surprised you should listen to him."

"I can't see why he should be jealous of Marc, since he's leaving the office himself."

"He's only leaving because men like Marc have bested him."

"Now, Felicia, that's not worthy of you. I think I know a bit more about our associates than you do. After all, that firm has been my life, my family."

Felicia looked away from those large haunted eyes. She felt frenzied with impatience and frustration. Wasn't it bad enough to be pecked at by the old witch of a tramp upstairs, who reveled in fantasies of the sex life of her husband's subordinates, without having to endure the damp sympathy of this sublimated faggot who could not even understand that his principal motive for practicing law was to be in a position to enforce the confidences of handsome young men? Why the hell didn't the two of them go to dirty movies?

"What do you want me to do about it?" she exclaimed.

"Something very simple. I want you to come home. I can arrange it. I know the head of your organization. I even gave him some money. He's planning to set up a New York office, anyway. I can fix it that you'll be the advance scout. You can have temporary quarters at Shepard, Putney and Cox. You . . ."

"Mr. Ehninger, has it ever occurred to you that people might like to lead their own lives? Even if they make messes of them?"

"My dear young lady, I'm only trying to help!"

She sighed in exasperation at the simple pain in those gray-green eyes. "Maybe you are. Maybe I'm unfair. But damn it all, can you really think I'm obliged to go back to my old life, just because my husband's such a weakling that he takes to the bottle thirty days after I've got a new job?" She knew that Beeky would never help her now, but she also saw that he sympathized. Maybe that would be enough. Maybe the shock of shoving the truth into the white, rabbity blankness of his love-thy-neighbor look would give her the courage to live alone. "Must I sit by and watch while he works day and night for money I don't want and don't need, sweating for causes I don't believe in? Do you expect me to turn into a zombie, like his mother and grandmother? Acolytes at the altar of a god who has ceased to exist, even for them? Oh, Mr. Ehninger, what a life! Have *you* liked it?"

"But I live more for my firm than for the law."

"Well, I don't!"

"I can see your problem, but I can't see that you have explored all the alternatives."

"Can *you* get Marc to see a psychiatrist?"

"If I ask him to go to a psychiatrist, his pride will make him ask you to go to one. There's no end to that. What we need is something immediate. Something practical."

"Excuse me, Mr. Ehninger. Do you claim to represent my husband?"

Beeky's smile made him look even more foolishly boyish. "Only on one condition. That I represent you, too."

"You seem to forget that Marc and I are both lawyers."

"How could I forget what's precisely the trouble? Now you listen to me, young lady. I am determined not to let you and Marc ruin your careers *or* your marriage. They seem to me to go together. You're both lawyers to the marrow of your bones

— and you're both in love. Oh, yes, you are, Felicia. If the law can't solve your problem, then I say with Mr. Bumble that the law is a ass. I propose that we draw up a simple contract in which you agree to respect Marc's desire for a corporate law practice and he agrees to respect your desire for a public law practice, provided only that you both agree to practice in New York. The rest is detail. You will each be allowed two nights a week to work until midnight. There will be similar stipulations for weekends and vacations and for the allocation of social life between the clients of each."

"Are you serious?"

"Perfectly serious."

"Do you actually think such an agreement could be enforced by a court?"

"I'm not such a dope. It would simply provide the guidelines for the conduct of two honorable persons during a period of difficulty. Once you know it has worked, you can tear it up. Let me try my hand at it. What can you lose?"

"How do you propose to try?"

"By sending you each a draft of the agreement before the end of the week. If nothing else will bring you together, contempt for my draftsmanship may."

"You make me feel like the law. A ass."

"My dear girl, you have a problem that would baffle any woman. Just say you'll agree to read my draft, and we'll speak no more about it."

"How can I say I won't read a draft?"

That afternoon Felicia did not pretend to work. She sat in the library gazing out the window over an opened volume of *The Federal Reporter.* Around her, above her, in hundreds of big books and loose-leaf folders, red, blue, brown, gray, black, was the accumulation of thousands upon thousands of ideas of how men should live together: whom they might take from and not take from, whom they might kill and not kill, whom they might hurt and not hurt. Perhaps she had been guilty of arrogance in thinking that the law could not work out her problems. Perhaps she had been like some grave priestess, exhorting the multitude to righteousness while nursing a secret atheism. What was Beeky asking her to do but to let the law, the law of sane men, enter into her own life and govern her own actions? What was he asking Felicia and Marcus Currier but to open the door to their private cellar of self-pity, all jammed as it was with the cherished old furniture of fantasies of pride, and clean it out?

"No!"

She rose in sudden passion and strode back to her own little office. She slammed the door and stood with her hands resting on the desk, her eyes tightly closed. Oh, that agreement of Beeky's, how she saw it now, with all its remorselessly priggish little phrases! With its demure little party of the first part, its prurient little party of the second part, agreeing not to molest, not to interfere, not to sue, not to make claims. She saw all the tight, empty little clauses designed by lawyers to protect women like Marc's mother and grandmother from the natural consequences of their sexlessness. Well, she wanted no such protection. She wanted no hollow relic of long discarded ecclesiastical law to rule her life. What was Beeky's contract but a source of emotional pollution?

As she put her hand on the telephone to call the Mayfair it rang. It was Marc's voice, tense and excited.

"Felicia, have you talked to Mr. Ehninger?"

"I just had lunch with him."

"Did you agree to read his draft?"

"I did, but I was just about to call him to say . . ."

"Felicia! If you'll accept it, I will!"

She had a vision of a thousand movies unrolling their reels

into her mind, miles of celluloid on which were stamped multitudinous images of nice young husbands and nice young wives making up, saying these things to each other, blurting out "I love you!" overcoming their pride, their self-pity, melting into each other's celluloid arms. Could she be big enough, or fool enough, to give in to him?

"Can you tell me that you love me, Marc?"

"Darling, I love you."

"And that you really want me back on those terms?"

"Yes!"

"Then I agree to read the draft."

When she hung up, she was panting with the passion of her defeat. She understood now why Mr. Ehninger had drawn up his little agreement. After all, he was no fool.

VIII

Shepard & Howland

BEFORE HE BECAME A LAWYER, Beeky Ehninger had never done any real work in his life. At school he had used his frail health and frequent absences and a worried mother's indulgent interferences to avoid the more taxing subjects, and at college he had elected courses in literature and art appreciation where a bit of taste and a nice turn of phrase could command average grades. But at Harvard Law School and afterward, in the office of Judge Howland, he had to learn to toughen his mind. There were even moments when, without the judge's encouragement, or perhaps without his fear of incurring the judge's scorn, he would have dropped out altogether and taken the easy sinecure that his father held open in the Means estate office.

Once he had actually started clerking on Wall Street, he felt more secure. From the beginning he was Howland's chief assistant, preferred over clerks of greater seniority and with far better law school records. That was Howland's fashion. He ran Shepard & Howland, now that Elias Shepard was retired, as an absolute despot. It was perfectly understood and received without audible murmur by his rather broken associates that young Ehninger should occupy a special, even a filial position.

The judge practiced law in an old-fashioned, rather violent

way. When he took up a matter, a will, a corporate merger, an appeal, even a divorce, he liked to concentrate on it altogether, and one of Beeky's functions was to see that other cases were taken care of by substitutes. He was almost more of a secretary than a lawyer, for he had to keep track of all Howland's clients and the exact status of each of their matters. Howland would never talk on the telephone, never lunch with a client, never leave his big, shabby, book-filled office except to go to court. But Beeky was more interested in his boss than in the law. He would rather have been Howland's Boswell than his own Johnson. He had the judge's single published volume, the classic *Essay on Equity* mounted in sumptuous morocco. But the old man simply snorted when he showed it to him.

"I always thought that golden reliquaries and jewel-studded missiles heralded the decline of faith. For the true believer, isn't the word enough?"

"But if one wants to honor the word?"

"You do me too much honor, Beeky. It's not right to put a man on a pedestal. All he can do is fall off."

"Oh, sir, you could never do that!"

"At times, young man, you revert to the state of asininity from which I have endeavored to rescue you. Kindly remember that you are not at the Beach Club at Southampton. And when you feel inclined to goggle at such a poor thing as *my* prose, pick up a volume of Maitland and adjust your sights."

Unhappily, Beeky's god was not always benevolent. There was a dry kindness in Howland, an almost unexpected supply of sensitivity and sympathy behind his rigor, but this facet of his nature was more than balanced by an irritability that under some provocations could border on cruelty. Howland was savagely intolerant of inferior work. There were days when Beeky had the mortification of seeing his suggested

amendments to a brief demolished with a contemptuousness
which reminded him — if reminder were needed — that no
matter how high a ledge he might occupy in his superior's
craggy heart, he was always within reach of the stinging whip-
lash of the unyielding perfectionist.

Howland's high standards, of course, deeply affected, actually shaped the office. He cared as much about the general
welfare of his employees and junior partners as a great opera
diva might have cared about that of the stagehands and choruses who made up the background of her performance.
Beyond a vague general benevolence and a waspish eye for
error, he was totally above what he evidently considered the
degrading and menial details of office administration. Had he
taken the trouble to analyze his attitude, he might have said
that the law was a profession for individualists, to be learned
by example. To have watched Hobart Howland was privilege
enough. The wise clerk would then break away and practice
on his own. And the best did, too, which was why Shepard &
Howland was ultimately staffed with subdued, resigned, middle-aged, salaried specialists from whom the spirit of ambition
had passed.

One of these came into Beeky's office on a cold winter
morning to tell him that the judge had a new client, a "real
dude."

"He said you were to go in at ten. He seems tickled pink
over some new real estate job. From the way he kept growl-
ing about 'Attila the Hun,' I wonder if he hasn't found his
chance at last to tackle Joe Lazarus."

"Who?"

"You've led a protected life, I see. Joe Lazarus is trying to
be the landlord of Manhattan. Howland hates his guts. I
sometimes think the old boy keeps his biographer in mind. He
seems to be collecting cases for chapters, one for each great

victory. Well, he hasn't got one yet in real estate. Maybe that's what that dude has brought."

Beeky, entering Howland's office, thought that the old man *did* look rather foxy. But when the "dude" turned around, his heart fell.

"Why, Father! What are *you* doing here?"

"Is it so surprising, Beeky, that I should avail myself of the wisdom that bubbles from this famous font?"

"Your father, Beeky, in his high capacity as chairman of the board of the Church of the Resurrection, has seen fit to retain our services to fight the new barbarians."

Beeky was aware of two sarcasms. There was the sarcasm of Duke, who probably saw himself as a treat to shabby clerks in green eyeshades perched on high stools, a Dickensian milord with shiny boots marching through dingy legal corridors, bringing a vision of Tudor parks and country houses, a lung-filling sense of hounds and halloos. And there was the sharper sarcasm of Howland, bitingly polite, pretending to give the views of his caller his deepest consideration, while privately consigning him to the shelf of fools who had only just brains enough to select the right counsel to save them from the consequences of their foolery. Yet Beeky was soon aware of a third factor. Howland was different. Politer? More compliant. Ah, yes, because Duke was a client. It was not toadyism — far from it. So might a great surgeon benevolently beam on a poor creature with a malignant tumor.

Two of the firm's real estate men came in now, and the judge proceeded to explain, in broad outline, the problems of the Church of the Resurrection. One of New York's oldest, it was also one of its richest, endowed with several dozen acres near the East River below 42nd Street, occupied by business and cheap housing. In the past year the signs of erosion in the area had turned into symptoms of a well-known cancer.

Easements and options had been quietly picked up; leases sublet to undesirable tenants; janitors unaccountably negligent. It was clear that Joe Lazarus was preparing a raid. Under a sleepy management the enemy had infiltrated every unguarded nook or cranny of the Church's title and possession. And now had come the sorry proof: the insulting offer of purchase from a known Lazarus subsidiary.

"Taking a case like this is virtually a public service, gentlemen," the judge exclaimed, tapping a map of the area that was draped unevenly over the piles of paper on his desk. "When I read the manager's sorry report last night, I saw at once that we were up against the most vicious predator of our time: the realtor. And do you know something, my friends? Even a man as vile as Lazarus dare not show himself except in the guise of public benefactor. So deep is the mystique of our sentimentality that he must prate of progress, of adapting the city to the multitudes of the future. He even presumes to put models of his wretched developments in museums! Yet what is his aim in sober fact — what is the aim of any of his kind — but to buy land on credit and pay for it by jacking up rents? He is a parasite, pure and simple."

Duke smiled broadly at his son, basking in the approval of the latter's worshiped boss. "And now the holy church militant, through her faithful servant, Hobart Howland, will deal with the blaspheming Jew!"

"I don't suppose religion is involved, Father," Beeky retorted. "Or is it the Christian slumlord against the Jewish?"

"My son Beeky is a liberal, Hobart. We must watch our tongues. I observe for the record that the rent roll of the Church supports our foreign missions."

Howland glanced from father to son with what struck Beeky as a mischievous look. "Of course, religion is not really involved, Duke. I must agree with Beekman there. Lazarus would march against a synagogue as briskly as against your church. But even such a liberal as you, Beekman, will have to admit that the trade of the realtor is one that seems to have particular appeal for the Hebrew."

"Only because New York is so largely a Jewish city." Antagonism to his father had made Beeky bold. "And I do *not* agree, sir, that all realtors are parasites. They build as well as buy. Even Lazarus, you say, builds."

"Only when his tenements aren't big enough for the maximum rent roll. And then he would tear down the Parthenon itself to put up the biggest, barest box in which to cram his victims."

Beeky said nothing further, but when his father had left and the judge had taken him to lunch at his regular corner table at the Lawyers Club, he asked the waiter to bring him a drink. Howland greeted this unprecedented move with the impassivity that he accorded to the grossest breaches of decorum.

"I'm sorry, Judge, but I'm upset. My father is apt to have that effect on me. He's so awful."

"Calm down, my boy. Remember that I know all about your father. I knew him long before you did."

"Oh, yes, you know everything about him. Everything and nothing. You know that he's small and snobbish and prejudiced. But what you don't see is that he's . . . dead."

"And what has killed him?"

"Well, for one thing, his anti-Semitism."

Howland's eyelids flickered with amusement. "Some of my best friends are anti-Semites."

But Beeky's mood was for blacks and whites. He had no answering smile. "*You* have no such prejudices, I hope, sir."

"Do you think I'd admit them if I had?"

"My father's anti-Semitism is part of his religion. It is a religion of exclusions, shared by his whole caste. It's what has destroyed them."

"Aren't you being a bit dramatic? Every social caste is built on excluding minorities."

"But father's excludes majorities! Maybe if he and his kind lived in Cleveland or Cincinnati or someplace where they were less special, they might be better. Can't you feel the dryness of their mean little world, Judge? They've cut themselves off from the rich, life-giving stream of the real New York."

Howland was decidedly amused. "You're talking about my world as well as your father's. Do you really think we would be richer and more alive if we cultivated men like Lazarus? Richer perhaps."

"But Lazarus is not typical!"

"No, he's smarter."

"Oh, Judge!"

"There's something more important in this, Beeky, than the attitude that you and I may take about the Lazaruses of this world. You should realize that your father is trying to make up to you for parental deficiencies that he is big enough to recognize. He is not a man to whom sentiment comes easily, but in his own way he is very fond of you and anxious to do the right thing. That is why he has brought his church to this office. We are not the regular lawyers for the Resurrection, you know. Sloane and Sidell are. Your father has persuaded his board to retain me as special trial counsel."

Beeky reflected bitterly, as he turned to his salad, that Duke, as usual, had managed to have the last word. Now he had to be grateful to him for getting the church the best lawyer in New York.

As in other litigation matters, Beeky was only indirectly

concerned with the Lazarus affair. He had to attend the conferences where his father was present and to keep generally abreast of what Duke odiously described as the "last crusade." Beeky soon made out Howland's grand strategy: it was to carry the war into the enemy's territory in every way that he could. The judge repudiated all contracts or other agreements made with Lazarus' paper man and sued their principals directly for a malign conspiracy to destroy the value of the Church's holdings. Many of his charges were tenuous, but the campaign had a simple object: to gain time. Howland knew that his opponent always operated on credit. He could never afford extended hostilities.

The rivals offered a striking contrast at the negotiating table. Lazarus was much the younger, young enough to have been Howland's son had such a relationship been conceivable; he was still in his early forties. He seemed to be affecting the pose of the languid, bored heir, lending a reluctant attention to his family's tiresome business managers. He had long, wavy hair and a long, Modigliani face; his suits and ties were of rich material and vivid colors. Indeed, the uninitiated onlooker might have surmised that it was he who represented the Church of the Resurrection and that the real Joe Lazarus was the granite old man with the hooked nose who seemed to exude an air of Old Testament prophecy.

Lazarus' lazy eyes took in everyone. He even seemed to divine the relationship that existed between Beeky and his boss, or a facsimile of it. Beeky found himself distinguished by the realtor: greeted by name, subjected to little jokes, even invited to lunch. His suspicion that he was to be used for the kind of private talks that Lazarus vastly preferred to Howland's open meetings was confirmed one evening in the back seat of the enemy's Rolls Royce, as Beeky found himself transported to his doorstep, despite his plea that he preferred the subway. Lazarus was profuse, fatiguing, insistent. He praised the judge unstintingly.

"They don't make them that way anymore. They broke the mold with that old man. The way he holds himself! The air of superiority! The scorn! He's the most magnificent old ham I've ever seen."

"Ham? He wouldn't thank you for that."

"Oh, wouldn't he! Do you think he doesn't know he's a great actor?"

Beeky reflected a moment. "Are all great lawyers that?"

"Hell, no. He's the rarest of comedians. Or should I say tragedians?"

"You mean he's not sincere?"

"Oh, sincerity. What has that to do with art?"

Beeky was tired from his long day, and now he was peeved. "He's sincere about one thing. He certainly doesn't like *you*."

"Of course, he doesn't. Where would he be if he did? That wouldn't be his style at all. I wouldn't want him to. A Hobart Howland who liked Joe Lazarus would be a depreciated product. A pale, diluted, modern liberal kind of thing. No taste. No tang. No guts. No thank you."

"Style is everything? Even if it's the rankest prejudice?"

"Style is everything."

Beeky didn't care after this what he said. "And life is nothing but amateur dramatics? In which one man plays Lear and the other Shylock? It only matters how well they act? Never what they mean? Or even what they say?"

"I like your way of putting things, Beeky. Only why amateur? I think both Howland and I ought to resent that."

Beeky decided that he would say no more on the subject, and he stopped listening to his chattering host. So fixed was his mood that it was several minutes before he realized that

Lazarus had changed the subject and was now actually offering him an overall settlement of the Church case. It was all he could do to keep from gasping as he made out the terms. A new corporation was to take title to everything in the area owned by the Church or by Lazarus. The Church was to have 25 percent of the stock. The suits were to be withdrawn by both sides, and the Church was to be paid a compensation of one million dollars over ten years. Financially, it seemed dazzling.

"Do you think for a minute the judge would consent to such a partnership?" Beeky asked, in as stiff a tone as he could muster.

"Saint Peter himself knew something about compromise."

"All I can do is transmit your offer."

Which he did that same night, only an hour later, in Howland's apartment. The judge received him in the library, sitting under his huge illuminated Thomas Cole: "View of Mount Etna from Taormina." It seemed to open a whole side of the darkened chamber to a mysterious Dantesque world. Howland's face was a gray mask as he listened grimly to the end.

"I don't suppose you will be interested," Beeky concluded.

"And why do you assume that?"

"Because I doubt that you will wish to become a partner of the man you have consistently described as Attila the Hun."

"And who said *I* would be his partner? Would I own so much as a share of the proposed corporation?"

"No, sir. But everyone will know that it's your creation. Morally speaking . . ."

"And who are you to speak morally, you young jackanapes?" Howland was thunderous. "Is it our duty to make moral decisions for a client?"

"Why not? If he's incapable of making them himself?"

"You say that of the Church of the Resurrection? Of your

own father? What impudence! Let me tell you something, Beekman Ehninger. It not only isn't our duty to make such decisions. It *shouldn't* be. How intolerable it would be, in a free society, if every man's lawyer were his parson! No, sir! My duty is clear. My duty is precise. When my client is threatened, I must put my client in the strongest position that the law permits. How he conducts his business thereafter must be his affair, and his alone."

Beeky felt almost the judge's equal now. "Very well, sir. But I wonder if the day won't come when people will begin to wonder if it is for the good of society that brains like yours should be the simple tools of men like my father. And men like Lazarus!"

Howland looked as if he were about to annihilate him, but then he changed his mind. He simply snorted. "Oh, go home, Beeky. Go to bed. You're talking like a bolshevik. I was wrong when I told you to be a lawyer. You should have been a monk."

It seemed to Beeky, walking home through the spring night, that his father and the judge, as contemporaries, might have more things in common than they had differences. It was as if the past, by being the past, supplied in the end the greatest common denominator. For just as in seventeenth-century engravings the peruke seems to make all society kin, and to bracket a great scientist like Newton with a gossipy snob like Saint-Simon, so now did the two old men who had dominated Beeky's life begin to merge in his mind.

o

It was ten years later, after both their deaths, that Beeky discovered that even as a lawyer he had been more right than his boss. For Joe Lazarus had made a great thing out of the land of the Church of the Resurrection whose share in his company he soon bought out. At a political fund-raising dinner, where he and Beeky found themselves side by side on the long dais, he told him how carefully he had planned that crucial parley in the Rolls Royce.

"You see, I had made a thorough study of you, Beeky. That's how I do business. By psychiatry. By flair. I *knew* that my deal with the Church would shock you. I knew that you would go and denounce it to the old man as a pact with Satan. I counted on you to make him so goddamn mad that he wouldn't see it was a bum deal for his Church. And he didn't. He bit, the old goat. Hook, line and sinker — he took it all!"

Lazarus threw back his head and uttered a peal of happy laughter at the memory. Beeky wondered if the old judge could hear that laugh in Purgatory.

IX

The Novelist of Manners

ONLY A YEAR AFTER he had been made a partner in Shepard, Putney & Cox, Leslie Carter, at thirty-one, was sent abroad to take charge of the Paris office. In the 1950s this post had been regarded as a sinecure, to be held by a semiretired partner with a taste for Gallic life and a secretary who could get theater tickets for traveling clients. But with the boom of American investment in Europe all this had changed, and by 1972 the position required an expert in international corporation law. Leslie Carter not only fulfilled this requirement; he had always believed, with Oscar Wilde, that when good Americans die, they go to Paris.

He had originally wanted to be a writer. As a Yale undergraduate he had majored in English, specializing in the "lost generation." The Paris of Hemingway and Fitzgerald had seemed to him a paradise in Technicolor. Like so many of his contemporaries, he had interpreted the postwar malaise of these expatriate novelists, their disillusionment and mordant cynicism, their haunting doubts as to their masculinity, as mere romantic poses adding the final titillation to a world that seemed as colorful as modern America was dull. Leslie wrote his own *Gatsby* in his senior year, and it was the shock of finding his typescript-baby born dead that had precipitated his decision to go to law school. And for all his success there and afterward, for all his editorship of *The Yale Law Journal* and early partnership in Shepard, Putney & Cox, he had continued to nurse a secret dream that one day he would awaken with an idea for a novel as perfect as *Madame Bovary* or *The Ambassadors* and would shut himself away in the proverbial garret to write it out, in a sacred rage, from the first page to the last. It was only a dream, but it was serious enough to keep him from marrying.

Paris did not give Leslie the idea for a novel, but it gave him another. The explosion upon his senses of the City of Light was dazing. He had so long crossed off his physical surroundings in New York as useless to the imagination that he now found aesthetic adventures in every street corner. Was it his destiny, after all, not to write about life but to live it? He occupied the firm's beautiful apartment in the seventeenth-century Hôtel de Lucigny in the rue Monsieur, where he was ministered to by a discreet valet and a perfect cook. After only a few months he began to lose that look of cellar whiteness that half a dozen years of overwork in New York had produced. The image in his shaving mirror still had black circles under dark eyes, but it struck him now that his thick, inky hair was more lustrous, his pallor almost romantic. As he crossed the courtyard in the evening on his way out to one of the dinner parties that were now a regular part of his duties, he would liken himself to an elegant young man in an Ingres drawing, a Lucien de Rubempré or a Eugène de Rastignac, ready for the conquest of Paris.

Nor was this fantasy wholly absurd. If the representative of Shepard, Putney & Cox enjoyed no great position in the French capital, he still had easy access to many worlds. This would have been of small benefit to a dull legal specialist with a frumpy wife, but when the word got about that Mr. Carter was young, single, personable and that he spoke quite passable

French, he became the favorite *jeune américain* of many host-
esses.

Hubert Cox called him one late afternoon at his office.

"We hear you're a *succès fou*," came the sarcastic voice from
across the Atlantic. "I hope you still have time to mind the
shop."

"I was here at eight this morning. And I stayed last night
till seven. What do you want? Blood?"

"You're doing fine, kid. Just fine. But I've got a little job for
you. You've heard of Dana Clyde?"

"The novelist? Of course I've heard of him. He was the
only thing I read in three years of law school besides cases.
He lives here in Paris."

"Yes. His publishers have retained us to defend a libel suit
brought by Giles Stannix. The Washington lawyer-lobbyist."

"Oh, I know Stannix. Robin Hood in reverse. He robs the
poor to give to the rich. And saves his soul by defending an
occasional Red in the Supreme Court."

"You're worse than Dana Clyde. Anyway, Stannix claims
that Clyde libeled him in his last novel, *Mary Bell*. With a
character called Ebenezer Kline. Look it up. Talk to Clyde.
We think Stannix will settle for an apology."

Leslie was thrilled. Dana Clyde was his favorite contemporary author. If he did not number him among the great, he
put him in a more beloved category: those who wrote fiction
as Leslie Carter might have written it — if Leslie Carter could
have written fiction. When he put through a call to Clyde's
apartment in Neuilly, he had the good luck to find himself
talking to the great man himself. Clyde's voice was bland,
aristocratic, bored.

"Look, my dear fellow, it's absolutely preposterous. This fellow Stannix is a notorious shyster. It can't be anything but a
nuisance suit."

"Very possibly, sir. I still think it would be helpful if you could come to the office to see me."

"But you know, Mr. Carter, I'm a very busy man. As you are too, I'm sure. Couldn't we just chat on the phone?"

"I'm afraid that won't be enough."

"Oh, very well. If I must, I must."

In the weekend that had to elapse between this call and their appointment, Leslie reread not only *Mary Bell* but several earlier Dana Clyde novels. If they now seemed a bit dated, they were still wonderful fun. In an era when the term had not been pejorative, they had been called novels of manners. The opening chapters were usually set in some great Connecticut or Long Island estate, at a brilliant house party presided over by a witty and charming hostess with a mind wide open to all points of view. Her guests would consist of a radical daughter, her surly Red lover, a Joe McCarthy senator, an evangelist aunt, a Pentagon general and so forth. Everybody would be very much aware of who everybody else was, what clothes they wore, what income they enjoyed, what ancestry they boasted of or concealed. There would be passionate arguments and passionate resentments, usually based on each character's anticipation of a snub by another. But the talk was the great thing, the wonderful, frothy, scintillating talk that splashed and sparkled and finally piled up into waves and breakers that overwhelmed the last chapters in such a riot of fantasy that the end would seem to come in a vapor of bubbles. Dana Clyde was a literary magician, pure and simple.

At their first meeting, in Leslie's office on the boulevard Haussmann, Clyde sprawled in the armchair before the desk, smoking an English cigarette. He was one of those men who seem to bloom in their late fifties. There was an odd boyishness in his high clear brow, in his furtive eyes, in the ease of his motions, in the surprising raucousness of his laugh. He made Leslie think of a slim, gray, aging Pan.

"This whole business shows how utterly people misconceive the true nature of fiction. My character, Ebenezer Kline, is a universal type. As a matter of fact, I'm a bit ashamed of him. He's one-dimensional. He lacks flesh and blood. In Restoration comedy he'd have been called Miles Malpractice or Sam Simony. It shows what a guilty conscience Stannix must have if he sees himself under that label. All I can say is — if the shoe fits, let him wear it."

"Unfortunately, you saw fit to endow Ebenezer Kline with some nonuniversal characteristics. Was it necessary to your plot that Kline should be twice divorced and married to a girl half his age? And that he should live in a yellow colonial house in Georgetown?"

"I had no idea what color Stannix's house was. On my honor!"

"And did Kline have to have the habit of twisting his hair in back into a tiny ball?"

"Pray tell me, Mr. Carter, whose side are you on?"

"I'm preparing your defense, Mr. Clyde. Sometimes we lawyers have to be novelists, too."

Clyde chuckled. He was obviously a man who hated to lose his temper. "But there's still no basic similarity. My character is a bigger man altogether. He has wit and charm, whereas Stannix is only a cheap wisecracker. To tell the truth, Mr. Carter, if Kline is Stannix, it's the greatest compliment Stannix has ever had."

"He doesn't seem to appreciate it. He alleges in his petition that your branding him a shyster has cost him one of his most important clients."

"But everyone *knows* he's a shyster!"

"So it *is* Stannix."

"Oh, of course, it's Stannix," Clyde retorted impatiently. "I have to get my characters somewhere, don't I? The point is, it's Stannix bigger than life."

"I'm afraid that won't help us. There is, however, one possible out. We've had a veiled hint from plaintiff's counsel that he might consider a public apology in lieu of damages."

"Never!"

"Think it over, anyway."

"Never!"

Leslie had learned to let time rather than argument take care of clients' questions of principle. Their meeting ended on a pleasant note.

o

Leslie next met his client at a dinner party given by Mrs. Kenyon, part of whose dividends as a large stockholder in Clyde's publisher was the supply of authors as guests of honor. She took it as much for granted that her shares in a literary venture should make her literary as she did that her residence in Paris should endow her with its luminous qualities. Leslie, obviously, was there on duty as a lawyer, but he wondered why Dana Clyde should have bothered to accept. Surely he was too successful to have to please Mrs. Kenyon. With all Paris to choose from, what did he see in that handsome, banal, Louis XVI apartment with its handsome, banal view of Parc Monceau and its handsome, banal, expatriate guests of long-practiced sociability? The food and wine were good, to be sure, but no better than Dana Clyde could get elsewhere.

Yet he was obviously enjoying himself. The whole table listened and laughed as he described the ridiculous scenario that he was writing for an historical movie called *Nero and Poppaea*.

"My inspired director, Mr. Millstein, has moments of pure

genius, particularly when editing my script. Take, for example, his contribution for last week. The heroine's mother, a patrician Roman but a secret Christian, is giving a select soiree for others of the unavowed persuasion. At an imperial party in Golden House she murmurs in the ear of a prospective guest: 'Do come in tomorrow after dinner. Just a few of us. Quite informal. Peter and Paul are coming.' "

Leslie, even at the risk of being conspicuous, declined to join in the roar of general laughter. Later, in the library, where the men had assembled for brandy and coffee, he was surprised when Clyde took him by the shoulder and propelled him to an empty corner.

"Let us have a little private moment. I detest the American postprandial habit of knocking their President."

Leslie swallowed half his brandy. He was ready now. "I have to tell you, sir, how upset I am that you should throw away your genius on the kind of hokum that Millstein churns out."

"My dear fellow, you're very flattering. But I assure you there's no better place for my poor old 'genius' today. Nobody wants to read my kind of novel any more. It's passé. I've said goodby to fiction."

"But it's only five years since *The Lifeline* was a national best seller."

"And only one since *Mary Bell* was a flop. With the critics, anyway. Oh, I have a following yet, I grant. There are plenty of old girls and boys who still take me to the hospital for their hysterectomies and prostates. But the trend is against me. The young don't read me. The literary establishment scorns me. It's better to quit before one is kicked out. Society is intent on becoming classless, and the novel of manners must deal with classes."

"There still are classes! All over the world. Most of all at home."

"Well, maybe there are. But not my kind. Oh, you know what I'm talking about, dear boy. Don't pretend you don't. I have always dealt with the great world. The top of the heap. How people climbed up and what they found when they got there. That was perfectly valid when the bright young people were ambitious for money and social position. But now they don't care about those things. They care about stopping wars and saving the environment and cleaning up ghettos. And they're right, too. When the world's going to pieces, who has time to talk about good form and good taste? What are such things but pretty little blinds to shut out starvation and mass murder? Do you know what I call the young people today? I call them the moral generation. They're the first that have ever showed a genuine social conscience."

Leslie wondered if those bland gray eyes were laughing at him. "Even conceding all that, does it mean there's no more room for beautiful things? Must literature be confined to the politics of survival while Dana Clyde writes *Nero and Poppaea?*"

"Oh, that's just a game I play. I do it for the money, of course. I confess to an incorrigible sweet tooth. I like all this." Clyde waved an arm to take in the paneled library with its gleaming shelves of sets, the big table of glinting decanters, the softly talking, black-garbed men. "The *douceur de vivre*. I'm damned if I'll starve for a muse — or even go hungry for one. I like driving my Silver Cloud Rolls and seeing my little Boudin over the mantel in my den. I want my wife to be smartly dressed. When my children were young, I had to have them at the best schools. You don't do those things on a pittance, you know."

"You could still write a great novel."

Clyde's smile was glorious. "Still?"

But to Leslie the occasion was too rare and the issue of too high a seriousness for ordinary compliments. "Oh, you've written beautiful things, wonderful things — there's nobody like you. But you still haven't written your *Madame Bovary*. I may be just a lawyer, but all my life I've wanted to write novels. I can't. That's my tragedy — or my pathos, or bathos, if you will. But you can and must! And *now* is the time. Now is always the time!"

The other men had risen to join the ladies, and Clyde got up, too. In the intensity of his emotion Leslie remained seated, staring up at his client and new friend.

"It's not the time, it's far too late," Clyde protested mildly. "And now we really must go into the other room." Yet when Leslie rose, Clyde put out his hand to catch him and hold him back for one more moment. "I'll tell you one thing, my friend. I *could* have done it once. I could have been as good a writer as any in the world. So you see, I'm not modest. On the contrary, I'm vain indeed!" He still paused, hesitant. "All right. Tell me something, my brash young man. What would I write this great novel about?"

"Paris, of course!" Leslie stretched an arm toward the window. "Look about you. Where else do the individualists congregate: the artists, the movie stars, the maharajas, the ex-kings, the Greek shippers, the Texas tycoons, the super crooks, the last saints? All over the globe equality in mediocrity triumphs. Even the East has succumbed to highways and supermarkets. What used to be called American vulgarity is a universal virus. America was the first victim, that's all. Paris, of course, is doomed, too. But Paris will be the last to go. There's your subject!"

"My God, it might be. It just might be."

Leslie noted an odd gleam in his eyes, but only for a second, and then Clyde released him, after a friendly squeeze of his fingers, and sauntered across the parlor to their hostess.

o

After that night it was tacitly taken for granted that Leslie Carter should become an intimate of Dana and Xenia Clyde, or at least of the former. Xenia was a dark, small, silent, rather formidable woman to whom Clyde was ostensibly very devoted, but out of whose presence he seemed sometimes to skip with the bound of a schoolboy leaving his classroom. On the excuse of the lawsuit he lunched frequently with Leslie and took him afterward to private viewings of art shows or to galleries of museums not generally open to the public. He seemed determined to impress the younger man with the full range of his sympathy and wit, and indeed it was a rare performance. Even after the settlement of the lawsuit, premised, as Leslie had known all along it would be, upon Clyde's apology and retraction, the relationship continued.

Leslie was flattered by the great man's attentions without being overwhelmed. He understood perfectly that what Dana Clyde really wanted was a disciple. All Clyde's professed resignation at his own diminished role in the modern world was an arrant pose. Underneath he yearned, he panted, for the tributes of the young. And Leslie was perfectly willing to represent his own generation and to give Dana Clyde all the laudations that he could swallow. But on one condition: that Clyde should write the great work that Leslie could never write. For Leslie was perfectly clear now on the nature of the mission that had awaited his arrival in Paris. It was *not*, after all, to live. It was not even to write. It was to save Dana Clyde and make him compose his masterpiece.

Xenia Clyde regarded her husband's new friend with unconcealed suspicion. She had black bangs and thin, tight lips, and tiny hands that were always on the move — but her agate eyes seemed to indicate an intelligence quite the equal of Clyde's. One night at Mrs. Kenyon's she and Leslie had what was almost a row.

"I want to know what you're up to," she began crisply.

"Do I make any mystery of it? I want your husband to go back to his real work."

She appeared to consider this carefully. "He tells me that I should like you. That you help him."

"Dana has charming manners."

"He has to make up for mine. Somebody said that Dana always approaches a new acquaintance placatingly — on the presumption that he has probably, at one time or another, been insulted by his wife."

"Do you always insult people?"

"Only when they have pretensions. What do you want Dana to do that he hasn't already done?"

"I want him to write a great novel. An immortal masterpiece."

"You don't consider *The Lifeline* that?"

Leslie shrugged. "Then I want him to write another."

"Why are you so sure he won't? Without your prodding?"

He glanced impatiently about the room. "Because he says he won't. And because he spends so much of his time at parties like this."

"What about you? Don't you feed in the same trough?"

"But I'm not an artist!"

Xenia seemed mollified by this. Her countenance relaxed, and she resumed the needlework that she was never without. "Of course, you must think Dana and I are fearful snobs."

"Not at all. I only wonder if you see the danger in the life you're leading."

"I see what you see." She paused to study her work with a judicious eye. "But I also see something you don't. This kind of party is not a bad compromise for Dana. Literary people drink too much and argue too much and never go to bed. He requires good food and regular hours. Social life like Mrs. Kenyon's is a kind of cordon sanitaire. It protects his genius."

They were suddenly both aware of Dana Clyde standing behind their chairs. "It protects my genius to have a good night's sleep," he said with an easy laugh. "Come, Xenia, it's time you took me home. I shall need all my energy for the great task that Leslie has set for me."

"Does that mean you plan to embark on it?" she asked sharply.

"Shall I tell you both something? I just might. I really just might." He put his long fingers on his wife's shoulders. "What would you say, my dear, if I asked you to hole up for a year in Vichy or Aix while I composed what Leslie likes to describe as the last great novel of manners of the western world?"

Leslie looked from Clyde to his silent wife. "You're making fun of me."

"On the contrary," Clyde retorted. "I have never been more serious. I shall retire, like Proust, into a cork-lined chamber to write my masterpiece. No more jokes, please! Do you remember, Leslie, what that delectable priest, Talleyrand, whispered to that fatuous ass, Lafayette, as he stepped forward to celebrate the revolutionary mass before the mob in the Champ de Mars?"

"What?"

"'Ne me faîtes pas rire.'"

o

Dana Clyde was good to his word. He and Xenia went to Málaga where they leased a little white house on the summit of a high hill overlooking the Mediterranean and for a year saw none but a few intimates. Leslie was not included in the latter group, although an early postcard had led him to expect an invitation. None came. There were two more cards, and then silence. He had the mortification of hearing only from others about the Clydes. Even a direct appeal remained unanswered.

Leslie at first assumed that the novel must be going badly, and that Xenia, holding him responsible for her husband's useless sacrifice and disappointment, had shut off communication with him. But then reports began to filter in that, on the contrary, the novel was going well. Xenia, apparently, was writing everyone that it would be his masterpiece. Leslie could now think of no other reason for his disgrace than that the Clydes did not care to be indebted to him for Dana's finest hour. He hated so to judge them, but no other theory seemed to fit. Disillusioned but resigned, he tried to dismiss the matter from his mind. Fortunately, a case involving the French government and the mining rights of an American company in Nouméa came into the office and occupied all his time. For six months he was unable to dine out. Paris was like New York again. But at least he was distracted.

One morning, some eighteen months after the departure of the Clydes, Leslie found on his desk the galleys of *The Twilight of the Goddess* by Dana Clyde sent air mail from New York by his publishers to be checked for libel. Leslie at once told his secretary that he would see and talk to nobody and locked his door while he read the novel at a sitting.

It was certainly Dana Clyde at his best. It was the story of the many husbands of a great American heiress: the handsome boy from next door in the early days before the fortune is made, the designing lawyer who handles the first divorce, the mortgaged Italian count, the stony-hearted French communist.

With the communist the heroine moves to Paris where she buys a vast hotel in the avenue Marigny and assembles at her international parties the world that Leslie had suggested that the author delineate. And there she meets her fifth husband, Gregory Blake, toward the end of the book.

Leslie's feelings, as he recognized the model for Gregory Blake, were not bitter. It was a relief, after all, to have solved the riddle of Clyde's silence. His involvement with the latter's "genius" needed at least the dignity of a third-act curtain. It was better to know that Clyde would not face him because he *could* not face him than to speculate that Clyde was ungrateful. It was better to have the novelist wicked then petty.

And wicked he had certainly been. He had torn his poor disciple to ribbons. The character, Blake, was an American lawyer in Paris, pathetically if absurdly in love with the glamour of the city's past. The old Duchesse de Foix, the heroine's social mentor, says of him: "I'm gonna wash that Proust right out of his hair." But she can't. Gregory sees the other characters cleansed of all their tawdriness, arrayed in a glory appropriate to their wealth or titles or talents. For this reason he enjoys a passing popularity in the social world. He is a kind of panacea against revolution and taxes, against death and decay, against the gray future of a mechanized, socialized universe. It is as if by touching him they may save themselves, redeem their silly souls. The heiress, vicious but still beautiful, woos him and marries him. But Gregory is impotent. After his wedding night, he commits suicide.

Leslie finished the book by lunchtime and then reread the publisher's letter. Mr. Clyde, it informed him, was staying at the Crillon.

In the lobby of that hotel he ran into Clyde himself, but the latter hurried by him with averted eye. Leslie was not even sure that Clyde had seen him. The boy at the desk, however, informed him that Mrs. Clyde would receive him in her suite. He found her engaged, as usual, with her needlework.

"Why did he do it, Xenia? Why did he want to hurt me like that?"

"He always takes his characters from real life. You *knew* that, Leslie. Why didn't you stay away from him?"

"Oh, it's not being in the book I mind. It's not even being made such a fatuous ass. That was fair enough. But the impotence and the suicide! They seem to show actual malevolence, as if he was out to get me. Why?"

Xenia's brief silence indicated some inner debate. "If ever I saw a man put his head in the noose, it was you. I tried to warn you off, but you stuck like a leech. Still, I admit, he treated you abominably. Even for him. Tell me something. What did you think of the novel? Other than the character of Gregory Blake?"

"I thought it first-class. First-class Dana Clyde, that is."

"But is it a great novel? Is it that last great novel of manners of the western world?"

"It is not."

"You say that very positively. Didn't you assure him it would be?"

"I was a fatuous ass. I was Gregory Blake."

"I'm afraid you were worse than that, Leslie. You badgered Dana into writing that book. You never stopped to think it might hurt him. Well, it did. It hurt him terribly. That's what he can't forgive you."

"But I never meant it to hurt him!"

"Of course, you didn't. You're not a sadist. But it still did. You see, Dana had a secret fantasy. He liked to think of himself as a genius, but a genius manqué. He liked to tell himself that if it hadn't been for his love of the good life — the *douceur de vivre,* as he always called it — he might have been another

Flaubert. 'Ah, if I could only work as he worked,' he used to say. Well, he worked at Málaga. He really did. And you see what he produced. He sees it, too. He can no longer kid himself that he could ever have written Madame Bovary. So he took his revenge."

Leslie stared. "But can't he persuade himself that he simply started too late? That if he *had* worked hard enough, early enough, long enough, he *would* have been a Flaubert?"

"No." Xenia laughed her dry little laugh. "Because a genius, even a genius manqué, could never have written anything as magnificently second-rate as *The Twilight of the Goddess*. But don't worry about Dana. He always gets through. It's you I'm worried about. I hope that my husband's silly book isn't going to ruin your young life."

Leslie looking at the tough little woman before him, felt a surge in his heart of something like joy. For a moment he was so full of the sense of life that he could not even articulate an answer to her suspicion that his share of it might be slight enough to be affected by the likes of Dana Clyde. He turned away from her and went to the window to look down on the Place de la Concorde and its eddies of darting traffic.

"No, I'm grateful to Dana. He was wrong about the novel of manners. It *does* still have a function. If only to prove to a poor thing like Leslie Carter that he doesn't want to write one anymore."

X

The Last of the Barons

BEEKY EHNINGER always believed that his life might have
been a greater thing had Judge Howland been a dozen
years younger. For then his own conversion from dilettantism
to hard work, which he liked secretly to compare to the spiritual deepening of his hero, Franklin Roosevelt, through the
trial of polio, could have been followed by a master-apprentice
relationship long enough to have left him a master himself.
But there had been no time for this. By the end of World
War II Howland was in the grip of a sclerotic condition that
made him peevish, arbitrary and forgetful.

Sometimes he would threaten to fire the whole staff because
a file had been mislaid. At others his wrath would fix itself
persecutingly on a single unfortunate, and the harsh voice
would be heard thundering down the corridors: "If you, sir,
have the brains to find your hat — which I very much doubt —
and the sense of navigation to locate the front door — which
seems even more dubious — pray find your hat and find said
door and go, *go!*" Beeky would have to run after the shattered
young clerk and tell him that he hadn't really been fired, that
all would be forgotten in the morning.

Only Beeky seemed able to handle him. Not yet thirty and
the most junior partner of Shepard & Howland, he found himself nonetheless virtually in charge of the office. The others

were like so many Bob Cratchits waiting for the growl of Scrooge. Howland had never bothered to train a successor, and now it maddened him to be assailed with administrative questions by men who had never learned to take responsibility. He referred them impatiently to Beeky for everything, from the setting of a fee to the hiring of a secretary. Only in legal questions did he reserve his old dominion, although it was just here that he needed most help. He was beginning to make mistakes, and Beeky, without consulting anyone, had taken out, in the firm's name, a substantial insurance policy against malpractice.

Even clients were not immune from Howland's bad temper. Old age had increased his disenchantment with the worldly world. A testator's failure to make provision for charity in his will or sufficiently to provide for a spouse could bring down on his head the thunder of the judge's denunciation. A tax scheme that Howland found shoddy, a pension plan that struck him as scanting old employees could cause its proposer to imagine that he had ventured into the kirk of John Knox rather than the office of his own attorney — and one to whom he was paying a stiff retainer for the privilege of receiving such rigorous comminations.

Members of the Means family started asking the receptionist for Beeky instead of the judge. They would even slip in the delivery entrance and scurry furtively down the corridor to Beeky's office to avoid passing the great man's door. If the latter happened to come in while they were there, they could expect to be dressed down as if they were schoolchildren caught smoking. And this, too, was the best that could be expected from the encounter. The worst was that the clients would go elsewhere.

When Beeky's old cousin, Nathan Means, richest of the surviving clan, walked out of Howland's office after hearing him-

self described as the "stingiest white man south of Canal
Street," Beeky realized that the time had come to implement
the desperate plan that for six nervous months he had been
privately debating. He went to the two stars of his class at
Harvard Law, Hubert Cox and Horace Putney, and proposed
that they leave Sloane & Sidell to become the managing partners of Shepard & Howland.

They were interested. They were quick enough to see the
chance that was offered them. For although they were sure of
ultimately becoming members of Sloane & Sidell, that firm
was controlled by a group of partners only then in their forties
and fifties. It might be twenty years before two men of Cox's
and Putney's age should find themselves in the position that
Beeky offered them now. Of course, Shepard & Howland was
a much smaller firm, but then there was no reason, with the
carte blanche that Beeky proposed, that they should not build
it into something great. It was not only, as Beeky put it, an
opportunity. It was a challenge.

He supplied them with all the financial data of the firm. He
promised to invest his own money in physical improvements.
He summoned his partners — all but one — to a secret meeting
in his home in which he made them swallow the humiliation of
accepting this proposed promotion of two young clerks. They
all knew that Shepard & Howland was disintegrating; they
had no real choice. Beeky wrote memorandum after memorandum implementing his plan with a feverish industry to hide
from himself the ghastly specter of his unbelievable disloyalty.

Late one afternoon Hubert Cox called. "I've just had a long
talk with Horace. I think we're ready to answer you. How
about dinner tonight? I told Sophie I'm staying in town."

"Will you dine with my family? It'll be a treat for the old
folks. We can talk freely. They know all about it."

But when he and Hubert were seated opposite each other in
the middle of the long refectory table in the dim, medieval
banquet hall of the Fifth Avenue house, with Elise and Duke
Ehninger at either end, silent and vaguely beneficent, she intent on her little vials of pills, he nodding in his wheelchair,
Beeky regretted that he had not suggested a club. The
thought of Hubert's cheerful cottage in White Plains, of Sophie and all the noisy children, offered a dismal contrast to this
bachelor life of his, trapped at home with age-stricken parents.
He felt a sudden savage flare of resentment against the senil-
ity that seemed to be besieging him both at home and in the
office. He heard his voice take on an uncharacteristically
harsh note.

"We have everything at Shepard and Howland but leadership. We have brains, expertise, character, integrity. We can't
galvanize it, that's all. With you and Horace to do that, the
future should be wonderful!"

Hubert's steady smile was that of the amiable bargainer who
is never going to be lured into the error of premature enthusiasm or the worse one of temper. "Let's leave the wonder of it
to the future. I think the time has come at last to try the
sticky wicket. Don't look so surprised, Beeky. I mean the one
that you have been so carefully avoiding all along. What do
you intend to do about Judge Howland?"

Beeky opened his mouth but no sound was heard. He drank
his wine. "Isn't that routine? Don't we make him 'of counsel'?"

"Now, look here, Beeky, you can't shove a man like that
under the rug. You and I both know that it would be impossible to carry out a single change with a personality the size of
his around. Horace and I are absolutely agreed about it. Howland must be out of the office altogether. I'm sorry if that

sounds heartless. I can't help it. We couldn't even afford to allow him a desk."

Beeky's palms were moist. "If you'll agree to come, I'll agree to take care of Howland."

"You mean you'll get him to retire? Altogether? Before we come?"

"Leave it to me. I promise to work it out to your satisfaction."

But Hubert was inexorable. "He will have retired, then, before we come in?"

"Oh, Beeky, he never will!" his mother intervened with a soft gasp. "Don't promise Hubert more than you can deliver."

"Beeky *can* deliver it. He can *make* Howland quit!"

The other three turned to Duke Ehninger in surprise. The stroke that had crippled him at seventy-five was supposed not to have affected his mind, but it had obliterated all of his old aggressiveness. He had retired from life, from his family and seemingly from himself. He rarely read and talked little. His nurse always wheeled his chair into the room when there was company, and the visiting daughters, all now married, after kissing him and telling him how well he looked, would ignore him as they chatted with their mother. It was impossible for Beeky to tell what went on behind those catlike eyes. They appeared to take in every spot on a wall, every tear in a rug, every maid who dropped an ashtray or chipped a glass, but whether it was with a grim satisfaction to see the collapse of the old grandeur, the tackiness of the contemporary world, or with simple indifference, no one could say.

"There's no reason that Howland should have things his way until the end," the firm, soft voice continued. "Just because *he* has been spared a stroke."

"Father, you forget my obligations to the judge."

"I do not forget them. I deny them! Hobart Howland has

used you as a convenience. He has made you his office boy.
Well, the time has come to set the record straight. For decades he has sneered at me as a parasite of the Means family.
What the hell does he think he's been himself? Now that he
sees the end approaching, he prepares to make a bonfire of his
life and law practice. To go out in a Roman blaze! But I do
not propose to let him sacrifice you to that luxury. He owes
his business to the Meanses. He can leave it to a Means."

Beeky had not heard his father speak so much at a time in a
year. "I think I can handle him, Father. I've been turning
over in my mind how best to do it."

"Which simply means that you've been putting it off. Oh, I
know you, Beeky. You could never bear the idea of hurting
people. But in life one has to be ready to hurt people at times.
This may be the making of you, my boy. And if you *don't* do
it, I shall have myself wheeled into Hobart Howland's office
and do it myself!"

"Duke!"

"You shall not stop me, Elise! Interference will be idle. If
necessary, I shall call the police."

"Never mind, Father. I'll do it. I promise."

Beeky was silent and moody for the rest of the meal.
Hubert chatted with Elise about his children. Duke seemed
to be dozing. It was bitterly ironic that the parent whose
moral code Beeky had always despised should now be the person to give him the pep talk to gird for the great moral duel of
his life. Could it mean that he was wrong? That it was a
higher duty to let Howland destroy the firm that Howland,
after all, had created? But it was too late. He was committed.
"Dear God," he prayed, moving his lips silently and squeez-
ing his knife in the hand under the table until he had cut
the palm. "Send one of your blessed strokes from heaven to
take your servant, Hobart Howland. Make it a quick, clean

one. Please, God! Do not leave him in a wheelchair like Father. Take him all. Take him now!"

○

The next day it seemed as if Beeky's prayer would be granted. Judge Howland suffered a slight heart attack. He recovered, however, almost immediately, and his doctor said that he could go back to work in a month's time. During this period, very trying to the impatient old man, Beeky called every evening, and on Saturday afternoons he took him to art galleries where the judge added an occasional painting to his collection of American nineteenth-century landscapes. On the last Saturday before the Monday of Howland's scheduled reappearance in Wall Street, as the two men sat in a private room at Wildenstein's before an overwhelming Frederick Church panorama of what seemed to Beeky nothing less than the whole Wild West itself, he told his sinking heart that he could postpone his task no longer.

The judge's concentration while he studied this candidate for his collection was total. All his energy seemed transferred to his staring eyeballs.

"It's perfect. So calm. So serene. So free of hate. But where would I put it? I have no room that size."

"You could get a larger apartment."

"Don't be an ass, Beeky. You know I'm too old."

Beeky said nothing.

"What a bliss of peace," Howland continued. "What modern painter could do it? They're all cranks, you know. Rotted by politics."

"Why don't you buy it and give it to a museum? Then you could get a tax deduction and see it whenever you wanted."

"I never go to museums. You know that."

Beeky looked at the picture. The judge had taught him how

to look at American landscapes. There was always a tree or a bush in the foreground, almost life-size, to provide a gauge for the viewing distance, usually close to, as if one were gazing out of a window. Now he divided the painting and examined it section by section. He took in the prairie, the Indian village, the forest beyond, the immense Teton Range. The judge was immobile, except for one slowly blinking eye. Couldn't he die? Then and there? Oh, God, please!

"Well, all I can say, Judge, is that those of us who can't afford to collect *have* to go to museums. How else would we know great art? How many people see your pictures in a year? Me. Your butler. Your cleaning woman. An occasional dinner guest."

"*I* see them. And I make up in intensity, young man, for the herds of vulgar cattle who chew their cuds before Rembrandts and Titians, trying to guess the price."

"But after you're gone, what then? Don't you have to leave them to some kind of institution? What else is there?"

"I'm leaving them to you."

"To me!"

"As my executor. You will sell them and add the proceeds to my residuary estate. It goes to Harvard Law School."

"Sell all your beautiful pictures! Why?"

"Because that way they will go to people who care for them."

"That way they'll go to fat cats who want them for social status."

"Even fat cats can love art, my friend. The best way to appreciate a picture is to buy it. I know no lesson like that sick turnover in the abdomen when you know you've been had. Give me the collector's eye against the curator's any day."

Beeky studied the painting again. Something was going on in that Indian village. Were they roasting a missionary? Was that the point? The contrast of nature's vast peace with man's tiny malignity?

"I once read a book on Indian tortures. They were very ingenious in cruelty. But no more so, I suppose, than we are."

"You are sententious today, Beekman. It usually means that you have something on what I shall be polite enough to call your mind."

"I wonder if you can't read it, sir."

"If you can't say it, it must be nasty."

"I'm afraid it is." Beeky did not turn, but in the tense silence that immediately followed he was uncannily aware of the abrupt withdrawal of sympathy at his side. When he heard the judge's voice at last, it was low and grating.

"Ah, then, I guess!"

Beeky felt the thongs in his wrists, on his brow. Around him brown, stinking bodies writhed in a thumping jive. Where had the painter Remington found *his* noble Indians? He still could not look at the judge.

"I think, sir, that the time has come for you to retire. We have discussed it in the firm, and we are all agreed. It kills me to tell you."

There was another pause. Then the terrible voice at his side sounded again, a stranger's, icily hostile. "You look very well for a corpse. Have you concluded that I am incompetent to practice the law?"

"No, sir. But we want you to quit before you are."

"You don't mince your words."

"Do you wish me to?"

"And who, pray, is to run the firm? *You?*"

"Hardly. We need help from outside. You know my friends, Cox and Putney. They are willing to come in."

"Two brash young clerks from Sloane and Sidell? Take *my* place? Is *that* what you think of me? Somebody's incompetent, never fear. Are you sure you have the right fool?"

"They're brilliant men, sir. I know I can't expect you to see it. I haven't slept a full night in two months trying to decide how to tell you. But finally I concluded it didn't matter how. There are things that just have to be told, and that's that."

"Thank you for not binding my eyes. What makes you think that I'll do as you tell me? How do you know I won't kick the lot of you out?"

"Because, sir, at eighty-two you can't go it alone. You know that. Your only chance to protect the investment you have in the firm is to let me try. And I can only try in my own way. But I must have a free hand! There you are. I've said it, and I'm numb. I don't care anymore."

He had thought, when the savages had lit the fire, that it would be soon over. He was wrong. There was nothing like the pain of this. Nothing. When he turned at last to face Howland, he saw the old man's hard eyes harden further in contempt for his tears.

"My only stipulation is that my name shall not appear in the reconstituted firm."

Beeky choked. "I hope you realize, Judge, that you've been the light of my life."

"That's the Means's blood in you. How well I recognize it! You all have to have your cake and eat it, too. You want me to resign and to love you for making me resign. But I *don't* love you. Get that through your silly valentine of a head."

"Judge! Forget the whole thing! Nothing is worth this."

"You're a slop pot, Ehninger, and you always were. You're not even a very good lawyer. But I daresay you know something about law firms, and that may get you through. You have a murky sense of teamwork. Only remember this. Never fight your own natural ruthlessness. God created you for a hatchet man. The sentimental always make the best ones."

"We can't leave it like this, sir. I can't bear it, that's all."

"Oh, you'll bear it, and lots more. Only I don't care to have anything more to do with you. I shall negotiate my terms on Monday with the others. They will be stiff ones, too. You can count on that! And then I shall set up a little office in East Hampton where I can take an occasional case if I choose. Which is what I had all along planned to do when I retired. For I *had* been planning to retire, sir. Only *you* couldn't wait! No, no. Stay where you are. I can find my car alone."

Beeky, left with the pictures, perceived that nothing dreadful, after all, was going on in that Indian village. Perhaps the smoke only meant that they were cooking supper. But man's greatness had gone with man's malignity. Beeky was alone with nature.

When he rose, twenty minutes later, he found that he was utterly depleted, that he actually staggered. But by the time he had reached the street he was walking normally again. He began to wonder if the dull new calm that was settling in his heart might be a sign of permanent relief that his terrible mission was over. He had loved the old man, of course, but had anything in his life ever been worse than his dread of the scene that had just taken place? Might he not be almost happy, living without the love and without the dread, rather than daily beset by both? He even began to be conscious of a smarting little resentment of the judge for having been so savage. Could his great legal imagination not encompass the agony of a disciple who had had to do what Beeky had had to do? Was it too much to demand of his mighty intellect that it distinguish Saint John from Judas? Then, abruptly, he broke away from such thinking. Indeed, it might be too much. A part of Hobart Howland died every day as his arterial condition degenerated. The man with the cruel granite face was not the man who had rescued Beeky from frivolity by the curling breakers of Long Island's south shore.

o

The judge was good to his word. With the consistency of the senile, he refused to speak to Beeky again, even in the office. But his East Hampton project was never realized because he died of a second heart attack that spring, in the same week in which Duke Ehninger succumbed. Six months later when Beeky and his mother were sitting for the last time in the dining room of the Fifth Avenue house before moving to their new apartment on Park Avenue, he asked her if his father would have really carried out his threat of forcing Howland to retire had he himself failed to do so. Elise was emphatic.

"Oh, yes, he felt it his duty. He said that if he'd been the kind of father you had needed and wanted, you'd never have turned to the judge. How he hated Hobart Howland! He always claimed he had robbed him of his only son."

"Then, Father really cared, after all," Beeky murmured.

"Oh, he loved you. He always loved you."

How she said that! As if it were an emotion just a little beyond her comprehension, something for mortals and not (here perhaps with a touch of high regret) the privilege or duty or even the preoccupation of those not superior but certainly more complicated female creatures whose destiny was to sing in the Sistine Chapel of Heaven. Elise Ehninger in the end had to give a man, a mortal man, his due. What more, in the last analysis, could she really do for him? And Beeky now saw that he was going to be haunted by *two* ghosts. He shook himself, half in apprehensiveness, half in exasperation. He could only pray that they would keep themselves company.

XI

Oberon and Titania

I T IS A TRUTH that at least ought to be universally acknowledged that some of our most painful afflictions, to wit,
hay fever, hemorrhoids, diarrhea, chronic hiccoughs and any
sexual disfunction, are greeted with the snickers of our dearest
friends. In this respect we are never far from the primitive African oarsmen who, in Alfred North Whitehead's anecdote,
shouted with laughter when one of their crew, a good friend
and neighbor, "caught a crab" and was hoisted from the boat
into the jaws of a passing crocodile. When the tragic has the
ill grace to walk hand in hand with the ludicrous, it must not
expect attention.

The long friendship between Hermione Stoutenburg and
Jeremiah Blakeman was looked upon with just such smirks by
their associates at Shepard, Putney & Cox. For a while it had
been believed that they would marry, and then the smirks had
been smiles. All the bar loves a lover. But that had been ten
years ago. Nobody believed it any more. Jerry was forty-
seven, Hermione, forty-three; they had to be confirmed celi-
bates by now. Why then did he escort her to every office social occasion, take her with season tickets to the opera and
Philharmonic, spend his vacations in a cabin on her mother's
camp in the Adirondacks? What *was* their relationship? Did
they or didn't they? Could they or couldn't they?

In a *désoeuvré* society, as described by Proust, where the pursuit of sex is an accepted profession for a gentleman, the great lover occupies stage center. But in a working world, with little time for the refinements of jealousy and the gradations of ecstasy, the crowd is apt to be more taken with the fool. What everyone *can* do is pretty much the same. It is the nondoer, the can't-doer, the buffoon, who diverts. Perhaps his failure helps to convince the majority of ordinary copulaters that they are on to something worthwhile.

Hermione Stoutenburg was the more popular of the pair; without Jerry, she might even have been the office sweetheart. Tall, thin, with a long, strong, elegant stride, high-heeled, big-breasted, tassled and beaded, with red, touched-up, crisply set hair, merry eyes and a small, pursed mouth that seemed undecided between a laugh and a playful reproach, she was a welcome figure in every department. Her cheerful, rasping voice, her quick, jerky movements, her confused air of rush and hesitancy, of drive and indecision, put one in mind of some gaudy tropical bird fluttering from an obscure hurt. Hermione was loved for her heart and sympathy, if deplored for her loquacity and repetitiousness. She was perfectly content with her position as "queen of wills," the office expert for testators, and had never expected to be made a member of the firm.

Jerry Blakeman, on the other hand, resented having been passed over in what he called the "rat race for partnership." He was head of the firm's small real estate department, an expert in a limited field, but the business had not been big enough to warrant the ultimate promotion. Jerry, however, had preferred to see himself as the victim of a mysterious, even a sinister discrimination. He was a big, blunt man who might have been handsome had there been some delicacy in his large rounded chin and brow. His thick, glossy hair, always smoothly parted to the side, his white lineless skin, his straight, stocky build made him seem youthful, but not appealingly so. He was too loud of voice, too violent of manner, too stentorian, too emphatic. He carried to offensive proportions the lawyer's mannerism of hitting key words with an oral hammer. Hearing his voice down the corridor when he was telephoning, one might have thought that he was discharging rather than advising a client. Fortunately, in the real estate world bad temper, or the appearance of it, is taken quite for granted.

The serene amity between Jerry and Hermione might have lasted for their joint lifetimes had the gods not seen fit to send a dart to part them in the shape of a young associate, Nick Huston. Rejected by the corporate and litigation departments, this blue-eyed, curly-haired, baby-faced clerk ended up working half the time for Hermione and half for Jerry, and was dubbed "Trouble in Paradise" by the office wags, for both his new bosses appeared to have been struck with a sudden infatuation for him. Did Nick need coaching for the bar exams? Jerry would devote his Saturday mornings to it. Did he need new curtains for his apartment? Hermione would go shopping. They might have been a fussing father and a clucking mother, nervously pushing along a slightly retarded only child. And their fights! They quarreled noisily and publicly over the allocation of Nick's working hours. "You had him all day yesterday at that safety box opening, Hermie!" "You kept him a week on that Queens closing, Jerry!" Beeky Ehninger caused general hilarity by comparing Nick to the "lovely boy" in *A Midsummer Night's Dream* who causes the dissension between Oberon and Titania.

And Nick? What did he think of Hermione? What did he think of Jerry? Nobody knew. Nobody seemed even to know how he had got his job in the firm. He would look at the person who tried to explain a legal matter to him with a benevolent blankness, an amiable incomprehension, until he seemed at last to get, not so much the point as some hidden, ironical point of his own, at which his smile would broaden slowly until it erupted into a contagious yet vaguely mocking laugh. Nick, the younger clerks insisted, was as far from being a fool as he was from being a cherub.

o

Hermione frowned as she read over the draft of Mr. Phelps's will that Nick had prepared. He sat by her desk, looking at her, his hands folded in his lap, impassively prepared to see his work annihilated. His wide eyes, blue, gray, opalescent, shifted away whenever she glanced up. At such moments Hermione would be vaguely disturbed by a subtle shift in their relationship. Ordinarily so gentle, so pleasantly flattering, so impudently intimate, her young associate would then betray a faint diffidence, a sense of being importunately sought. And yet it was not as if he, Nick Huston, were avoiding the advances of her, Hermione Stoutenburg. It was not nearly so personal. It was more as if an instinctive sense in him reacted protectively against the inevitable awareness in others of his beauty.

"You can't use 'so long as' in the sense of 'provided that,'" she observed, running her red pencil through the phrase. " 'So long as my son's wife shall live,' yes. *Not* 'so long as she shall be his wife at the time of his death.' Didn't they teach you any English at college?"

"They taught me poetry."

"Well, it sounds like poetry. Modern poetry, anyway. Now, where is the precedent I gave you for the condition about a daughter-in-law living with a son at the time of his death? Obviously, you never read it."

Hermione pulled out the long file drawer of her precedents. It was an office joke, of which she was rather proud, that she had clauses for every possible wish of a testator from a trust for canaries to a foundation for lepers.

"You can be reading that while I check the residuary clause," she said, handing him the needed form.

Hardening her voice, she sought to re-establish their former relation. But as she read into the residuary clause, her frown deepened.

"What have you done here?" she demanded with a little wail. "You haven't provided for what happens if Mrs. Phelps dies first. Look, here's your subdivision A: 'If my wife shall survive me.' Now where's B? You've left it out!"

"Oh, have I?" Nick was shaken from his detachment. "I can't have."

"Well, where is it?" She thrust the page at him. "Just point it out to me, will you, please? Oh, Nick, you've *got* to take more care of these things."

"It's only a draft."

"Only a draft! Don't you realize that I have to report on your work to Mr. Ehninger and that I'm supposed to be on *his* side when I do it? Suppose I showed him this?"

"But you wouldn't, Hermie."

"But suppose I did?"

"Well . . . he's not such a bad guy. Anyway, Mrs. Phelps is ten years younger than her husband. She's not going to die first. And if she did, he could always write another will."

Hermione considered bleakly what even a man as kind as Mr. Ehninger would say to any such excuse as *that*. "Look, Nick. What a will draftsman is paid for is to cover *every* contingency. Any testator of average intelligence could provide for the ordinary ones himself. The idea of being a lawyer is to think of things laymen don't think of. Now if . . ."

"Oh, come off it, Hermie. Quit flogging a dead horse. You're never going to make an Oliver Wendell Holmes of me, and you know it. Christopher and I are giving a cocktail party this Saturday. Can you come early and stay late? We'll have a cold turkey."

Hermione began to fuss again with her precedent drawer, caught between irritation at this cavalier rejection of her good advice and the excitement that any invitation from Nick and his roommate always engendered in her. Nick had a way of smiling with an air of radiant surprise as he opened his apartment door to admit a guest. He would introduce Hermione to his friends with a gently mocking exaggeration, a caressing impertinence, which was to her the headiest of praise. "This is Miss Stoutenburg, my boss, my mentor, my Egeria. Treat her with respect. Handle her with love." Entertainments, parties, that, of course, was *his* world, one of the many, one perhaps of the all, where a beautiful youth outranked a middle-aged spinster. Yet how lightly he wore his higher rank! It was not even, she reflected, with a sudden, jagged twist of tension that caused her to tear the top off one of her precedents, that he was particularly nice. He was only amiable. Amiable in the soft, catlike, meaningless way of his brand of bachelor. For however much she clung to a rather tattered innocence of mind, Hermione could not help but recognize the boy who sported with both sexes. She knew that he was in love only with himself. But how could he not be?

"I can't discuss social engagements in the office," she protested primly. "You ought to know that by now. I'll have to let you know later about Saturday. In the meantime I suggest we get on with the work in hand." For several minutes more she continued to read his draft. Then she threw it down on

her blotter with an air of final defeat. "You haven't even provided that the taxes be paid out of the nonmarital deduction
trust!"

"Oh, skip it, Hermie, let's call it a bust and let it go." Nick
rose to his feet. "I'm so worked up over these bar exams, I
can't think of anything else. Do you know that Jerry's got me
signed up for a cram course four nights a week?"

Hermione was at once solicitous. "Can't you take a couple
of weeks off until the exams are over?"

"I asked Jerry that, and he said no. He said nobody else in
the office took off time to cram, so why should I?"

"But nobody else in the office has failed them twice before!
Jerry must know how nervous that makes you. I'll speak to
him."

"I doubt that argument will appeal."

"Why?"

"Because Jerry believes that passing the bars is a test of
manhood. One shouldn't degrade it with special indulgences."

"Well, then, I see no reason you should take the bars at all
this year. You don't have to be admitted to do the work you're
doing for me. *Or* for what you're doing for Jerry."

"You still miss the point, Hermie."

"What point?"

"The point, as Mr. Blakeman so graphically puts it, that a
lawyer who's not admitted is a man without balls."

Hermione abruptly smoothed out the will draft on her blotter. Then she picked up her red pencil. "I'll finish this, Nick.
Why don't you get on with Mrs. Phelps's will? That should
be simple enough. 'All to my husband.'"

When he had gone, she leaned forward and covered her
burning cheeks with her hands. Had Phaedra felt this way before Hippolytus? Had he, returning, bare-shouldered, bare-
foot, from the hunt, set the poor queen aflame with some disin-

genuous reference to male genitalia? Hermione shuddered at
the violence of her interest, the intensity of her reaction. God
in heaven, what did all of *this* have to do with the wills of the
Phelpses? And why Phaedra? Phaedra had had Theseus; she
had had children. What had Hermione Stoutenburg ever had?

Not even Jerry. For seven years now she had carried the
memory of the night that no amount of reason, no amount of
prayer, no amount of wishful thinking or of lectures delivered
from the inner rostrum of a desperate common sense could
eradicate. She had been ready, tense but still so ready, ready
as only a virgin of thirty-six could be ready, clad in a silk
dressing gown, and he with less than that, ready too, passionate, vigorous, forceful, fast, too fast, and then suddenly had
come the horrid damp all over her, not in her, and the
screeching anticlimax of a farce that she could not even raise
in her own excuse-seeking mind to the dignity of tragedy. Yet
even that had not been as bad as Jerry's dry sobs, his torrent
of excuses, his plea that with her he had believed it was going
to be different, his threat, not even believed by her in such a
crisis, of suicide.

Oh, she had pulled things out. She had saved the friendship. She had even half persuaded Jerry that she was the one
to blame. Her panic, the ancient panic of being touched, the
dread of reaching hands and poking fingers, could have hardly
encouraged him. She had told him what she truly believed:
that without her friends she would simply wither away, that if
he would only continue to give her his blessed friendship, he
would have given her more than any lover, more than the
greatest lover could give, that he would be positively sexy,
that he would be all the man she had ever wanted.

And Jerry had been just that. And it had been a lot better
than nothing. She took out her compact now and went to
work on her ravaged face to restore the Hermione of the office

legend: the perennial good sport, the efficient, compassionate, briskly stepping lady of the legal corridors with the helping hand for all, the liberal thinker who became angry only at the vision of cruelty, the girl who could laugh at herself and then laugh at herself laughing at herself, but who could be very grave indeed at the enunciation of first principles, of funda- mental loyalties such as those to her old mother in Flushing, her sister in Brooklyn Heights, her many wonderful friends and, of course, Jerry. Life could be wonderful if one took ad- vantage of one's opportunities. Did it really so much matter what those opportunities were?

As she pulled the lever of her Dictaphone and began dictat- ing the missing subparagraph B of Nick's residuary clause, she tried to console herself with the reflection that she was not, after all, a total failure. She was a technician. She had made a place for herself in a male world, a godless world. She had sought to keep abreast of the new thinking: in economics and politics, in law and sociology, in ecology, in psychiatry . . . well, no. She had to pull up here. She could not honestly claim that she had kept abreast of psychiatry.

"Maybe that's your trouble, Hermie," she told herself gloomily. "Maybe you should never have given up going to that terrible man."

Doctor Fellowes had been her second great failure. After the dreadful episode with Jerry, she had gone to Beeky Ehnin- ger, the most sympathetic yet also the most worldly-wise of the partners, to ask him about psychiatrists. He had told her frankly of his own analysis by Doctor Fellowes and had of- fered to recommend her to the great man. An appointment had been made, followed by others.

At first she had almost liked it. Determined to be objective, candid, up-to-date, she had held forth loquaciously, discur- sively, about her childhood, her early fears and hopes, her family, almost forgetting at moments the large, bland, brooding presence behind the couch. It had been as if she were composing her oral memoirs, and there had been times, after a particularly well-phrased reflection, when she regretted the absence of her office Dictaphone. But the doctor did not long permit this uninterrupted flow of autobiography. He soon began to interrupt her, quietly but authoritatively, suggesting that she amplify her tale in precisely the places where she had least desire to amplify it. She began to wonder if his reputed genius did not consist in his ability to spot the rare subjects on which babblers did not care to babble.

Of course, she had understood that this was his job. Over her infant years, a long habit of fear had stitched an impenetrable veil under which, as with the curtain of an amateur theatrical performance, could be glimpsed, but ominously, the heavy feet of stage assistants. It was obviously Doctor Fellowes' intention to lift that veil, but Hermione recoiled in abject horror before her anticipation of the wiggling, writhing things that might lurk behind it, the fingers, the eels, the snakes, the long-necked, long-billed birds, the spindly-armed, spindly-legged marionettes, the whole turning, tumbling mess of her phallic nightmares. Oh, yes, it was obviously his job to try to piece together from these fragments the memories that she had repressed — provided (as she candidly hoped) that she had not obliterated them altogether — the ancient episodes of grinning, impertinent milkmen or handymen, the sly intrusions of older cousins, the insinuations of siblings, possibly (O horror of horrors) the hand of an even closer relation. Hermione had a recurrent dream, of which she had a particular dread, that she was shipwrecked on a coral island with the corpse of her mother, and that her older sister, Muriel, knife in hand, pale and priestlesslike, was trying to persuade her that it was their duty to survive by eating the maternal flesh. Muriel was very fine about it, very high-minded, even very convincing; she compared the proposed act to the communion service. But in the end of the dream Hermione turned away to the easier fate of the sea. It was so much simpler to die, to awaken.

It had not been, however, this attempted lifting of the veil that had put the end to her therapy. It had been her terror of having to articulate reflections that were personally insulting to the doctor. He was uncanny in his ability to sense when one of these was taking place, and he always insisted that she tell him, very explicitly, what it was. The morning that she had received his Christmas card in the mail she had known that she could never go back to his office. It had been a banal, elaborate, lacy card with a stout Santa whose girth had reminded her of the sender's own. Hermione had seen at once that on the couch that round red figure would fill her mind to the exclusion of other images and reduce her to a guilty silence until she confessed. But to tell the poor man who had committed the simple kindness of sending her a message of Yuletide cheer, not only that his card was vulgar but that it suggested his own adiposity, was simply beyond her courage. She had never gone back.

Some time later, when she confessed this to Beeky, after several cocktails at a firm party, he exclaimed:

"But Alan probably sent you that card on purpose! It would be just like him. To force his patients out of their reserve."

"Well, he didn't force this one," Hermione muttered, for all the world as if she had scored a victory over the psychiatrist.

But except for this, she tried to reassure herself, turning back once more, with a sigh of exasperation at herself and at Nick, to the latter's wretched draft, she had made a good enough life. And soon she should be over the worst. Old maids, after a certain age, could become "characters," no longer snickered at, but respected, loved, admired. The beau-

tiful Nick Hustons would be less and less upsetting. Ultimately, they would scarcely cause her a pang. She would be
quite self-sufficient with her friends, her law practice and her
multitudinous photograph albums, constantly arranged and
rearranged. Married people, in such compilations, like to
show their posterity. Hermione devoted hers to her forebears,
projecting herself backward instead of forward so that the big
volumes were filled with photographs of the dead, of their
family gatherings and places of abode. Their plain, long-for-
gotten faces, with brooding eyes and funny hats, lived again in
a strange survival for which no god but Hermione Stoutenburg
had provided.

Her nerves were still so taut that she jumped up when Jerry
Blakeman, in his rough way, flung open her door.

"What were you doing? Plotting a murder? You look
ashen."

"No, no, don't be silly. Come in, Jerry. What's up?"

"Nick says you don't think he ought to be taking the bar
exams. Don't tell me you've joined the lunatic fringe that
wants a nonlawyer on the U.S. Supreme Court? Could *that* be
the chair you're keeping warm for your protégé?"

"*My* protégé? When is he that? When you allow him to
sandwich one of my codicils in between your mortgage extensions?"

"You had him all last week! Is that why you don't want him
to take the bars? Because you've too much work for him to
do? You'll keep him an apprentice for life, is that it?"

"Oh, Jerry, you're ridiculous! I simply happen to think that
Nick is too tense to take the bars now."

"You baby him, Hermie. Sooner or later that young man
has got to learn to stand on his own feet. And there's no test
like the bar exams. Nick is a fine fellow. I couldn't like him
more. But he's got a soft side; let's face it. You think you can

cure that by mothering him. I suggest he's too old to be mothered."

"He needs a father, I suppose."

"Well, if he needs a parent at all, I think it had better be a male one!"

Hermione was angry now. "I know all about your appeal to his virility," she said cuttingly. "He even quoted your locker-room phrase. I cannot help thinking that a man who has had his own difficulties in that line might have a little more sympathy."

When Jerry's complexion whitened as she had never seen it do before she realized what she had done. "All right, Hermie. Have it your way."

"Jerry! Forgive me."

"I'm sorry to have taken your time. Tell Nick to do as he pleases about the bar exams. I couldn't give less of a damn."

Hermione, now on her feet, caught his arm as he was leaving. "Jerry, we're still going to the opera tonight, aren't we?"

"Give my ticket to Nick. He won't be going to the cram class now." And he slammed the door.

Hermione sank back in her chair and wept. The erotic images that Nick had suggested to her mind were all blown away, helter-skelter, before the fierce blast of this threatened loneliness. It was suddenly unthinkable to peer into a future that had no evenings with Jerry. It was even unthinkable to contemplate the one that was now pushing its way on to the face of the silver clock on her desk, a present after fifteen years with the firm. She had seats for *Giovanna d'Arco*, which was to be given concert style at Town Hall. It was to have been the climax of their year's study of Verdi operas: at the Metropolitan, at the City Center, on radio, on discs. They had loved it, too, each playing the accustomed role: she, the enthusiastic musical amateur, apologizing for knowing more than he, apologizing for gushing, indulgently simplifying plots and historical events, closing her eyes, even taking his hand during the loveliest arias, and he, the mocking male, superior to Italian long-haired goings on, putting it on a bit, covering over the genuine kick that he got out of the thumping choruses. And all that was to be over? Because she had been unable, like Elsa in *Lohengrin*, to resist the temptation to shoot down the gay little bird of her precarious happiness? Because she had been unable to keep her big mouth shut?

"I can't bear it!" she cried aloud as the mail boy opened her door. Pushing past him, leaving him to stare after her, she hurried down the corridor to Jerry's office.

"Jerry, please. *Please!*"

In consternation he jumped up to close his door. "For God's sake, Hermie!"

"I can't stand it. I just can't stand it! Tell me you'll go to the opera with me. Please! Tell me things will be as they have been. I can't lose our friendship, Jerry, and I don't know what'll happen to me if I do. I'm scared. Tell Nick to take his bar exams if you want. I'm sure he ought to, anyway. I'm sure you're right. He *is* soft, and he needs a man like you. A *real* man. I mean that, Jerry."

As she looked up at Jerry's averted face, she sensed the full impact of his inner battle. There was the old side of him that wanted to forgive, wanted to be loved, and there was the dusky side of his self-commiseration. But there was also an umpire: his fear of scandal.

"Of course, I'll go to the opera with you, Hermie. Only don't make it a soap opera."

It wasn't much, but she would have to make the best of it. At least it was a truce. And talks followed truces.

*

2

Jerry shook his head as he reviewed the contract of sale.

"No, no, Nick, you can never get away with a loose clause like this: 'The sale is to cover all personal property now on the premises except such items of sentimental value as the seller shall choose to remove before the closing.' For Pete's sake! Mrs. Murphy could strip the house of every light bulb under that one. What's the point of a contract with a loophole the seller can drive a truck through? You're supposed to be representing the purchaser, man!"

"But there's nothing on the place that either of the ladies really cares about. It's just a beach house at Montauk. I put that clause in because Mrs. Murphy thought there might be some old albums or other family junk in the upstairs closets. They're both *ladies,* Jerry."

"Ladies! What kind of talk is that for a lawyer? I want an Exhibit A to this contract listing every goddamn album or other piece of junk that the seller wants to keep out of the sale. Or else I want a memo in our files, initialed by the purchaser, stating that Shepard, Putney and Cox are exonerated of all responsibility for personal property removed from the premises prior to the closing. Take it from me, Nick, you'll find Mrs. Murphy claiming that a fire extinguisher is an heirloom under your clause. They'll do it every time."

Nick was obviously not convinced. Over his usually docile countenance had moved a reserved expression, a new detachment, as if he might be coming at last to the end, so to speak, of his legal rope. He had always shown a happy admiration of, a flattering submission to, Jerry's leadership, but more recently the continued poor quality of his work, and Jerry's exasperation with it, had begun to affect their relationship. It might have deteriorated altogether had not a horrid little growth made its unwelcome, secret appearance on Jerry's side of it.

"I've got to rework this fire clause," Jerry grumbled. "No, don't go. You can wait. I may have questions."

Nick looked out the window toward the Statue of Liberty.

When Hermione had mentioned to Jerry, two weeks before, with the false casualness of the would-be-sophisticate, that of course she supposed that he and she both supposed that Nick and his roommate Christopher were lovers, he had wondered, in his first moment of outrage, if she might not be trying to degrade Nick in his estimate in order to have the young man all to herself. But such malignity would have been quite uncharacteristic of her, and, besides, it became apparent, in the rather heated discussion which ensued, that Hermione was essentially indifferent to the issue she had raised. Like all women, she had no morals in such matters, only a perfunctory jealousy that any male should prefer his sex to hers. She had spoken, in the old pattern of their friendly rivalry, to show him that she was more liberal than he. And indeed she was, and welcome to it. Jerry had been as violently disgusted as he had been rapidly convinced by her theory. Dirty little bugger — no wonder he had no inclination for a man's work. It was faggots like that who made the world so conscious of pansydom that even a bachelor as virile as Jerry Blakeman was not safe from raised eyebrows and muttered innuendoes. God!

But later that week, as he had thought it over and over, as pictures of Nick in all kinds of erogenous attitudes with his roommate Christopher had kept flashing up on the dark screen of his mind, his disgust and indignation began to be tempered by a stealthy curiosity, a shocking pseudosympathy, a guilty half-tolerance. Before his apprehension of Nick's deviation, his vivid affection for the younger man had been qualified by his envy of the latter's good looks, by the gnawing idea that Nick could have all the girls that Jerry had never had, that the ju-

nior clerk had been born to be loved and embraced by beautiful nymphs while his older, wiser mentor was condemned to
look through mental peepholes at the sport of cherubs. But
now Jerry's heart found itself softened by the image of a less
happy, a less blessed youth, one who was sentenced to be a
kind of outlaw, who was the slave of shameful urges that he
had to conceal from his family and office associates, and who,
far from scorning poor old Jerry Blakeman, might even be secretly drawn to a man so much bigger and stronger. And
Jerry blushed with an odd thickening in his tongue and throat
at the fantasy of Nick coming to his office, closing the door behind him, standing silently for two or three moments before
blurting out a feeling that he knew could never be returned.
And Jerry saw himself smiling, sympathetic, putting his arm
around the young man's shoulders and explaining that he
would have to sublimate his feeling into something finer and
better, that he would have to put it on a plane where he,
Jerry, could properly return it, where they could be like the
two Greek warriors, the youth and the man, who loved each
other without carnal indulgence in Mary Renault's beautiful
Last of the Wine (which Hermione had made him read) and
went out happily together each morning beyond the Athenian
walls to kill barbarians.

But no. It was not turning out like that. It was not turning
out like that at all! Jerry was beginning to feel other things,
dirty things, things that made him pant with an exhausting
mortification in the silence of his room, behind his closed
door. Warriors were not meant to do *that* to other warriors.
He saw a bright, blinding image of himself kissing Nick on the
lips, and all his mind darkened. Damn sex! Would there
never be an end to the humiliations and agonies that it im-
posed on innocent, virtuous men?

"No, no, Nick, damn it all, you *can't* just say that half the purchase price will be defrayed by 'a first mortgage on the premises.' You have to spell it all out. 'By a first mortgage on the premises, executed simultaneously with the deed, a copy of which is attached hereto.' And then attach your mortgage. You *know* that, Nick. Or should have known it."

"I can't think, Jerry. You couldn't either if you were about to take bar exams you'd busted twice before." Nick was cooler and more assured, in the funny way he had in arguments with his superiors. He would suddenly toss aside his shy-little-boy demeanor as if, at a certain point in any negotiation, it was necessary to cut the pantomime. At such moments he seemed older, shrewder, even a bit nasty. "It isn't much fun to be the only one in the office with that kind of record. People snigger and make jokes about it. 'I'll pay you when Nick Huston passes the bars.' Oh, I've heard them! And if I fail again, how do I know how the partners will feel? You may back me up, Jerry, but I don't suppose I'm hurting your feelings when I point out that you're not exactly Mr. Cox." Jerry was hurt. He looked away, flushing, from the young man's cool stare. "And supposing I get the ax? Do you think I could get a job in any decent firm? Of course not. I'd have to go back to Kansas City and work in the old man's tool company. A fate worse than death!"

"What's wrong with the tool company?"

"Oh, come off it, Jerry. I've told you all about that. You know I don't hit it off with my old man."

"And I don't suppose dear Christopher would care to move to Kansas City, would he?"

Nick's face was inscrutable. "No. I don't suppose he would."

Jerry stared down at the blurred type of Nick's miserable draft. Had he really asked that? Had that been he, Jerry Blakeman, who had made so clumsy a thrust? Had this whole thing — whatever the hell it was — turned him into a sadist? "Look, Nick. You can't solve your problem by running away from it. Take the bars, but take the rest of the time before them off. That will give you thirteen full days for review. Jeepers, you could *learn* the law of New York in that time!"

Nick rose. "Okay, Jerry." His tone was not conciliatory. Still, he paused in the doorway. "If you're not doing anything on Saturday, would you care to come to my place for cocktails? Hermie's coming."

"No, she's not. Because you're not giving any cocktail party. You're going to work, my boy. Get it?"

Alone, Jerry rubbed his dampened brow with fingers that still trembled. Maybe he should go back to that psychiatrist. He knew that Doctor Fellowes was still in practice because he saw his plaque every morning on Park Avenue at 86th Street when he walked to the express subway. Jerry had consulted him once, at Hermione's urging, after the terrible episode of their fiasco, and he still heard the hearty voice that had seemed to carry his shame into the busy avenue outside:

"Mr. Blakeman, you suffer from one of the commonest of male sexual disfunctions: premature ejaculation. The cure of this can be very simple or very complex. It can vary from the mild therapy of a few talks with a doctor to a complete psychoanalysis. Sometimes it disappears without treatment, if the patient meets up with a sufficiently imaginative and understanding partner. But that is rare. In the incident that you have just described to me, your partner was obviously herself the victim of a sexual disfunction: frigidity. Coitus under such circumstances is almost impossible. I suggest that we have further exploratory sessions. But be of good cheer. Your case is curable."

Jerry had never gone back. The idea of exposing his most private thoughts and fantasies to a man so obviously, so almost aggressively, normal, was simply unbearable. The doctor's very lack of prejudice, his failure to make any moral judgments, seemed condescending, almost insulting, as if such poor creatures as Jerry Blakeman could not expect to be condemned for their vices. If he had only put his hand on Jerry's shoulder and murmured, like a priest: "Come, my sinning son, let us pray together to exorcise the devil which is in you," Jerry could have fallen to his knees. But this way! And "premature euaculation!" To have the long tragedy of his life summed up and tossed away as if it were some vulgar form of Asian flu, against which he was simply a fool not to have been inoculated, was atrocious. No, he had preferred to live with his ailment rather than risk losing his personality, his very soul in the horrid green office of Doctor Alan Fellowes. Had he not read that some of the greatest artists and statesmen of history had owed their driving life force to a neurosis? His had been a free choice. He had continued his practice of going once a week to a house where the girls did not object to his affliction. Indeed, some of them seemed relieved by it.

o

Two weeks later, at noon, just when he was about to pick up his telephone to call Hermione for lunch, she loomed up in his doorway, her face darkly grim with evil tidings.

"I hope you're satisfied now."

"What are you talking about?"

"Haven't you heard?"

"Hermie! What is it?"

"Nick was caught cheating in the bar exams by a proctor. He and a friend exchanged notes. He's gone home to Kansas City. Of course, he can never be a lawyer now. He's lucky not to be indicted." She stamped her foot. "But what does any of that matter to you? So long as he becomes a man?

Does cheating prove that? Does cheating prove poor Nick has balls?"

"Oh, Hermie. Please. This is terrible news."

"You made him take the bars!"

"Take it easy."

"You did. You can't deny it. You made that poor desperate boy take a test he *knew* he was going to fail. For your own crazy reasons of virility. It was you who put him in a position where he was forced to cheat." She started to sob. "But why do I rail at you? *I* was just as bad. I gave in to you!"

Jerry could only watch her with eyes of carefully assumed penitence as she ranted on. He was afraid that she might become hysterical. But after only a few moments of sobbing she seemed to regain control of herself. Did she perhaps suspect the giddy tide of relief that was pulsating through him? To be delivered forever from the sight of Nick Huston! A stern, benevolent god must have intervened to save the worthy Jerry from the fiendish imp. Bless him!

"Well, there it is. It's done now," she said flatly.

"Why don't you go home?" he suggested eagerly. "Let me come to your place after work. We'll have a drink and talk this whole thing out. If I'm guilty, I've got to face it."

"What for?"

"So that I can learn to be more sympathetic to young associates in the future."

Having said it, he was afraid she would find it corny, but she didn't. Hermione's sentimentality was a life jacket that she always wore puffed. Besides, her old dread of any break with a friend was already asserting itself.

"Very well. Come when you can."

Jerry had lunch with Beeky Ehninger, who had had a telephone conversation with Nick's father. Beeky had been afraid that office pressure about the examinations might have been a factor, but Mr. Huston had entirely reassured him.

"He must be a remarkable man, Jerry. He said that, far from blaming the firm, he considered that we had acted with the greatest generosity in giving Nick two weeks off to study for the bars. He was very candid about his son. Almost too much so. I couldn't help wondering if a father who really cared for his offspring would have been quite so open. He said that Nick had lied and cheated since childhood. He was thrown out of two schools and at least one college. All of which he must have suppressed in his application blank to us. Mr. Huston seemed to think the whole thing might be a blessing in disguise. He's delighted to get Nick away from New York and its 'degenerate temptations,' whatever he may mean by them."

Jerry coughed. "Who ever hired the guy in the first place?"

"You're looking right at him. I interviewed Nick twice and then told him that his marks weren't up to snuff. He fixed me with those big boyish blue eyes and said: 'Mr. Ehninger, do you care about marks or do you care about human beings?' And I, like a fool, fell for it."

Jerry laughed uneasily. "I guess you weren't the only one."

"No. Hermione was, too, wasn't she? I think she had rather a crush on that young man. I wanted to talk to her about it, but I was told she'd left for the day. Will you be sure to tell her, Jerry, what I've told you — that it wasn't anybody's fault?"

o

At Hermione's that night, he decided that he would wait until their third cocktail before telling her about Nick's record. Each knew precisely the other's alcoholic need and capacity, for they had consumed together some thousands of gallons in the decade of their friendship. They were accustomed to plan carefully ahead just what each evening called for, in order to permit the maximum enjoyment with the minimum conse- quences for the following morning. If they were going to a se- rious play or an opera, for example, the limit for each might be as low as two and a half cocktails and a half bottle of wine; if they were dining at home on a Saturday night, it might be as high as four cocktails, a full bottle of wine and three or four Scotches afterward. Neither of them ever got really tight. Their spacing was too expert. But that evening everything seemed to go wrong. Hermione became maudlin after the sec- ond drink. Jerry suspected that she might have begun well be- fore his arrival. And when he told her what he had learned from Beeky, she burst into violent sobs.

"You mean I'm not even to have the consolation that I was at fault?" she cried. "I can't even tell myself that I meant *that* much to Nick? I was always just a silly sentimental old maid who bored him to tears? Oh, God, what a destiny! To mean nothing to anybody! As empty as a valentine one little girl sends to another before she learns about boys."

She became incoherent. When she got up to pour herself another drink, she stumbled, and if Jerry had not caught her, she would have fallen. She still insisted on the drink, and when she had finished it, she seemed to pass out. He had to undress her and put her to bed. When he was about to leave, however, she caught him by the arm. She had not, after all, been quite unconscious. With a sigh, he lay down beside her. Anyway, if she had planned it, the failure would be on her head.

Maybe it was the transfer of responsibility that made it work at last. Lying awake afterward he listened to her snores. Did they indicate content? Satisfaction? Had it been a cli- max or an anticlimax? Was *this* what it was all about? Had he enjoyed it? Or was he simply happy to have made the grade? Could she still have a baby at her age? A wild hope for paternity suddenly shook him. Or would he be laughed at? Would people shriek their heads off at the old office lovers who, after a decade of sighs and tears, a decade of Verdi and Donizetti and Wagner, had finally succeeded in accomplishing the simplest of all human acts? Did he care? Yes! No! As he settled himself for a night of sleeplessness he suddenly realized, very clearly and very simply, that what he would have to fight in the future — and fight it for his very life — would be the temptation of his mind to dwell morbidly on all the wasted years. For he was bound to suffer nostalgia for a condition that had become too much a part of himself to come out, all at once, without a pang. He wondered if Hermione would have to fight the same thing. Or were women different? Perhaps they were. After all, who was snoring?

XII

The Foundation Grant

THE NASTIEST PART about the whole business was that Beeky had smelled a rat from the beginning.

The Herman Hussey Foundation, run by five old cronies of the late Mr. Hussey, including his accountant, his dentist and his maiden sister, had twenty-five million to give away and no guidelines beyond a vague limitation to the area of New York City and a testamentary suggestion that the known tastes of the decedent be given due consideration. Beeky, as chairman of the board of the Colonial Museum, the yellow Greek marble temple on Riverside Drive that housed the Beekman collection of pre-Revolutionary Americana and the relics of the Eastern Indian tribes, had made several visits to Mr. Hussey in his lifetime, but had signally failed to inscribe his beloved institution among the objects of the latter's bounty. The old bachelor, round and bland, puckering the high brow under his moppy chestnut hairpiece and touching his fingertips together, had kept reiterating, in a high singsong voice, how absolutely certain he had to be that each of his donees was the "real, right thing," until Beeky, exasperated, had retorted that philanthropists who fussed too much about that sort of thing always ended up giving their money to the faddiest causes. This had ended — and abruptly — their final interview.

But then, only a year after the indecisive old gentleman's

demise, with the fortune about which he had so fretted himself still virgin to the philanthropic pruning knife, the bewildered persons on whose shoulders he had bestowed his responsibilities approached Beeky to inform him that they were considering a grant to the Colonial Museum! They had discovered minutes in their late founder's handwriting indicating that he had discussed the Museum with Beekman Ehninger, but no minutes indicating what his conclusion was. Now if Mr. Ehninger could only confirm this indication of Mr. Hussey's interest by some evidence in his own files . . .

Beeky, with death at his heart, telephoned Director Turner to institute the search that he knew in advance had to be futile. All curators were instructed to go through every file in their possession, not relying on labels or numbers, but opening every folder to be absolutely sure that no document had been misfiled. After three days of this Turner telephoned Beeky to say that he was hurrying down by taxi to One New Orange Plaza.

"You don't mean you've found something!"

"Pure gold, Beeky. Or almost pure."

An hour later, Dick Turner, with green, darting eyes and wavy black hair that he kept shoving back from his high pointed forehead, faced the chairman of the board across the latter's desk at Shepard, Putney & Cox.

"Well?" he kept asking, as Beeky tried to concentrate on the document that he had handed him. "Well? What do you think of *that*?"

Beeky shook his head to enjoin silence as he studied the memorandum typed in purple ink that lay on the blotter before him.

"November 16, 1968. Herman Hussey called again. He won't talk to Mr. Ehninger anymore. Who could blame him? I went to Hussey's apartment. How bleakly the new rich live!

We talked of cabbages; we talked of kings. And a little of silver. Silver and then more silver. Silver and Santa Claus. We
drilled and redrilled all the old ideas. To what avail? Ah, to
what avail?" Here followed a crude drawing of what appeared
to be a goose. "Good resolution for today: Must learn to keep
my temper with Mr. Turner. Is it so hard? Remember, God
made fools — though they bored his son."

"And you say this is from Miss Dunham's journal?" Beeky
asked.

"If you call it a journal. Our former curator of silver was in
the habit of typing notes to herself."

"I'm afraid it's not very complimentary to you."

"There are worse entries. Violet was not an easy woman."

"Dedicated virgins rarely are. Let me see. November of
nineteen sixty-eight. It must have been just before her stroke.
Is there any point my going to see her?"

"None whatever. This week she thinks she's a sea gull. Last
week it was something rather worse."

Beeky sighed. "Well, it certainly shows that Mr. Hussey
had some idea in mind of making us a grant for the silver
collection. If only it weren't for that dismal 'To what avail?'
But I'm surprised that Violet shouldn't have told me of her
visit to Hussey. She knew I'd been after him."

"She also knew you'd quarreled with him. He may have
told her not to tell you."

"It's possible. Anyway, you'd better take it right over to the
Foundation."

The memorandum was received there with undisguised excitement. The late Mr. Hussey's visitors' notebook not only
confirmed the visit of Miss Dunham on November 16, 1968, it
showed a subsequent one. Because Mr. Hussey had so rarely
asked any representative of a cultural institution to call upon
him more than once, and because his death had occurred only

three weeks after Miss Dunham's second visit, the board of directors decided to award three hundred thousand dollars to the decorative arts department of the Colonial Museum. In their opinion a persuasive case had been made out of a donative intent frustrated by the double tragedy of the silver curator's stroke and the founder's demise.

Beeky and Dick Turner embraced each other in joyful congratulation in the street outside the Foundation headquarters.

"If only poor Violet could know," Beeky said sadly.

"You must remember to drop Ludy Dean a line of thanks."

"Ludy?" Ludovic Dean had been Miss Dunham's principal assistant and was now her successor. "A letter of thanks? Don't you mean a letter of congratulation?"

"Well, that too, of course. But don't forget it was Ludy who discovered the journal entry. *After* Violet's secretary had missed it."

Beeky discovered that he was walking down the street with an accelerated stride. "Oh? Violet's secretary had missed it? Nobody told me that. Wasn't that rather careless of her?"

"You can't trust these girls today. If you want something done right, you've got to do it yourself. Ludy has always been a great one for finding needles in haystacks."

"I see. Good. Well, I shall certainly write him."

o

Ludovic Dean was a bony, gray, cadaverous man who might have been any age between thirty and fifty. His origins, his family, were constantly obscured, not by the paucity of his references to them but by their contradictions. In his smiling, wheedling, sourly breathing manner, as he moved closer to his interlocutor than the latter could possibly want, he managed to imply, with his hoarse, gasping, almost noiseless laugh, that he was mocking himself quite as much as his listener. He

claimed to be descended from Ludovico Sforza. All that anyone knew for sure was that he had an M. A. from Boston Uni-
versity and a small independent income on which he managed
to furnish his single floor of a brownstone with a surprising
number of exquisite things.

Beeky had always known that Ludovic Dean's humility was
as false as Uriah Heep's. What provoked him was that Dean
so obviously intended him to be aware of it. The mask of his
toothy, open-mouthed, eye-glinting admiration of the chairman of the board was so crudely a mask as to be almost insulting. Beeky smarted under Ludovic's comments on his comments:

"I guess there can't be many curators, Mr. Ehninger, who
have the good fortune to serve under a chairman who knows
that Duncan Phyfe was not a musical instrument . . .

"Actually, Mr. Ehninger, you're very close. It's not early
nineteenth century but early twentieth. No, no, I'm not being
sarcastic. Even the cognoscenti confuse the Putnam County
version of *Hudson River Bracketed* with *Art Deco* . . ."

It was universally agreed on the staff and board of the Colonial Museum that Ludovic Dean was its most brilliant star and
that if he had not so persistently concealed his light under a
bushel — refusing to lecture, to publish or even to visit other
institutions — he would have been grabbed up by the Metropolitan or the National Gallery. Ludovic's noncompetitiveness
was actually aggressive. He draped his rejection of what he
called the "cultural rat race" under the scorn of his uncontami-
nated aestheticism.

"Of course, you know why I resent Ludovic so," Beeky observed to the blank green wall of Doctor Alan Fellowes' office.
Behind his chair the psychiatrist brooded — unless he were
reading his mail. Beeky never knew how much attention Fel-

lowes paid to him on these quarter-annual checkups. *"Do* you know why I resent him, Alan?"

"I think I do. It's because he makes you feel a failure. But that's just his game. Nothing exists for Ludovic Dean but eighteenth-century silver, so he tries to convince himself that's all there is in life. And like so many fanatics, by convincing himself, he convinces others. Until you put him in the right perspective."

"Ludovic doesn't believe I could *ever* be his equal. Even if I became Chief Justice of the United States!"

"That's what I mean by his being a fanatic."

"And the funny part of it is that, deep down, we're probably not so different. I'll bet our basic problems are much alike. Yet I have a sneaking admiration for his solutions, and he has nothing but contempt for mine."

"That's you all over, Beeky. You're always so determined to see the good in people."

"Oh, shut up, Alan. Like all psychiatrists, you have no morals. You sneer at goodness. But to me it means something. It means working at your job, and helping your charities, and loving your fellow man. And I try to do those things, too, damn it all! It's a bit of an accomplishment, if you stop to consider what I started from: the browbeaten, only son of a bully, an asthmatic, stammering . . ."

"Stop. You're breaking my heart."

"Oh, don't think I'm trying to kid *you.* Where would that get me? But it's still true. And what I really hate about Ludovic Dean is that he *sees* all that. He sees what I started with and what I've achieved. Only *he* thinks I was better off in the beginning. He sees my whole life effort as a farce."

"You mean, you *imagine* he sees those things. He hasn't said so, has he?"

"No, of course not. How could he? I'm chairman of his board. But his whole manner implies it. And the worst of it is that I agree with him! I can't get away from the gnawing little notion that there's a dignity in his solutions that mine totally lack."

"Is that why you think he's a forger?"

"Probably! To get rid of the image of his superiority."

"Well, it's too bad for your theory that it wasn't a better memorandum. If Ludovic had forged it, he'd have done a better job. Because, if he's so brilliant, how could he have put together a document that's subject to the interpretation that Miss Dunham had applied for the grant and been turned down?"

"But it worked, Alan! That memo was our open sesame. It convinced the Foundation's board that Hussey had been interested."

"Yes, because they happened to read it that way. But they might not have. They might perfectly easily have read 'To what avail?' as a cry of despair in the face of a flat refusal. No forger in his right mind would have deliberately introduced an ambiguity like that."

"I suppose you're right."

"You know I'm right. If you want to hook Mr. Ludovic Dean, you'll need some better bait than that."

"Oh, of course, I don't want to hook Dean. Don't you think I want to keep that money?"

Beeky felt a good deal better about the matter after talking to Fellowes; indeed, he almost succeeded in dismissing it from his mind. But all his doubts came back, two weeks later, when the Foundation's check arrived on his desk, and he read the exuberant press release that Turner sent down with it. In the middle of the following night he awoke suddenly with a little cry.

"What's wrong, dear?"

Annabel was still reading in bed. Beeky slept in a dressing alcove off her bedroom. Getting up he walked to the French double bed in which her great mound, in black lace, dimly lit by her reading lamp, was vaguely outlined to his blinking eyes.

"You remember Violet Dunham's journal entry?"

"Oh, Beeky, forget that. You've got it on the brain. I agree with Alan Fellowes. It's obviously genuine."

"But the phrase at the end, Annabel. Do you remember it? 'God made fools — though they bored his son.' Ludovic said that! He whispered it to me at that board meeting when he reported on the new acquisitions, and one of the trustees asked if the George the Second punchbowl had belonged to George the Second."

"And what of that?"

"But don't you see? It proves he forged it."

Annabel put down her *Vogue* with a sigh of exasperation. "Why should it? Didn't he work cheek by jowl with Violet Dunham? Wasn't it one of those old maid-faggot palships? It's only natural they should borrow each other's little phrases."

"Maybe. But it sounds more like Ludovic than Violet."

"And didn't they both detest Turner?"

"I suppose they did."

"Really, Beeky, you're working yourself into one of your states. What does it matter if the paper was forged or not? You've got the money, haven't you? Do you think anyone's ever going to check on it? Why don't you destroy Violet's journal? Then you'll feel safe."

"Safe? From my conscience?"

"Oh, your conscience. Don't be such an egotist. What earthly difference can it make to anyone — including the mem-

bers of the board of the Foundation — whether or not silly old
Herman Hussey liked your silver collection? The money's
gone for a good purpose, hasn't it? A lawful purpose?"

"Yes. But it might have gone to another museum."

"Beeky, go to bed. Take a sleeping pill. You're making no
sense."

He saw that he was dealing with a moral issue which would
never exist for Annabel, which would never, indeed, exist for
most of his world. He went back to bed, but the next day,
which was that of the monthly board meeting of the Colonial
Museum, he went up to Riverside Drive an hour early and
slipped into Violet Dunham's old office on the ground floor. It
was a tiny, circular, high-ceilinged room, with one tall bay
window looking over the Hudson and a beautiful American
pewter chandelier. On the shelf over her desk was the tin box
of her now assembled journal. Beeky was not surprised, when
he thumbed through the 1968 entries, to find the one he
sought missing.

"Can I help you, Mr. Ehninger?"

He turned to the little wisp of a secretary in the doorway,
hump-shouldered, stooped, scared, yet lavender-haired and
wearing absurdly high heels. "Yes, Miss Egan, you can. I am
interested in how you happened to miss that entry in Miss
Dunham's journal. You went through the drawers of her desk,
didn't you? And collected the cards?"

"Oh, yes, and very carefully, I thought. It must have been
just one of those things, Mr. Ehninger. Perhaps two cards
were stuck together."

"But I'm sure you sorted them out carefully."

Miss Egan's shrug implied a universe of fallacies.

"Did Miss Dunham ever speak to you about her interviews
with Mr. Hussey?"

"Well, she implied that she was having a pretty tough time with him."

"Did she say she'd been turned down?"

"Oh, no, Mr. Ehninger. How could she have done that? When we know she wasn't?"

"You're begging the question, Miss Egan."

"The question that should have been put to *me*, I think," came the grating voice of Ludovic Dean from the doorway. "May we excuse Miss Egan, Mr. Ehninger?"

Miss Egan needed no further bidding. She hurried out the door, which Ludovic closed behind her. Then he turned to Beeky with his broad, toothy, hostile smile. "Now, sir?"

"I'd like to see that journal card, please."

"Which journal card?"

"You know the one." Beeky's heart was doing all kinds of nervous things, but it was obvious now that he was suspected of suspicion, and there was nothing to be lost.

"I suppose you refer to the one that was sent over to the Hussey Foundation. It was returned, but it has been somehow mislaid. Fortunately, we have Xerox duplicates. Shall I get you one?"

"I want the original."

"As soon as it is located, you shall have it. In the meantime I should think a photograph would suffice."

"A photograph cannot be tested to show the age of the typed indenture on the paper."

Ludovic smiled as if he were now thoroughly enjoying himself. "What game are you playing, Mr. Ehninger?"

"Need I tell you?"

"Are you implying that the page was recently typed? And that it might not have been typed by Miss Dunham?"

"I'm implying that it was typed by you."

"Then I guess you'll never know the truth."

"Why not?"

"Obviously, because the card has been lost."

"Lost or destroyed?"

Ludovic's shrug reminded Beeky of Miss Egan's. It was like that of a vulture poised for flight. "Does it matter?"

"You destroyed it, Dean!"

"I advise you, Mr. Ehninger, not to poke around too much. Those dogs are asleep. Let them lie."

Beeky's ire had now obliterated his tension. All he was aware of was how much he hated the ugly, grinning creature before him. "You not only destroyed it, you forged it!" he cried. "You cheated the Foundation out of that money!"

"Cheated? Oh, Beeky, please." There was superb insolence in Ludovic's drawling, unauthorized use of his nickname. "The Foundation *has* to give away the money, doesn't it? All I did was to remove a stumbling block in the form of a ridiculous prejudice on the part of the late Mr. Hussey. It is perfectly true that he turned Violet down, but then he used to turn everybody down. Why should we lose a grant that would otherwise go to some museum that *hadn't* been turned down only because it was too lazy or too ignorant to apply?"

Beeky became aware of a little green pit of sickness in his stomach. He had not realized until then how intensely he had been hoping that Dean would *not* have done it. "So Hussey *did* turn her down," he almost whispered. "As you had the termerity to imply in your forgery."

"Ah, but that was just the stroke of genius! I knew that Violet had failed. She told me so with tears, with terrible bitterness, the poor dear. I'm sure it brought on her stroke. But when, three years later, I learned that the Foundation had actually *solicited* an application from the Museum, I realized that Hussey could never have made a record of his negative decision. Perhaps he even had the grace to be ashamed of it when he heard she had been stricken. Still, even a board that wanted to make a grant was bound to suspect a self-serving diary entry — particularly one in typescript. So I had to make that memo seem indisputably genuine. And to do that, I had to make it equivocal. Even at the risk of losing the grant."

"It's a pity you went to such trouble," Beeky said drily. "Because the money will have to be given back."

Ludovic's interminable smile now became almost satanic. The only reaction that he seemed never able to express was surprise. Ludovic Dean, to the very gates of hell, had to be one pace ahead of the world. "You'll tell the Foundation? What if I deny it?"

"Then they can choose which of us they will believe."

"I see. You want me to go to jail. You've always hated me. I've felt that."

"No. I shall simply instruct the Foundation that incontrovertible proof has come to light that Miss Dunham had failed to interest Mr. Hussey in making a grant to the Museum. That there is no evidence in our files to contradict the presumption that he had weighed us in the balance and found us wanting. With that I shall tender the money back. There will be no reason for them to suspect actual fraud. My information will be perfectly consistent with your forged entry. You need apprehend no prosecution. All you will have to do is submit your resignation. On grounds of health, if you choose. It will, of course, be accepted."

Ludovic's smile was at last converted into a laugh. But it was not the gasping, silent laugh that Beeky knew of old. It was a high, strident, crackling noise, suggesting smashed glass and ripped fabrics.

"How satisfactory for you, Mr. Chairman. To get rid of a poor wretch who might really care about anything as unimportant to the downtown world as old silver. Or who might even know something about it. Perish the thought! Museums are for board members, for prestige, for puffs, for status, are they not? Imagine a man so low as to care enough about a few miserable artifacts as to commit a crime for them! A crime for himself, that would be understandable. Where else would Wall Street be? But a crime for beauty? Burn him!"

"I hope this expostulation makes you feel better, Mr. Dean."

"It does make me feel better, Mr. Ehninger. It makes me feel better to be able to tell you that, if you hate me, I despise *you*. Oh, I know your type. You've never cared for anything in your whole blighted life but the medals you wanted stuck on your thin white chest. Beeky Ehninger, the wise fiduciary, the honest little fellow, the widows' darling. What would a plaster-cast man like you know of beautiful things? What would you know of passion or sacrifice? When you come creeping into the temple of art to grab another medal, you should be exterminated ruthlessly with a moral DDT!"

"A moral DDT, Mr. Dean? What do you know of morals?"

"Ah, yes, you think that's your department, don't you? Your specialty? But spiritually you can't even spell the word."

Beeky felt suddenly depleted. He sat down and turned away from his accuser. "As the young people say today, we're not communicating. I must do what I must do."

o

The reception room of the Hussey Foundation seemed designed to remind the waiting applicant that nobody behind the closed doors of the president's office was committed to him or his cause. The light yellow and pink of the chairs and curtains appeared to deny that he would even be listened to seriously. The crude reproductions of van Gogh landscapes had the look of proclaiming that they were good enough for him. The antiquity of the magazines prohibited diversion.

But Beeky did not so much as glance at the magazines or look at the pictures on the wall. He stared out the window and saw in the blank white sky the drawn features of blind old Guy Fletcher, retired chairman of the board of the Colonial Museum, as he had appeared at yesterday's meeting of the Executive Committee. Fletcher had rocked in his chair; he had shaken his head; he had seemed to be searching for something on the table with his sightless eyes.

"You ask us, Beeky, if we want to keep money acquired by a crime. We cannot argue about that. We cannot hear ourselves say that we will. We cannot even accept your offered resignation from the board. We have to answer: 'Stay with us, Beeky, and do what you must do.' But we can still ask you a favor. We can still ask you — without argument, without discussion, without hypocrisy and without pretense — to forget this whole wretched business. Let us, for God's sake, go on as if nothing had happened."

"You ask too much, Mr. Fletcher. I have offered to resign from the board and keep my mouth shut. If I stay, I must go to the Foundation and tell what I know."

What else in the name of the late Hobart Howland *could* he have answered? If he remained chairman of the board — and they had insisted that he do so — he had to act in the only way a decent man could act. What other? What?

"You're right, Judge!" he cried aloud, for he thought he was alone in the dismal waiting room. "It *is* easy to be honest! It just takes a little guts, that's all. A refusal to be soft-soaped."

But the receptionist had come in. She looked frightened.

"Did you call me, Mr. Ehninger? Mr. Ashton will see you now."

Harold Ashton, with thick curly hair and a grin and eyes that seemed dance partners in the exploding sincerity of his sunny demeanor, rose to greet Beeky like the foundation president in the closing sequence of a happy dream. But as Beeky came closer, he saw that something was wrong.

"We were so sorry to hear the bad news, Mr. Ehninger."

"You mean you *know?*"

"Your director told me this morning, when I called about the tax exemption letter for the grant. It's a tragic business, but I always say that people who do that kind of thing must be a bit off their heads."

"That's very charitable of you, Mr. Ashton. But I'm extremely upset that any names should have been named. I really think Mr. Turner had no business speaking to you about it. What did he expect to gain by telling that sorry story? Your sympathy? So we could keep the money?"

Mr. Ashton stared. "I wonder if we're talking about the same thing. I was referring to what Ludovic Dean had done."

"Of course. And I was asking you if our director was pleading to keep the grant which we obtained through his forgery."

Very slowly Mr. Ashton resumed the seat that he had quit to greet his visitor. "Perhaps you had better tell me exactly what happened, Mr. Ehninger. Step by step. I seem to have missed something."

As Beeky told the simple, sordid tale, he marveled at the impassivity of his listener. Young as Ashton was, he must have heard many applications to have developed so tight a mask.

"And what do you propose, Mr. Ehninger, to do about this unfortunate situation?"

"Do about it? Why the only thing a decent institution *can* do. Give back the money."

The mask flew off at this. "But you can't do that! We've started a new fiscal year. All our forms would be screwed up!"

Beeky burst out laughing in the gaiety of his sudden relief. Why had he not foreseen this perfectly normal, totally anticipatable reaction? "I'm perfectly happy to keep the money, of course. Just so long as you recognize that it was obtained under false pretenses."

"I hope you're not going to make me go to my board of directors with this." Ashton's handsome gray eyes were vivid with alarm. "I'd look like a pretty ass!"

"No. My conscience will be perfectly satisfied with this report to the Foundation president. I take it, then, that we may keep the money?"

Ashton was on his feet again, but his face was flushed. He seemed suddenly indignant that his visitor should have the impunity of departing with a clear conscience, leaving the stinking little corpse of his scandal in the very center of his unspotted white blotter.

"Well, don't you think he's earned it?"

"Who's earned it?"

"Don't you think Ludovic Dean has earned the money?"

"By committing forgery?"

"No. By dying!"

Beeky reached for the edge of his desk. "Dying? What in God's name are you talking about?"

"You mean you didn't know? Ludovic Dean shot himself at your Museum this morning at nine o'clock."

o

Annabel was a woman who rose to emergencies. Beeky sometimes suspected her of enjoying them. She insisted that night that they dine in her favorite French restaurant, the Diane de Poitiers, but they occupied a table in the furthest corner. "It's good for you to have people about," she said. "It keeps your mind on how you look, not how you feel." She had cocktails, and he had wine. Annabel was at her discursive best on the subject of the marriages of the people she knew who happened to be dining there that night. But she interspersed her anecdotes with little paragraphs of consolation.

"The man was half nuts, anyway," she observed, as she critically examined her quail. "I've always known that. Do you remember our cocktail party last year for the Museum staff? He told me, in all seriousness, that the only proper way to rate the Presidents of the United States was by the additions to the White House silver in their terms of office. Kennedy first, then Jefferson, then Hayes, and so on."

Beeky ran the tip of his tongue over his lips to take up the lingering essence of the velvety Haut-Brion. His stomach felt almost in order again, numb, but at ease.

"Annabel, darling, you're wonderful. Your kindness is limitless. When I need you, you're always right there. But tonight I have to confess I'm a bit of a fraud. I don't need your help as much as you think I do. Because I don't really consider myself responsible for what happened to poor Ludovic. Of course, he wouldn't have killed himself if I hadn't discovered him, but it was he who lit the powder fuse, not I. He chose to commit his crime. When he made that choice, he made himself responsible, morally and legally, for the normally anticipatable results of his act."

"The *what?*"

"I'm sorry, dear. It's a legal phrase. Ludovic should have anticipated that he might be discovered by a person to whom his act was morally abhorrent. He was even in luck. Most such persons would have denounced him to the police. I didn't do that. I made it perfectly clear that there would be no prosecution."

"But you told him he'd have to resign his curatorship!"

Beeky, even at such a moment, could smile. Annabel

wanted him to be consoled, but not at the expense of failing to recognize his own priggishness. "Oh, I told him that, yes. How could we keep a man who had practiced such deceit?"

"But if the Museum was his whole life, Beeky!"

"Was it my fault that he placed such a burden on us? No, Annabel, it's sheer sentimentality to avoid doing the right thing because somebody may get hurt. Had I known Dean was going to commit suicide, I suppose I should have wavered. But I would have been wrong. I sincerely hope that in the end I would have done what I did do. And so long as I hope that, I am determined that I shan't feel guilty about it. So there!" He picked up his glass that the waiter had refilled. "I drink to my independence. To my strength of mind. I shall *not* be mawkish!"

As he and Annabel clinked glasses, he wondered if he could not make out the gleam of something like admiration in her eyes. "You're a man, Beeky. Whatever else you may be, you're a man."

His first anguished concern, as he leaned over to pretend to be rereading the label on the wine bottle, was how to conceal the violence of his reaction. He had a sickening vision of Alan Fellowes' grinning face.

"Don't say that, Annabel. Doing the right or the wrong thing has nothing whatever to do with being a man. *You* would have had the same obligation as I."

"Oh, no, honey, we leave all that to the boys. It makes you feel so good. And when you feel so good, you can make *us* feel so good!"

Beeky debated taking refuge in the men's room, but the mere name of it was enough to put him off. "You mean only men are Christians?"

"How many of the apostles were gals?"

Beeky began to feel the surge in his chest of something like hysteria. "What about all those virgins in the Roman arena that the academic painters loved?"

"Exhibitionists all. And here and there a lesbian."

"Annabel, you're impossible!"

"Sweetie, I only want to cheer you up. You know you need it, too. For all your boasting."

Desperately he gripped her plump hand under the table. In his flaming mind he saw himself and Ludovic Dean, like two black apish creatures silhouetted against a fire, locked in a death struggle for the mate who wasn't there.

XIII

The Merger − I

As Hubert Cox sensed his sixtieth birthday moving stealthily up behind him like a child in a game of "statues," freezing every time he whirled around, but only to glide instantly forward again the moment he had turned his back, he deplored his financial prospects. For despite three decades of a successful law practice, he had built up only a meager capital, and Shepard, Putney & Cox had only a meager commitment for retiring partners. The partnership agreement, to be sure, had the saving grace of not obliging him to retire at any fixed age. He could stay on till he dropped in harness. But what if he survived the drop?

In bitterer moments Hubert would attribute his failure to make better provision for himself to a reprehensible softness in dealing with his offspring. When his daughter Lila had claimed that it was against her principles as a liberated woman to take alimony from her rich, unfaithful husband, it was her "chauvinist male" father who had given her the money to support her four children. When his son Jack, the bankrupt victim of unscrupulous partners in a discotheque venture, had decided, in a rare moment of bourgeois scruples, to pay off his creditors, it was the "wolf of Wall Street" who had enabled him to do so. And finally, when his youngest son Franz had run over and permanently lamed a child, it was the "inhuman imperialist" who had compensated the parents for Franz's inadequate insurance. It gave Hubert a wry amusement that his children, in using him to pay the price of their own consciences, should still stoutly maintain that he himself was not possessed of one. In their lively, if rather shrill family discussions, he would have happily joined in the hue and cry against himself as an apostle of greed had he only been a rich one. Sophie, of course, defended him, Sophie who would have lived happily in a hut, but none of the children ever listened to her.

And now, at last, came hope. Now, at last, just as he had been abandoning anticipation, just as he had been reaching for his hat under the seat as the drama of his career seemed to be approaching its finale, what should descend from the ceiling but a big, breezy *deus ex machina* in the shape of Franklyn Sidell of Sloane & Sidell, with an offer of merger. The larger firm, which had employed Hubert when he was first out of Harvard Law and which he had often secretly regretted leaving, was proposing, unsolicited, precisely the second chance that he needed. For the combined organizations would be big enough for all things, and not the least of such a total was a proper retirement plan.

When Hubert discussed it with Beeky Ehninger, he was already so convinced of its marvelous possibilities that he was exasperated by his partner's failure to take corresponding fire. Beeky walked stubbornly up and down the big Chinese rug that was the glory of Hubert's office, his hands in his pockets, his eyes turned away from the early evening view of the harbor, the expense of which had prompted, two years before in 1971, his lone dissenting vote against the firm's move from Wall Street.

"If Sloane and Sidell are so keen to merge, we must have

something they want. If that is so, why shouldn't we keep it for ourselves?"

"Beeky, that kind of grudging Yankee suspicion is out of date. Granted, there are plenty of old farts around looking for young ones to do their work for them. But this is different. Sloane and Sidell are bigger than we are, and richer. What Franklyn Sidell is looking for is symbiosis."

"What?"

"Don't you remember your biology? Symbiosis is where two organisms come together for mutual benefit."

"I thought that was called something else."

"Very funny. Listen to me. They have a large municipal bond department; we, a small one. They're low on corporations; we're high. They're the big thing in real estate; we're nominal. And so forth and so on. It's the most fantastic mesh you ever saw. We come together like two parts of a picture puzzle. And united we'd be big. As big as Davis Polk or Sullivan and Cromwell. We'd be one of the great firms of the city."

"On the theory that you can put a great firm together with a pair of scissors and a roll of Scotch tape. I don't believe it, Hubert. A great firm has to grow. With handed-down traditions. With one generation teaching another. With precedents. With young men coming in it from law school and working their way up and . . . and, well, *loving* it." Beeky stamped his foot. "Yes, loving it, damnit all! And how can any man love a law firm where any day he may see himself arbitrarily passed over by somebody brought in from the outside?"

"Maybe law firms don't have to be lovable any more. You seem rather conveniently to forget the way you brought me and Horace into this firm."

"That was a blood transfusion. An emergency. The patient was dying!"

"We're all dying. The question is how soon. Look at the little retail stores you see closing all over the city. They've got
to go supermarket or bust. Only the big can survive. Okay.
Let's go big!"

"What a noble ideal. What an inspiring goal."

"Look, Beeky. If you'll agree to this one, I'll see it your way
in the future. Always."

"My way? With twenty-five new partners? And the precedent of this merger? What will my way amount to?" Beeky
tapped his finger on Hubert's desk. "Suppose we get to the
real point. Who has to be pushed off the sled to feed those
wolves you're looking back at?"

"What makes you ask that?"

"Because I know you. I know when you're holding something back."

Hubert contemplated his partner's earnest expression for a
moment of restrained exasperation. Friendship had not played
a great role in his life — he got on too quickly, too easily, with
too many people — but there was nobody, even including the
devoted Sophie and his irritating children (for he was no more,
basically, a "family" than a "friendship" man) of whom he was
fonder than Beeky. He accepted perfectly the fact that this
fondness was inspired in part by Beeky's greater fondness of
himself. But was that something, at his age, that he could afford to throw away?

"There's never any fooling you, Beeky. There *is* a rub.
Franklyn Sidell makes this point: that in any merger you're
bound to disappoint some people. So why be hanged for a
lamb? Why not get rid of all your deadwood at one stroke?
I've drawn up a list of duplicating associates in all departments. For example, we'd need only one accounting department, theirs, not ours. We could eliminate their tax litiga-
tors . . ."

"Hubert! Wait. You talk as if you were dropping some superannuated machinery. Am I mistaken, or are we dealing with human beings?"

"Oh, Beeky, nobody's going to starve. The job market's too good. We have no commitment to look after people for life. What do we even do for our partners? The point is that here we have a chance in a million to put together a perfect law firm. I *agree* with Franklyn Sidell."

"Whom I've detested ever since we were in Saint Andrew's School together."

"Can't we leave your school days out of this?"

"No. I learned too much from them. And let me tell you something else. My mother used to say, if I ever told her I'd been to a perfect dinner party, that my hostess couldn't have been a very nice woman. For what had she done with her frumps? Well that's what I think of your perfect law firm. What have you done with your frumps?"

"Maybe a law firm doesn't have to be like a very nice woman."

Beeky took another quick turn about the room. "Hubert. Let me put something to you. You know all my business affairs. One has to come clean to tax counsel. You know that I've taken care of Annabel and that I've more than enough for myself. My sisters are very well off. I owe nothing to anybody. There's no reason under the sun I shouldn't set up a trust fund for you and Sophie. It could provide you with a nice little income, and the principal could go to my foundation when you die. So you see, it would really cost me nothing."

Hubert's smile, aroused by the law firm and the "very nice woman," had become stale. "You take it for granted that I'm only interested in this merger for my private gain?"

"No. But I feel sure that Sloane and Sidell have better pension arrangements than we do."

Even in his disgruntlement, Hubert could admire the speed
with which Beeky had picked up the scent. "I'm not very flattered by your image of me. May I remind you that it was not
I who went to Franklyn Sidell? He sought *me* out. Should I
turn him down because his scheme happens to work to my
benefit? That would be the Beeky way of doing things, I suppose."

"I was only seeking to remove that factor from the temptations of the offer."

"Well, don't play God, Beeky. The role hardly becomes
you. There's always been something condescending in your
attitude of moral superiority. As if I were a kind of wild man
whom you had to tame and dress up for the drawing room. I
suggest that you consider the proposed merger on the merits
and not as a perpetual Saint Andrew's schoolboy."

"I resent that!"

"You were meant to. And now let's cut this embarrassing
scene. It's time I went home."

"With pleasure. But just remember this. While you're elim-
inating duplicating associates, you can cross off one duplicating partner."

"Beeky, don't be an ass."

"I mean it, Hubert!"

Hubert decided with a sigh that he did. All the irritation
that he had used to feel for Beeky in the early days of their
friendship hissed up in the back of his mind. He had always
objected to Beeky's "knight in armor" stands. Yet this irritation was so intertwined with his fondness for his partner that it
brought back a vivid nostalgia for the old law school days.
How could he not have been fond of Beeky? Beeky had been
so impressed by Hubert's brillance, so awed by his law review
editorship, so dazzled by his success with girls, so ashamed of
his own wealth. Hubert had used Beeky happily, outra-

geously, had borrowed money from him, wrecked his car, given drunken Saturday night parties for which the other had been only too glad to pay. And yet, for all Beeky's seemingly humble discipleship, there had always been something sticky about him, something one could never quite shake loose from. Like his great-grandfather, the tycoon, he seemed to get more out of people than they got out of him. But what? What had Beeky ended up with? Certainly, it did not show.

On nights when they were not entertaining or dining out Hubert and Sophie got into their robes and pajamas before supper. Afterward they read or watched television in bed. That night Hubert turned his light off early and lay gazing at the dulled yellow of the ceiling illuminated by his wife's reading lamp. There was no point talking to her about Beeky because she always took Beeky's side. She had from the beginning. Sophie, so loyal, so submissive, almost at times so mousy, had yet her independence in this. She insisted that Beeky was Hubert's better nature, his good genius. It was very provoking.

"You're worried about something," Sophie suggested.

"Well, yes. I have a project in mind which Beeky passionately disapproves of."

"Then you're wrong."

"Probably. But neither of you knows why. You're both so goddamn smug. You carry your little fetishes of Victorian morality like two old maids after a glass of sherry at an office party, pretending to do a Spanish dance with castanets. You don't see that you embarrass everybody."

"Whatever you're planning must be horrid. You've been dreaming up that metaphor all evening."

Hubert, without answering, put on his eyeshade and went to sleep.

The next morning, an early dentist's appointment took him

to an apartment house at Fifth Avenue and 62nd Street directly adjacent to the old Ehninger mansion, now an advertisers' club. He crossed the avenue after his hour in the dental chair to sit on a park bench and contemplate the worn, pink French Renaissance façade. Like most of its kind, now reduced to a few stately survivors, the house was still trying to look bigger than it was. Yet he could remember, in 1938, when those haughty Corinthian pilasters, those elaborate gray arches, that roseate brick had seemed to defy the surrounding brownstone of Manhattan with a sumptuous reminder of François Premier, of Catherine de Médicis. If a New Yorker of Beeky's father's day was rich, he built a house like that. How otherwise could people have told?

Hubert had never been asked to the mansion while he and Beeky were at law school. He had taken for granted that Beeky had not considered his new friend "social" enough for his parents and had not in the least resented it. That was simply the way those people were. But a year after he came to New York to clerk for Sloane & Sidell, he received a large engraved card from Mr. and Mrs. Ehninger inviting him for "tea and cocktails" on a Sunday afternoon at five. His logical mind was at once a fuddle of silly questions. That was the deplorable result of any contact with society people. They were trivial, but they made you trivial, too. Did five o'clock mean five o'clock? And what did you wear? A friend told him that Mr. Ehninger was famous for being "old world" and loaned him a tail coat. Did you address a girl to whom you were introduced by her first name or as "Miss"? Could you take her out afterward? And why did you care if you couldn't afford to, anyway, and if you were practically engaged to a penniless German refugee called Sophie Hoffman?

Hubert closed his eyes as he tried to bring back that afternoon. How had Proust done it? With a *madeleine?* And what the hell was that? But there was no real need, he soon found, for reflection, for searching, even for relaxation. He remembered every detail exactly.

o

He pushed open the heavy grilled glass door and slowly ascended the low, wide, closely spaced marble steps. He passed through a second grilled door opened by a footman in a red jacket into a dark hall lit only by lighted portraits and the gleam of armored figures. He moved cautiously forward, like some blinking, curious fish, and then seemed to swim up a circular marble stairway passing under the giant portrait of a lady with dark eyes and noble mien and a gown of billowing, tumbling, cascading scarlet onto a landing dominated by a great tapestry of some French royal hunt, all deep green and flashing blue, with vivid red-jawed hounds and a sadly bleeding stag. Was it right that so much splendor should be owned by one family? Here was a man's world!

Then he noticed something. Something decidedly unpleasant. Standing at the doorway of the white and gold paneled parlor whose mirrors doubled one's sense of its size, he made out that he was the only man in a cutaway. He turned at once to go back down the stairs, but his retreat was cut off by a short, plump little man, of nervous gesticulations yet of unmistakable authority.

"Where are you going, young man? You can't walk out just as you've come! You must be Hubert Cox. Beekman's always talking about Hubert Cox. He tells me you're the most brilliant lawyer of his generation. Don't think I'm laughing at you. I'm not. I believe my son implicitly — on certain subjects. If he had said you were the greatest wine connoisseur, or the wittiest conversationalist, or even the greatest lady-killer, I might have reserved judgment until I met you. For I know considerably more than Beekman does about those subjects. But in the law I bow to him. Take a glass of champagne, and let us stand apart from the throng. Tell me how you rate Beekman's chances to rise in your esteemed profession."

Hubert, taking the champagne glass, was aware of two things: first, that this fussy little man was not congenial with his son, and secondly, that he was patronizing his visitor.

"I was wrong to wear this monkey suit, sir. I won't make that mistake again."

"I'm sure you won't. I can see you're a man who will never have to be told anything twice. But do you know something, Mr. Cox? I *like* your coming to my house in a tail coat. It shows that you expected something of it and that you expected it to expect something of you. That's the way a young man with his fortune to make, coming to a great city, *should* feel. I'm afraid it's a sense most of us have lost with that son of a bitch of a cripple in the White House, scattering our wealth to paupers. A young barrister should be like the hero of a Balzac novel. Life should be romance!"

"I don't suppose many Balzac heroes tried to conquer the world in a firm like Sloane and Sidell."

"It wasn't the way to the top in the Paris of his time. But it may be in New York today. After the age of predators comes the age of small print. A lesser era, perhaps, but we can't choose our eras, can we?"

Hubert caught sight of Beeky watching them. He was talking to a girl in the parlor, and he had obviously taken in the cutaway. But Hubert recovered quickly from such things. He even looked a bit down on Beeky for minding, or rather for rating his guest so low as to think that *he* would mind. "If it's the right ladder for me, it should be righter for your son.

Beeky must have a great roster of potential clients in this room alone."

Mr. Ehninger sniffed. "Beeky was not born for the first rank. He has his mother's habit of moralizing. It is all very well to moralize, as the Victorians knew, so long as one is not afraid of hypocrisy. Beeky's problem is that he is. Like many misguided young people, he sees it as the principal vice of the world."

Hubert found such objectivity a bit chilling. "What you say may be true. But I find it rather sad. Perhaps the world ought to be the way Beeky wants it."

"He should take his lesson from Margaret Fuller. He should accept the universe."

"Does that mean he should accept his father's Wall Street?"

"Haven't *you?*"

"Oh, me." Hubert shrugged. "I have no use for moralizing. Or for hypocrisy. I want to get ahead, that's all."

"Does New York amuse you?"

"Very much." Hubert decided, after all, that it did — all of it, even this old peacock. "And this party amuses me. I amuse myself, turning up in a silly suit and making you leave your guests to put me at ease."

"I can't tell you how refreshing I find enthusiasm in a young person. Most of you are so disillusioned. I feel as if I'd spent my life as a court jester in a sort of Windsor Castle in perpetual mourning for Albert. My mission was to teach Americans to enjoy their money. It can't be done."

"Because they only enjoy making it?"

"Precisely. But as I say, we can't choose our eras. We must make the best of what we have. *You* will be happy, my dear fellow. You will make money."

"In Sloane and Sidell? I wish I could see it."

"In the law or in something else. Or if money ceases to be

the thing, you'll make whatever is the equivalent. You have that look about you. I never miss it. I'm sorry my daughters are all married."

"Really, Mr. Ehninger! Isn't this a bit sudden?"

Hubert's host seemed too absorbed in his thoughts to find this worth answering. "It's so curious that Beekman should have spotted you. It shows there *is* Means blood in him, after all. I had almost despaired. You're not married, are you, Mr. Cox?"

Hubert could not resist a chuckle. "Is one of your daughters coming back on the matrimonial market?"

"Not at all. Not at all. You mustn't joke about such things. You still, I see, have much to learn. I inquired because I thought, if you were a bachelor, you might like to move in here and share a floor with Beeky. We rattle around in this old barn." Here Mr. Ehninger caught sight of Beeky approaching them and stepped closer to Hubert, dropping his voice to a confidential tone. "No need to decide that now. We can talk of it later."

He trotted briskly off as his son came up, and Hubert decided he was living in a Beaumarchais world.

"What has the old man been telling you?"

"What does any old man tell you? That he'd like to be young again. That he'd like another chance to conquer the world."

"To conquer it or to marry it? Duke's world is gone!"

"What's all this then? Its ghost?" Hubert's gesture took in the marble stairway coiling below them and the dark lady in the gilded frame. "It looks pretty solid to me."

"Would you want it?"

"It might do. Till another came along."

"An oversized marble stairwell in a minor Horace Trumbauer house? With a bad Boldini portrait giving Grandma

Means a swan neck she never possessed? Don't look up or you'll see the ceiling needs plastering."

Hubert shrugged. "You see it that way because you're used to it."

"No! I see it that way because it *is*."

There was no mistaking the passion in Beeky's blinking eyes. Hubert understood now why it had taken him so long to ask him to the house. Beeky detested his father and dreaded the old man's attraction for his friends. It might be laughable, it might be ludicrous, to be so afraid of the lure of a pompous town house and a party of chattering fools, but there was no denying Beeky's state. Hubert grinned. After all, how cross could one get at a man who believed that Hubert Cox and his friendship were more valuable assets than any that being a Means could bring him?

"Have you never thought of your father as a romantic?"

"Romantic! A man who boasts that he's Balzacian because he married for money! Why, my father even finds romance in the novels of Dreiser. Any book or play about money unscrupulously made and vulgarly spent brings tears of sentiment to his eyes."

"I wonder if I don't rather admire that."

"Oh, I knew you and he were bound to get on. That's why I asked you here. To have it over with."

But this was carrying the joke too far. "Don't be an ass, Beeky. From where I sit, you and your old man are out of the same antique shop. His materialism and your idealism are like two Toby jugs on a modern mantelpiece."

Beeky stopped blinking at this. Then he changed the subject. "I'd hoped you'd bring Miss Hoffman. I wanted so much to meet her."

"Sophie? I didn't know I could bring a girl to a party like this. Why didn't you tell me?"

"I'm sorry. How idiotic of me. Of course, I should have."

"Then I'll give you a chance to make up. You can take us out for dinner."

Beeky clapped his hands. He really *was* a child. "You mean tonight?"

Four hours later, at La Rue, Hubert, Beeky and Sophie Hoffman were still drinking. At least Hubert and Beeky were. Sophie had had nothing all evening but one glass of beer. She and Beeky had hit it off wonderfully. The Teutonic in her, almost comically emphasized by her straight brown hair, her flat, pale, lineless face, her brilliant blue eyes and perfect teeth, expressed itself in protectiveness rather than assertiveness. She had divined at once in Beeky the man who was totally devoted to Hubert, and she was shameless in the way she flaunted her own adoration. Sophie objected to nothing Hubert did except when he took out other girls. Even then she was dumbly miserable rather than irately jealous. She made a poor living as a translator, and she and Hubert had been going together for five years.

Beeky was beginning to get drunk. "Hubert Cox, if you don't marry this girl, you're a greater ass than I am." He turned to Sophie. "I know I'm an ass because Hubert told me so this afternoon. He also said I was out of date. On the shelf. Kaput. Through."

"Oh, Hubert, you didn't! You couldn't have called your delightful friend an ass. He was only joking, Mr. Ehninger."

"Beeky. Beeky. You must call me Beeky. For the sixteenth time."

"Beeky, then. We Germans are so formal. You must forgive."

"Of course, I called him an ass. He *is* an ass. Don't fall for his blarney, Sophie. The only reason he likes you is that your

father is a refugee professor. Beeky's full of guilt feelings because he basically identifies his old man with Hitler."

"Oh, Hubert, dry up."

"Hubert, dear, you're horribly unfair."

"I know whereof I speak. Besides, Beeky, I can't possibly
marry Sophie. I'm under contract to your father. He wants
me to move into his house until one of your sisters needs a
new husband. Which, under the law of averages in your social
circles, should not be long."

Beeky's whiskey-softened eyes fill with alarm. "My father
asked you to move in with us?"

"Certainly. Anyone can see you need a tutor."

"But are you serious, Hubert?"

"Why shouldn't I be serious? Do you think *you're* the only
person who can appreciate me? Your father is simply exercis-
ing the ancient right of Roman emperors to adopt a brilliant
barbarian to take the place of an ungrateful son."

Beeky said nothing for several minutes and then went to the
washroom. He was gone a long time. Sophie, seeing that Hubert did not want to talk, was discreetly silent, leaving him to
whiskey thoughts. Was he really going to marry this girl?
Was he really going to sire such nervous offspring as were apt
to be his on that steadfast, cowlike creature? So far he had
had the best of two worlds. He had been perfectly free to
have affairs so long as Sophie insisted on her chastity. But
now she seemed willing to reconsider the point. And now she
was being hotly pressed by a young protégé of her father's,
also a refugee, whom her family, who disliked Hubert, wanted
her to marry. What he had to decide was whether or not a
man as all over the place as himself, and as loose and easy —
and as brilliant, goddamn it! — could afford to pass up a wife
as sound and efficient and loving as Sophie only too obviously

would be. He was so devoid of basic loyalties, so tempted by every temptation, good and bad, that he was already exhausted at twenty-five. It was ridiculous.

When Beeky returned, he was morose.

"Why should I stand in your way, Hubert? Of course you should move into our house. And I should move out. I will, too. You're the kind of son my father always wanted. Don't think he hasn't made me feel it! You ought to let him adopt you. You ought to let him make your fortune!"

"But I thought the money was all your mother's."

"Beeky, my poor friend, Hubert's only joking. Hubert, tell him you're only joking."

"I'm only joking."

"No, no. Tell him nicely. Tell him as if you meant it."

"I meant it."

"Hubert, you're impossible. But it's all right, Beeky. Hubert can't move in with your parents. He's really going to have to marry me one of these days."

"Who says so?"

"Darling, it's only decent. After five years!"

"Do you imply that I ought to make an honest woman of you? You slander yourself. And compliment me!"

Beeky looked from one to the other in a slow acceleration of surprise and wonder. At last he smiled. Hubert supposed that Sophie would have called it a beatific smile. All Beeky's moroseness was gone. "You mean that you two might really get married? Seriously?"

Hubert shrugged. "Stranger things have happened." Instantly, Sophie's knee was against his, and he was aware of the tense shock of her tremor. The *speed* of these things!

"How wonderful! Can I give the reception? Can I buy you a house?"

"You'll have your chance, never fear. When the time comes. Don't be pushy."

"Hubert, dear! You know what your friend is *offering?* How can you be so rude?"

"Well, I hope you're satisfied, Beeky. You were always afraid I might be the type to marry a girl for her money. Now look what's happened. A girl wants to marry me for mine."

o

When Hubert rose from his park bench, he noted that he had been sitting there for less than five minutes. Such was the efficiency of memory. The image of the young Beeky followed him into the subway. He saw again that wide "beatific" smile. He felt again the utterness of Beeky's absorption in his love life. He remembered all the loans that had made possible his and Sophie's marriage on the pittance that law clerks earned in 1939.

But he also saw something that he had never — at least fully — seen before. He saw the extent to which Beeky's fantasy had been to *be* Hubert Cox.

"In some ways he owes me as much as I owe him," he muttered to the image of himself in the mirror over the gum machine. "Well, if it's Hubert Cox he wants to be, let him go all the way."

At One New Orange Plaza he went straight to Beeky's office.

"I've had a visit from the Ghost of Christmas Past," he announced from the doorway. "Behold a changed man!"

Beeky looked up from his museum bulletin. "You've changed your mind about the merger? I thought you would. Basically, Hubert, you're a bigger softy than I am. Anyone who's watched the way your children have taken you knows that."

"Ah, but I'm not. Not nearly the softy you are. My children don't count. They're mere extensions of my ego. The most abominable monsters are good to their children. And I have *not* changed my mind about the merger. I have simply decided not to be your fall guy in moral matters. That is why I am resigning as chairman of the firm's merger committee. And that is why I am naming you in my place."

Beeky got slowly to his feet as he made out that his partner was serious. "Without my consent?"

"Consent? What do I need your consent for? You and I are agreed that we're both obliged to do anything within reason for the good of the firm, are we not? And who is more qualified to negotiate with Franklyn Sidell than his old school chum, Beeky Ehninger? You have always prided yourself as having been the architect of our firm. Well, here's your chance to do it again."

"But suppose I don't want the merger?"

"Then kill it!"

As Beeky took in how thoroughly he was trapped, he gave a little groan. "You Machiavellian son of a bitch," he murmured, but Hubert simply roared with laughter.

XIV

The Merger – II

B EEKY SOON DISCOVERED that negotiating with Sloane & Sidell was like negotiating with a delegation of oriental communists. The faces beamed, the lips curled in grins, the tones were dulcet, but at the end of each session he found himself right back where he had started. For the members of their negotiating committee seemed sublimely convinced that they occupied an unassailable position from which to dictate terms, and their only instructions, so far as Beeky could make out, were to dictate them as pleasantly as possible. He began to despair as he found himself beginning to be persuaded, by one after another of these suave, persuasive, reasonable men, that duplicating personnel had to be eliminated. What else would Mr. Ehninger seriously propose? And did he not have to agree that Sloane & Sidell should be the name of the new firm? How else could Mr. Sidell hope to retain the confidence of his municipal clients accustomed to seeing their bonds validated under that letterhead for eighty years? And could Mr. Ehninger really offer any reasonable alternative to the regrettable botheration of his firm's having to move to Sloane & Sidell's building on Broad Street? Had not he himself conceded that there was no more space available at One New Orange Plaza?

So it went. It was not enough that he should concede each

point, he had to do so gracefully. Not to such as he was accorded the luxury of grumbling. Beeky was not only going to have to sign what he considered the death warrant of all his high hopes and aspirations for his firm, he was going to have to affix the seal, shake hands with the witnesses and offer a toast to the new venture. Hubert's little scheme might have been fiendishly clever, but Beeky began to wonder if he would have the fortitude, in the last analysis, to see it through.

The social ratifications were even harder to bear than the business initiations. Dreadful was the night when he and Annabel had to dine with the Sidells. Franklyn Sidell had delegated the details of the merger to his juniors, but some recognition had to be made of his long acquaintance with Beeky, and the invitation was duly dispatched and ruefully accepted.

The very house oozed with superiority. It was only a brownstone, of the kind that in Beeky's boyhood had been a symbol of mere middle-class affluence, but such were now occupied, at least as single dwellings, only by the rich. The Ehningers soon discovered beyond its sober façade, as if hiding from the tax assessor, discreet evidences of wealth and taste: old paneling and marble mantels, parquet floors and Aubusson carpets. Here and there, a small Picasso, a Léger, a Dufy, winked at them to prove that the proprietors were at home in all times and in all places. Beeky would not have been surprised to hear his host answer, to a question of date: "The red buffalo on the sideboard? A beauty, isn't it? Fantastic how they knew how to use the natural shape of the rock. It's twenty thousand B.C."

There were other guests, but Franklyn Sidell drew Beeky aside in the drawing room to tell him what a splendid fellow Hubert Cox was.

"Of course we've always had an eye on him. After all, he started with us. It was you who snitched him away."

"You could have kept him."

"How?"

"By offering him a partnership before I did."

"Ah, no doubt. My uncle Jack Sidell was very stuffy about those things. He couldn't see any man becoming a partner of his before age thirty-five."

"A commitment to that effect might have done as well."

Franklyn seemed surprised at such persistence. "Perhaps. But it was harder in those antediluvian days to take a chance on a young lawyer with no connections. You forget how recent the Depression had been."

"Excuse me, Franklyn. I do not forget. *I* had no difficulty in foreseeing Hubert's brilliant career."

"Well you, my dear Beeky, have always been smarter than anyone."

Franklyn Sidell was not handsome, but he made one blush for recognizing that he wasn't. He had such a fine strong build, such a firm, frank handshake, such a big, brave nose, such a glassy, commanding stare that one was almost embarrassed for a God who had neglected to make him beautiful. And, even worse, there was something undeniably comic about him: in the stiffness of his pigeon-toed walk, in the goggling roll of his eyes, in the beaming benevolence of his too public smile. Frankly was a natural leader who was always going to be laughed at — behind his back. At Saint Andrew's School he had been head monitor and head boy, and Beeky should have been honored by his friendship, but the Sidell condescension had stripped the gift of most of its value. Franklyn, in making no pretense of concealing the long stairway down which he had climbed to his asthmatic little friend, had placed Beeky under yet another unwelcome obligation: that of applauding his lack of hypocrisy.

If the ex-head monitor of Saint Andrew's School had had the

grace to fail in afterlife, or even to limit himself to a middling career, he would have been forgiven and perhaps even loved by a grateful Beeky, even as the red-faced, stertorous drunks at the bar of the Patroons Club were forgiven. But no, rich as he was, big and brave as he was, Franklyn Sidell had had the crudity to become one of the foremost corporation lawyers downtown, greater even than his father and uncles before him, making the scant success of Beeky Ehninger seem even scanter. And now, into the bargain, he was going to swallow Beeky's firm.

Franklyn would not allow him to join the other guests. Still smiling, he barred his way.

"It'll be fun to be partners again, Beeky."

"Again?"

"Well, don't you consider that the sixth form at Saint Andrew's was a kind of partnership? We helped Doctor Agnew run the school."

"You did. I didn't."

Franklyn's raised eyebrows responded gently to such churlishness. "Anyway we were friends there, which is always a kind of partnership. I hope you won't deny that."

"We weren't friends. Not really. I didn't have any real friends at school."

But nothing, it seemed, was going to quench his host's willed benevolence. "I guess those years were pretty bleak for all of us."

"For you? What on earth are you talking about, Frank? You were the roundest little peg in the roundest little hole I ever saw!"

"Far from it. Do you know, I used to keep a calendar on my bureau so I could cross off each day of the term? And the day the number dropped to one digit, I'd celebrate by treating the whole dorm to ice cream."

Beeky was reduced to speechlessness. It had become so fashionable for childhoods to be unhappy that even Frank Sidell had convinced himself that his must have been so! No doubt all the savage joy that he and his gang had derived from persecuting wretches had dropped from the back of his mind like discarded scenery before a setting more appropriate to the new role of the homesick, sensitive Frank.

"Of course, the school's different now," Franklyn continued. "They all are. I've still got a boy there, you know. Our youngest. He graduates in the spring."

"I suppose he's head monitor."

"As a matter of fact, he is. But the kids today don't take those things as seriously as we did. Our new headmaster is a ball of fire. He's got the boys doing things about the pollution of the river and the garbage in the woods. I think they really enjoy school today."

"And why shouldn't they?" Beeky's voice was trembling. He knew that he ought to shut up, that if he went on, he would go too far. But, of course, he knew that he *would* go on, however far the mood might take him. "You don't need a genius to make boys happy. All you need is a man who doesn't go out of his way, like Doctor Agnew, to make life odious for them."

"You can't *still* resent Doctor Agnew, can you, Beeky?"

"Oh, can't I? That past is as real to me as this house is. As you are. More real!"

It was clear at last to Franklyn that he was dealing with a lunatic. "Dear me. Well, well. I think I see Alberta signaling to me. Dinner must be ready."

The oval paneled dining room was lit by candelabra and the bulbs over three Monet paintings of lily pads. Annabel was seated on her host's right. She was always at her worst at dinner, for she became tense with the shutting off of her supply of cocktails. Afterward, with brandy or whiskey, she mellowed again, but it was a sleepy mellowing. Beeky's heart dipped when he heard, down the table, the word "Vietnam."

Franklyn Sidell, like many cultivated, prominent members of the downtown bar, was something of a dove. He was one of those who tended to bury the strategic difficulties of the conflict under a profound head-shake and a grave muttering about "this terrible war." Annabel, on the contrary, was an unabashed hawk. She had lived in Hungary with her second husband, a State Department officer, and had seen communism, as she put it, "at work."

"You're as bad as the young people, Mr. Sidell," she was saying now, in a high-pitched tone. "You should know better. You have no idea how strong and ruthless an enemy you face. They always count on a majority of fools to underestimate the hell of communism — until it's too late!"

"But, my dear Mrs. Ehninger, I am the last person to underestimate communism. My uncle Barclay Sidell was a colonel in the White Army in nineteen nineteen. To me the vital question is not whether or not we oppose the Soviets, but how best to oppose them. I maintain that we fall into their trap when we allow them to select the battlefield. Everything favors them in Indochina."

"Where *will* you fight them, Mr. Sidell? In North America? Or is that too vast a territory to defend? In the United States, maybe? But two seacoasts — I suppose that's too much. How about New York — the city, I mean. Or are there too many boroughs? Why not narrow it down to Manhattan? Oops, I forgot Harlem." Here Annabel turned, smiling, to the table that she had silenced. "Ladies and gentlemen, I predict that our host will take his stand at last on the very doorstep of this beautiful house and fight to the death for Zip Code one-o-o-two-one. *C'est magnifique, mais ce n'est pas la guerre!*"

As she almost screamed out her French quotation, she closed her eyes and burst into a high, gasping laugh. Never had Beeky seen her so unattractive. The blond curls, set that afternoon, were tightly rolled, too close to her scalp; they made the round, powdered face and popping black eyes seem almost malignant. And worse yet, she was so sure that the whole unlaughing party was behind her. Beeky tried to play his old defensive game of imagining that he was in a dark auditorium watching a parlor comedy.

"I'm afraid you confuse strategy with cowardice," Franklyn muttered.

"Oh, I don't accuse you of cowardice, my friend. I am sure you are courage itself. Blindness is your trouble. If you had lived in communist countries, as I have, you'd see things differently."

"I served two years in the State Department, Mrs. Ehninger. I am not quite totally ignorant of these matters."

"Yes, but have you ever *lived* in a communist country?"

"Well, no."

"Then you see!"

Beeky began to wonder if the evening's events might not actually jeopardize the merger. Would it be the first time in business history that a deal had fallen through for some personal, petty, unacknowledged cause? As the conversation continued to deteriorate, the idea began to take firmer shape in his mind. He glanced with apprehension at the thin set line of Sidell's lips, at the dangerous flutter of his eyelids. Even if Beeky were sure that he wanted to kill the merger, was he sure that he wanted to do it *this* way?

"What an arrogant man your future partner is," Annabel whispered to him as they left the dining room. "But I guess I fixed his wagon. Remember, it never pays to start these relationships too humbly."

"I guess we haven't made that mistake," Beeky murmured with a sigh.

He left her and went upstairs to find a bathroom, a bedroom, anywhere to be alone. His host had told him to go to the third floor; he went to the fourth. In what seemed to be a child's former room, he sat by the bureau and blew cigarette smoke at his gray image in the mirror. Yet he felt no resentment of Annabel. Her performance had been no worse than his own. Between them they made up an antic pair, like two circus clowns cavorting between the acrobats and the elephants, pretending they were the real show. What right had they to stand between the merger of two great firms? Oh, no, there had to be an end to strutting, to buffoonery. And then the circus could go on.

When he came downstairs, he found the men assembled in Franklyn's den. He managed, with some difficulty, to get his host off in a corner.

"It's about the merger."

"My dear Beeky, can't it wait till the morning? I have my guests to think of."

"I'll be brief." Beeky took a deep breath. "It's about tonight. Of course, it's been horrible. I mean Annabel and I. We've been horrible. I've been sour as an old lemon because I was against this merger. I thought it was too . . . but never mind what I thought. My reaction only matters to me, and I'm not going to be around. That is, I'm not going to stay in the firm. No, no, wait. Don't say anything. It isn't because of you. I've got a lot of other interests — charities and family things — and I've plenty of money without practicing law. So the time has come for me to bow out. Oh, I don't say I won't rent an office in your new quarters, but basically I won't have to be counted. And now that I've made my decision, I want to tell you this. I think this merger is . . . well, inevitable. Hubert is right. Size is what counts in the world today. Together, Sloane and Sidell and Shepard, Putney and Cox ought to be great. Only don't be too tough about your title. Remember that a law firm is always known by the first two names on its letterhead. Like 'Root, Clark,' or 'Davis Polk.' So call the new firm Sloane, Sidell, Putney and Cox. You'll be known as 'Sloane, Sidell' and your bond clients will be perfectly satisfied. No, don't say a thing! Just put it up to your partners. I'm going to take Annabel home now. We're both dead tired."

Franklyn's smile was warm and welcoming. He reached out his hand. "I'll do more than put it to my partners. I'll recommend it to them. As to your retirement, we can discuss that another day. All I ask is that you give me the chance to talk you out of it! And now I think it's time we joined the ladies."

Beeky had no difficulty inducing Annabel to leave, particularly when he whispered that he would take her to a nightclub. Alone with the women, she had been exposed to the chill of Mrs. Sidell's reaction to her performance at dinner. At their table at the Plaza Beeky sipped champagne while she drank bourbon, and he told her of his plan to retire. Annabel was never surprised by anything he said.

"Of course, I've never shared your sense of the sacredness of Shepard, Putney and Cox," she observed judiciously. "But are you sure you'd have enough to do? You know what you've always said about men who retire too early: that after one giddy year they begin to rot."

"But I have no intention of giving up the practice of law. I thought I would start another firm."

"Oh, Beeky, no!"

"Wait till you hear my plan. I want to organize all the law-yers in our firm and in Sloane and Sidell who are going to be dropped when the merger goes through. Organize them into a new firm. I'd rent the office space and buy the library and hire the secretarial staff. I'd underwrite the whole venture for a year. Maybe two years."

"Are you out of your mind? It would cost a fortune!"

"It might cost a couple of hundred grand. Maybe more. But I might get it back, too. Suppose I lost it? We wouldn't be paupers."

"Oh, I'm not talking about that. It's your money. Do what you like with it. You've been more than generous with me. But what in God's name is the point of blowing good green-backs on a cartload of old crocks and incompetents?"

"They're *not* old crocks and incompetents. They wouldn't be where they are if they were. They're good lawyers, every one of them. They're duplicates, that's all."

"But would they be congenial? Would they get on? Would they make up a firm? You're always telling me how difficult it is to make up a firm. I don't suppose anyone ever tried to do it *this* way before."

"Maybe not. Maybe that would be just the fun."

"Ah, well, if it's fun." Annabel's shrug was tolerant, accept-ing, half-contemptuous. She could have explained to him very different concepts of the word. But so long as he put it on such a basis, she wouldn't argue with him, and she picked up her glass, smiling and waving as she saw an acquaintance across the room. The lights dimmed for the singer, and Beeky was glad to be alone to hug his project. Perhaps he had all along been wasting his ideals and energies on something that could never be realized. Perhaps this sudden, quixotic idea was of just the kind of law firm that Judge Howland, long be-fore, had vaguely discerned as being within the sphere of

things creatable by Beeky Ehninger. Perhaps his dim genius
was precisely for putting together a jerrybuilt organization like
the one now emanating from his whim.

And why not? What was the basic difference, after all, between the firm of his earliest vision and Shepard, Putney &
Cox or between either of them and the firm that he might
form tomorrow? Was it not a matter of the distance of the
viewer? He remembered the Indonesian Buddhas at the Asia
Institute, which even experts could not date within three
hundred years. To persons of the year 10,000 A.D. a Virgin of
Chartres and a Virgin by Picasso might be almost indistin-
guishable. The forms ultimately merged in the identity of the
aspirations. And what did the aspirations of lawyers boil down
to but the idea of practicing law in groups?

Oh, he had wanted much more than that! He had made
himself ridiculous, wanting it. He had tried to paint for a
bored bar the inspiring picture of what Hobart Howland had
been. And not even that. The picture of what his dream of
Hobart Howland had been. He was like Henry Adams, who
believed not in the Virgin, but in his concept of the Virgin, in
the memory of a fantasy.

"Annabel!" he exclaimed when the song was over. "Do you
know something? I *will* have fun. As much fun as even you've
ever had."

"Dream on, lover!" she cried with her old mocking laugh.
"What do you know about my kind of fun?"

Beeky was braced. He had learned that there was no tyranny like his old obsession that his amusements had to be
those of other people. He had digested the simple rule that
the most difficult of all lives to lead was his own. He had tired
of the compulsion to be moral in a world that was giving up
his kind of morals. From Hobart Howland to Hubert Cox —
he was ready at last to sweep the lares and penates from his

mental mantelpiece. And now he whispered to himself the words of a fierce little resolution. He was going to have as much fun with his crazy new law firm as Annabel had ever had in bed with Tom Barnes.